THE

LIFE

TARA SIVEC

The Simple Life
Copyright © 2018 Tara Sivec

Edits by KD Robichaux
www.facebook.com/AuthorKDRobichaux

Interior Design by Paul Salvette, BB eBooks
bbebooksthailand.com

A NOTE TO READERS

Ever since my first book, I've wanted to write about a character who owned a pumpkin farm. My grandparents owned the most well-known pumpkin farm in our area back in the day.

I pretty much grew up on it since my parents and all of my extended family worked there.

I have so many amazing memories growing up on this farm, and I used a lot of them in The Simple Life. This is 100% why Halloween is my favorite holiday, and fall is my favorite time of year. Please note: White Timber, Montana is not a real place. Don't try to find it on a map to hunt down Clint, Brooklyn, and the rest of this crazy group of people.

I hope you enjoy this trip down memory lane for me, and laugh your ass off!

Painting of my grandparent's farmhouse.

Prologue

*M*Y LIFE IS *amazing*.

I seriously want to pinch myself right now just to make sure I'm not dreaming. I've lived in New York City ever since I left home to go to college twelve years ago, but I can honestly say I have never loved this place more than I do right now. I have never loved my *life* more than I do in this moment, standing on a rooftop bar in the heart of Manhattan, looking out at the lights from the city, stretching as far as the eye can see. It's the end of April, and the first nice night of weather we've had since the winter that seemed like it would never end.

With a name like Brooklyn, it's no wonder I was obsessed with New York ever since I was a little girl and first found out I was named after a city here. I said goodbye to my weekly loans of all things Judy Blume and the Sweet Valley High Twins at the library, and said hello to every book I could find about the city that never sleeps. Growing up in the small town of White Timber, Montana, with a population of less than 1,000 people, I was fascinated by the fact that you could find things to do at all hours of the night in New York, and that you could walk the same city block every day at the exact same time for *years* and never see the same person twice.

In White Timber, everything shuts down at 5:00 p.m. sharp, every day of the week. If you realize you need milk at 5:05 on a Wednesday night, you should probably go out in a field somewhere and find a cow to milk. And since "downtown" White Timber pretty much consists of not much more than five blocks, you will definitely see the same people every day, who will stop and tell you the same stories you've heard a hundred times before.

When I was a teenager, I spent every waking moment dreaming about leaving that tiny town and moving to this big city where no one would remember that one time my freshman year of high school when I ran across the football field with the other cheerleaders, as well as the entire football team, at the start of the big homecoming game. I tripped over someone's foot at the fifty-yard line and landed flat on my face in front of the entire marching band, who had formed two lines for us to run between. That damn trip caused a domino effect with the football players who were running right behind us. I wound up at the bottom of a sweaty football player pile, and the town never forgot.

"Remember that time you ate grass at the homecoming game, Brooklyn? Boy was that hilarious!"

Yes, Susan, yes I do remember, because if was the most mortifying moment of my life. Thanks for bringing it up for the seventeenth time this week. And tell your shit stick nephew who played the trumpet that maybe he should have learned some manners and helped me up instead of just standing there, pointing and laughing at me.

Thinking about my hometown always puts me in a crap mood, and now is not the time for crap moods. I shake it off, and stare out at the sparkling skyline, thankful that I'm *here* and not *there*. I have an amazing job, amazing friends, and an amazing boyfriend. I really need to find another adjective other than amazing, but I'm too happy sipping expensive champagne, and schmoozing with the who's-who of New York to bother.

"I think I just saw Brad Pitt. God, we have the best jobs in the world."

I turn away from the view of Manhattan to smile at my co-worker and friend, Nicole, who snags a glass of champagne off the tray of a passing waiter and then gently clinks it against my own glass.

"I did all my research earlier today, and I've already written almost the entire article. All I have left to do is add a few things about the ambiance, what food and drinks were served, and throw in the quote I got from the owner right when I arrived, and it's finished. I basically have nothing to do the rest of the night but drink," I tell her with a smile.

"And I just finished taking the last of my photos," she adds. "I can't believe we get paid for this shit."

I nod in agreement, the word "amazing" floating around in my head all over again. Nicole and I both work at *Glitz*, the largest fashion magazine in the world, whose headquarters are here in New York. I'm what you'd call an "It Girl." I get invited to all the best places in the city. All the best restaurant openings, all the best club openings, every after party for Fashion Week, and anything else you can think of or might see on *E! News* during the weekend update.

I get invited, I get photographed walking the red carpet, Nicole takes photos of the event, and I write up an article about it. Not to pat myself on the back or anything, but everyone knows who I am at these events. They know they need to be nice to me and show me a good time if they want me to write a glowing article about their establishment or their event. I get to stuff my face full of expensive food and drinks for free, hang out with famous people, write a thousand-word article about it that takes me no time at all, and get paid handsomely for it. Tonight, we're celebrating the grand opening of a new rooftop bar on top of a hotel in the heart of Manhattan.

Say it with me: *Amazing.*

"I thought tonight might finally be the night I get to meet Stephen," Nicole states with a questioning raise of one perfectly sculpted eyebrow.

"He had a last minute conference call with Japan and couldn't get away." I shrug.

I keep my smile firmly in place even though this might be the one part about my life that isn't amazing. Not Stephen himself. He's the best boyfriend I've ever had. He's thoughtful, generous, romantic, and doesn't try to change anything about me. The only slight little snag in our relationship is how he cancels our plans at the last minute more times than not. And I refuse to be one of those whiny, clingy women who constantly complains about something like this. He cancels on me because of his job, not because he wants to hang out with his friends instead or some other bullshit excuse. His job is very important, and I totally get that. It just sucks that we've been dating for six months, and every time I make plans for him to *finally* meet one of my friends, something comes up.

At thirty, I've dated my fair share of losers and douchebags over the years. Every guy I've ever dated, I've met while working. Since I'm out on the town pretty much every night of the week, it's really the only opportunity I have to meet someone. I don't have time for dating apps, I'm always in too big of a rush when I'm grocery shopping to even glance at a guy in the frozen food section, hoping for a love connection over a Lean Cuisine, and I refuse to ever go on another blind date after the one Nicole set me up on two years ago. I stupidly let the guy come up to my apartment after dinner to use the bathroom, and he shit his brains out, overflowing my toilet, and used one of my good towels to wipe his ass, scurrying out of my apartment without so much as a "I had a great time tonight. Sorry I left my shit all over your bathroom floor!"

The only guys I meet at work functions are trust fund babies, who will never have to work a day in their life and don't understand why I can't just blow off a work party to go hang out in the Hamptons on their daddy's yacht.

Which is why I appreciate my relationship with Stephen so much and don't want to do anything to ruin it, like stomp my foot and complain that, at this rate, the first time my friends will meet him will be at our wedding. He made a comment the other night about a certain purchase he made at a jewelry store he found in Paris when he was there last month for a work trip, and I've been freaking out ever since, just waiting for him to pop the question. I thought tonight would be the night, at this beautiful rooftop bar with the glow of the city lights all around us, but I guess not.

I know we've only been together for six months, but when you know you've found the right person, you just know. Stephen Goodwin is thirty-nine, and it's the first time I've ever dated someone that much older than me. I want to kick myself in the ass for not doing it sooner. He's mature, well established with a wonderful job working as a trader on Wall Street, and owns the most beautiful penthouse I've ever seen. He's worked tirelessly to get where he is today. It wasn't just handed to him like so many of the other guys I've dated. He understands hard work, and he never cares how many nights a week I'm at clubs on the Upper East Side to interview an up-and-coming DJ, or hanging out with the rich and famous at a gastro pub in the West Village. He gets it, because he works just as hard, if not harder than I do. I just wish I could spend more time with him.

All of a sudden, the low hum of conversation all around us comes to an abrupt halt, replaced by the loud screeching of a very unhappy woman.

"Let go of my arm and let me through! I know she's in here!"

Nicole and I both crane our necks around the small crowds of people on the roof, trying to see what's happening. Everyone around us is pointing and whispering at the woman being held back by security, who stands right at the elevator that brings you from the lobby of the hotel straight up to the rooftop bar.

She's beautiful in a Barbie doll sort of way. Long, poker-straight blonde hair, tiny waist, and big boobs. She's dressed in a pair of dark, designer skinny jeans, a form-fitting purple, silk sleeveless blouse that I saw on the Dolce and Gabbana runway this past spring, and a nude pair of Jimmy Choo heels I instantly recognize. Stephen just bought me that same pair last week, and I'm wearing them right now. Even though this woman is still shouting and causing a commotion, I feel bad for her. She has good taste in fashion. If she wants to have a few drinks because one of her friends is here or whatever, they should let her in.

After a few tense moments where she finally lowers her voice and talks rationally to the security guard manning the elevator, he gives her a terse nod and lets go of her arm. Sadly, he points toward the elevator and my shoe twin is clearly being told to leave.

The blonde lowers her head dejectedly and starts to turn toward the elevator. Conversation around us resumes, and I open my mouth to tell Nicole I need to find a place to sit down, because as beautiful as these Jimmy Choo's are, they're killing my feet.

"Holy shit!" a guy sitting on one of the outdoor couches next to us shouts.

My poor feet groan in protest as, once again, I look toward the elevator just in time to see Fight Club Barbie throw her fist right into the security guard's stomach before racing around him, shoving people out of the way as she goes.

"I hope you're taking notes. This *has* to go in this month's magazine," Nicole says excitedly, her camera already yanked out of the bag on her shoulder and held up to her eye. The click of the shutter goes a mile a minute as she chronicles everything happening on the other side of the roof.

I start to laugh until I realize the blonde is heading

right in our direction. And her eyes seem to be locked on me.

"I think that's Felicity Kennedy. When did she go from brunette to blonde? Do you know her?" Nicole asks, slowly lowering the camera from her face, noticing this crazy woman is charging right for me, and I'm not just imagining the look of murder in her eyes.

"No! I mean, I don't think we've ever met. She's probably not looking at me. She's probably looking at someone behind me."

Nicole and I both quickly glance over our shoulders, and I realize there is no one behind me, because we're standing right by the glass railing at the edge of the roof.

So much for that idea.

Felicity Kennedy is one of the most popular social-ites in New York City. And yes, she's one of *those* Kennedys. She obviously comes from old money that she likes to flaunt and blow all over the city, and compared to her, calling *me* an "It Girl" is like calling The Empire State Building a shack.

For years, she was on the cover of every tabloid magazine week after week for making poor choices and partying too hard, until about ten years ago when she made a statement that she ran away and got married in a private ceremony. Her new husband was an average, every-day guy who didn't want to be in the limelight, and she asked for everyone to respect their privacy. The paparazzi pretty much laughed in her face and spent years trying to get a photo of them together and figure out who the guy was, but the joke was on them. They have never been spotted in public together, aside from one grainy photo someone snapped with their cellphone at the airport six years ago, of Felicity and some guy leaving the airport. He was hidden behind a big floppy hat, huge sunglasses, and a trench coat with the collar popped up to cover the rest of his face. No one even knows if that was really her husband or not. There have been rumors from day one that they don't even live together.

It's all very strange and the source of so much gossip it's not even funny. Some people think she just told people she got married instead of admitting she left the country to go to rehab. Some think she married her cousin and that's why everything about them is so hush-hush, because *eeeeew*. And my absolute favorite rumor— that Kurt Cobain is still alive, they met in a dive bar where he was in disguise playing new music he'd been writing since he faked his own death, and they have to keep their marriage a secret because Courtney Love would murder them both in a jealous rage. It's my favorite, because who wouldn't want to hear new Kurt Cobain music?

The crowd is now parting for Felicity as people start to recognize her, and she continues making a beeline straight for me. There are camera shutters clicking all around us from other news outlets, as well as people holding up their cellphones and recording videos for Snapchat and wherever else they feel like sharing them. I quickly start to panic when I realize that whatever is about to happen, it's going to happen all over social media.

"She probably has me confused with someone else," I whisper to Nicole hopefully as Felicity finally gets to us and stops two feet in front of me.

Her nostrils are flaring, and her eyes scan me from head to toe like she's trying to figure out the best way to slice off my skin and wear it as a dress.

"Are you Brooklyn Manning?" Felicity asks through clenched teeth.

"Oh, shit," Nicole mutters next to me.

It's fine. Everything is fine. Maybe I accidentally took a taxi she was waiting for earlier. Or maybe she's friends with someone I wrote about in one of my articles, and I'm confusing her "I'm going to slit your throat" face with her "Just wanted to meet you and say thanks" face. It's an honest mistake. Plenty of New Yorkers always look pissed at the world. I'm sure there's a logical explanation for why she crashed this party to find me.

"Um, yes. I'm Brooklyn Manning. It's nice to meet you Miss Kennedy…" I trail off, waiting for her to give me some sort of clue about what she wants with me.

"It's *Mrs.,*" she seethes, as she continues glaring at me. "Mrs. Stephen Kennedy-Goodwin. I believe you've been fucking my husband for the last six months."

There's a collective gasp that echoes from everyone standing within earshot. I don't even have time to let her words penetrate my brain and my heart, or the fact that everyone around us is losing their shit that this woman has finally gone public with who her husband is. Her fist comes flying at my face faster than a herd of women shoving through the doors of a designer clothing store during a sample sale.

The last thing I remember before my world goes black, is seeing Nicole leaning over me with her camera up to her face, clicking away at my amazing life that seems to have just gone to shit.

Chapter 1
Shitty Life

Three Months Later

MY LIFE IS *a dumpster fire.*

  Everything around me has burned to the ground and it smells like rotting flesh. Actually, that's probably *me* who smells like a corpse. I don't think I've taken a shower in four days. I look down at my coffee-stained Gucci T-shirt and Banana Republic skinny jeans, and have a vague recollection of putting them on Tuesday morning. It's now Saturday. Not only do I smell like a corpse from *The Night of the Living Dead,* I also look like one.

Pushing open the door to the bathroom, with nothing but thoughts of a long, hot shower running through my mind, my feet stutter to a stop in the doorway and I let out a scream that would make Jamie Lee Curtis proud.

Smacking my hand over my eyes before I see anything else that will give me nightmares for years to come, I let out a huff of annoyance.

"Dad! What the hell are you doing, and why didn't you lock the door?"

"What does it look like I'm doing? I'm emptying my piss bag. Try knocking next time," he grumbles.

When I hear the toilet flush and the rustle of clothing, I count to ten before slowly spreading my fingers apart and chancing another glance into the room. I find my dad facing me with his arms crossed over his chest, his bare, white ass no longer on full display. Dropping my hand from my face, I try to suppress a full-body shudder when I think about what I just witnessed.

"Stupid doctors making me take those damn pills that make me pee all the time," he complains. "I've had to empty out this catheter four times so far this morning. It's bad enough they had to saw my chest open like I'm some sort of Christmas tree; now they expect me to deal with a tube coming out of my pee hole that I constantly have to empty."

Welcome to hell, ladies and gentleman. Or as I like to call it, my childhood home in White Timber, Montana.

When I got punched in the face by my boyfriend's wife, it took all of seven-point-four seconds before that video of her fist connecting with my cheekbone, and me hitting the ground, to go viral. It took three days for *Glitz* to fire me, because having an "It Girl" who was accused of being a homewrecker wasn't good for business. They also received a million phone calls and emails from Felicity that if they didn't fire me, she would sue them for every penny they had, and own the magazine by the end of the week. If that wasn't bad enough, they took my article I submitted for the rooftop bar, added the story of the jilted wife taking her revenge out on the woman who stole her man, titled it *Hussy Homewrecker*, and my now ex-friend Nicole nicely provided two full-color, glossy photos to go with the article. One of Felicity's fist plowing into my face, and one of me passed out cold on the floor with my skirt up around my waist and my mouth wide open.

At least I was wearing a really nice pair of black, lace La Perla underwear.

I've never felt like a bigger fool in my entire life, wondering why in the hell I never put two-and-two together. But if the entire world didn't know the identity of Felicity's husband, how was I supposed to know? Felicity never went by any name other than Felicity Kennedy until that night on the roof, so it's not like the name Stephen Goodwin rang any bells when I met him. And of course that lying, rat bastard left that part out of the "getting to know you" portion of our relationship.

"My favorite color is red, my favorite food is beef bourguignon, and my favorite drink is whiskey straight up. Oh, and I've been married to the most famous New York City socialite for the last ten years, and if she finds out about you, she'll probably slit your throat. Are you ready to order dessert?"

I may or may not have drank two bottles of wine

one night when I felt particularly sorry for myself, googled that stupid, grainy airport picture from six years ago, and printed it out. I studied it for hours with a magnifying glass app I downloaded to my phone, to prove to myself I wasn't a complete idiot and couldn't have known it was Stephen in that picture. I learned nothing after staring at it for five hours, aside from the fact that two bottles of wine will make me sing "Careless Whisper" by George Michael over and over at the top of my lungs while snot-crying, until my neighbor pounds on my door and tells me if I don't shut up, he's calling the cops. I woke up the next morning with my cheek pressed to that damn picture, and a fucking ink outline of what may or may not have been Stephen the Shit Master imprinted on my face, which took two days to wash off. Two days I also spent not making eye contact with my neighbor every time I left my apartment.

For the next two and half months, I worked my ass off trying to find another job in the city with a different magazine, but it was useless. No one would hire the "hussy homewrecker." Once my savings started disappearing right before my very eyes, I even applied at three pizza places to wait tables, and eight bars with open bartending and hostess positions. As soon as I walked in the door to apply for the jobs, they took one look at me and started laughing. When I say everyone in the city knew who I was, I mean *everyone*. Especially after the home wrecking article was picked up by the *New York Times* and the pictures of me were splashed across the front page.

I couldn't even walk to my favorite coffee shop a block from my apartment without some dickhole asking me if I learned how to dodge a punch yet, or if I still had that lacy pair of underwear and would mind giving them to him as a souvenir.

That was the first time I ever had to use the pepper spray attached to my keychain since I moved to New York. In case you were wondering, they do still spray after twelve years of non-use, and if you accidentally spray yourself in the face first because you're too creeped out to make sure the nozzle is pointing away from you when you press the button, you might almost die from choking on all the snot and tears that pour out of your face.

With exactly fifty dollars left in my checking account, and not a stitch of furniture left in my adorable little apartment on the Upper East Side, because I had to sell it all to be able to afford the astronomical rent in that adorable apartment, I got a phone call that, at the time, I thought was lifesaving.

My father called and asked me to come home because he needed my help.

Which brings this happy little tale up to speed and the reason why I smell like death and walked in on my father emptying his "piss bag." That phone call from him really was a lifesaver, because it got me out of a city that I needed a break from, but it took ten years off my life when I found out why my dad needed me to come home. He decided to tell me four days after the fact that he had to have an emergency triple bypass, and he needed a ride home from the hospital. The phone call went something like this:

"Hi, Dad! Long time no talk. How's it going?"

"They cut my goddamn chest open, and they're finally springing me from the hospital tomorrow. I need a ride. You busy?"

"What? What do you mean they cut your chest open? What happened? Are you okay?"

"This hospital food sucks. They give you pepper but they don't give you salt. How's a man supposed to eat hospital chicken and rice without salt? Are you busy tomorrow or not? I booked you a flight at eight in the morning."

"I-I-I'm not busy. But I'm gonna need a little more information than this."

"I gotta go. Nurse is here and says I need to get up and walk. My nurse is a guy. Isn't that just the craziest shit you've ever heard? A guy nurse. I'm at Cedar Memorial. Room 801. Make it snappy when you land. I need a cheeseburger like nobody's business."

To say my dad and I haven't had the best relationship since I left for college is putting it mildly. He's never once called me in the twelve years I've been gone. I'm always the one to reach out to him if I want to know if he's still alive. I knew as soon as I saw his name flash across the screen of my phone that something was wrong; I just didn't expect it to be *this*.

I've been home for two weeks and I've done nothing but cook, clean, run errands, take my dad to the emergency room three times in the last week because of a bladder infection—hence the need for the current piss bag situation—and constantly argue with him about sitting his ass down and resting. I'm exhausted, I smell, and I'm stuck living in this tiny, crappy town where I swore I'd never live again after I left. But at least I have a roof over my head, food to eat, and, so far, my dad is the only person who knows what happened back in New York. Silver linings and all that shit.

"Why didn't you tell me you needed to go to the bathroom? I would have helped you," I tell my dad as I move out of the bathroom doorway so he can pass, reaching for his arm to steady him and make sure he doesn't fall.

He shakes my hand right off and glares at me before shuffling down the hall and back out into the living room, where he's been sleeping in a recliner since he got home from the hospital.

"I don't need help going to the damn bathroom. Stop nagging me," he grumbles, making me wince when he flops down in his recliner so aggressively that I'm afraid his chest will rip wide open right in front of me.

"I'll stop nagging you when you stop being a stubborn ass. You're supposed to be taking it easy and letting me help you when you need to get up and walk," I remind him, grabbing a blanket off the couch and tucking it around his legs.

He promptly yanks it off and flings it back over to the couch.

"Are you going to be okay while I run to the pharmacy to get your new prescriptions?" I ask, picking up the blanket and refolding it since he's clearly not going to use it.

I grind my teeth together when my eyes catch the framed photo sitting on the end table next to the couch, which I've shoved into a drawer a million times since I got here. It keeps reappearing when I'm not looking. That picture is like herpes. You think it's gone and you can finally live a normal life, and then *bam!* It shows up again to fuck with you.

Most normal fathers have pictures of their daughters on their graduation day framed in their home, or a few cute school yearbook pictures from back in the day, or maybe a sweet candid picture of the two of them together when she was little on a family vacation. Not my father. There's not one photo of me anywhere in the house, and there never has been. He's never showcased any of the thousands of articles I wrote for *Glitz* over the years, or any of the awards I won while working for them, but he sure as shit figured out how to print off that damn picture of me getting punched in the face from the *New York Times* article, and put it in a damn frame in his living room.

"I don't know. It's awful dangerous sitting in this recliner. What if it malfunctions when I pull the lever to put my legs up and it shoots me out the window, the glass nicks an artery, and I bleed out on the front lawn? What if I'm thirsty and don't know how to get up and get my own damn glass of water, and die from thirst in the whole thirty minutes you'll be gone? Maybe you should stay here and just stare at me to make sure I don't die."

He's my father and I love him. He's my father and I love him.

I've repeated this mantra in my head so much over the last two weeks that I can happily say I no longer roll my eyes when I think it.

"Oh, while you're out, you need to stop at the Hastings Farm. I got you a job interview," he mentions casually, grabbing the remote from the arm of the recliner and turning on the television that immediately blares to life so loudly the closest neighbors four miles away can probably hear the Wheel of Fortune theme song.

I snatch the remote out of his hand and mute the volume.

"What do you mean you got me a job interview?"

It's not like I'm planning on living here forever. This is just a temporary setback. Once my dad is back on his feet, the dust settles in New York, and everyone moves on to another scandal that is sure to happen any day now, I fully plan on going back and starting over. I can't stay here. The idea of me staying in White Timber for the rest of my life makes me want to laugh and throw up at the same time. I outgrew this town long before I moved away. I *kept on* growing the longer I stayed away. I'm not cut out for small-town life. I need the hustle and bustle of a big city. I need sirens blaring at two in the morning. I need traffic jams. I need to be able to walk to anything I might possibly need within a five-block radius at all hours of the night, and I need the comfort of being able to flip someone off when I'm crossing the street and they lay on their horn.

The White Timber Walmart, the one and only major chain store within fifty miles, has more parking spots for people who ride their horses there than they do for people who drive cars. And if I flipped off someone while crossing the street in town, they'd get out of their car and give me a thirty-minute lecture about how young ladies should never behave so crassly.

"You were really smart before you left for New York. That place knocked a few IQ points right out of your head, didn't it?" my dad asks with a shake of his head.

I'd argue with him, but I'm too busy being happy that he kind of, sort of paid me a compliment by saying I was smart. Compliments from my dad are few and far between.

I'm so pathetic it's not even funny.

"A job interview is what someone goes to when they have no money," he continues. "You put on some fancy clothes, lie to them about what your strengths and weaknesses are, kiss their ass, and then boom! You get hired and start making money."

I'm honestly surprised my grandparents didn't name him Allen Sarcastic Shit Manning. It has a nice ring to it. Much more fitting than Allen Michael Manning.

"I know what a job interview is, Dad. But I'm not planning on staying here forever. You know that, right?" I ask gently.

"Of course I know that. I just figured you should stick around long enough to at least learn how to block a punch and avoid getting another black eye. Never know when another fist might come flying at your face again," he replies with the first smile I've seen since I got here.

He's my father and I have to love him. He's my father and I have to love him.

"Besides, it's just a temporary job," he continues, leaning forward in his chair and grabbing the remote back out of my hand. "Just because I can't drive for the next two months doesn't mean you need to sit here all the time babysitting me. The Hastings are in a bind, and I told them you'd help out while you're here."

I let out a long sigh when he aims the remote at the television, presses a button, and Pat Sajak loudly asks the contestant if they'd like to solve the puzzle.

Honestly, I don't know how much more of this I can handle day in and day out. All my dad does is watch The Gameshow Network, play slot machines on his laptop I got him for Christmas a few years ago, and bitch at me for hovering. I know the Hastings family, and their pumpkin farm is only a few miles down the road. My best friend from kindergarten to our senior year of high school, Ember Hastings, lived there, and I practically lived there right along with her I spent so much time on the farm. We're not best friends any longer, but not a day goes by that I don't think about her. We're Facebook friends at best, at this point. Sometimes she'd like one of my pictures where I was attending an event. Sometimes I'd comment on a picture of her at her parent's farm, telling her how many good memories I had there, and so on and so forth. I know she still lives close by, never feeling the need to leave White Timber like I did, and I'm suddenly excited about the prospect of being home, working at the farm for a few months, and maybe catching up with her. Nothing makes you realize how fake the friends you had in New York were like a crotch shot in a major newspaper.

"I can't believe Old Man Hastings still runs that place," I muse, referring to Ember's father.

"He's the same age as I am. I don't know why all you kids felt the need to call him that when you were younger. It's insulting to our entire generation," Dad complains dramatically.

"Because he was a mean old son of a bitch. And you're just a delight, so there's no need to be insulted." I give him a cheeky smile, and it suddenly occurs to me that maybe *my* middle name should have been Sarcastic Shit as well. "What do they need help with?" I ask tentatively.

Sure, I wouldn't mind getting out of the house and away from my dad for a few hours every day, as well as being able to make some of my own money so I don't have to tuck my tail between my legs and feel like the biggest loser in the world every time I need to ask him for a few bucks to get toiletries and stuff like that. There's really nothing more humiliating than asking your dad for twenty dollars because you need tampons and Midol. But the idea of shoveling horse shit all day, or something equally as disgusting, doesn't make me feel all warm and fuzzy.

"I don't know, something to do with house management. You know how big that farm has gotten over the years. They're the biggest pumpkin farm in the state, and they're always busy with something or other. They've got so many employees now I've lost count. The job is pretty much yours. You just need to go over there and meet with… the employees you'll be supervising or some shit." He shrugs, looking away from me and at the TV.

Huh. House management. That's pretty much what I do here anyway. I could get away from my dad *and* get paid for doing the same stuff I do here all day. Plus, I'll have employees to manage. I do like telling people what to do. And since the farm is only a few miles down the road, if there's an emergency with my dad, it wouldn't take me any time at all to get back here to him.

"All right, I'll go. As long as you're okay with it."

"I don't know. This recliner is looking at me funny. Could shoot me out that window aaany minute now," he mutters under his breath, never taking his eyes off the TV.

"Jesus. Okay, okay, I get the picture," I tell him with a shake of my head, as I turn and walk toward the hallway that will take me to my old bedroom so I can shower and change, yelling over my shoulder as I go. "You're a big boy and you can take care of yourself. Just remember that next time you're screaming in pain for me to take you to the emergency room because it burns when you pee!"

"Nobody likes a smartass, Brooklyn Marie Manning!"

Said the king of the smartasses.

Chapter 2
WTF Life

PULLING DOWN THE long gravel driveway for Hastings Farm reminds me just how beautiful Montana is. Even though my dad's house is only seven miles away, Hastings Farm is seven miles closer to the mountains. As I drive past acres and acres of corn and pumpkin fields lined with a white picket fence, the giant white farmhouse comes into sight, along with a sprawling view of the mountains behind it.

I've been back to White Timber a handful of times over the years to visit my dad at Christmas and a few other holidays, but I've never gone anywhere except from the airport to his house, and then scrambled right back to the airport as soon as humanly possible. I'd break all the speed limits so I could get back to civilization and the nirvana of twenty-four-hour taco trucks.

As I pull my dad's red, beat up Chevy truck that he's had since Eisenhower was president up to the front of the farmhouse, I'm more than a little surprised at the sight before me. The Hastings' farmhouse was always huge and beautiful in its own way, but it was your typical Montana farmhouse that had been in the family for generations. The white paint was chipped all over the place until so much of the original wood was showing that the house looked more dark gray than white. The small front porch always had a few boards missing from the railing and seemed one footstep away from collapsing in on itself, and the roof would lose at least twenty new shingles every year that never got replaced. Since Old Man Hastings was always so busy with the farm, he never really cared much about landscaping or window treatments. Whenever Mrs. Hastings would complain about the state of the house, he would tell her "fancy curtains didn't pay the bills."

Still, I loved that house and the memories I made there with my friend. Growing up in a small, three-bedroom ranch home, being at the Hastings' farmhouse was like going to a mansion, no matter how dilapidated it looked on the outside. I had this weird idea that people who lived in houses with stairs were rich and cool and amazing. I was fascinated by houses with staircases, and this farmhouse had the most amazing set of stairs with a landing right in the middle of it.

As I get out of the truck and the rusty door creaks loudly behind me when I slam it closed, I stare up at the house in front of me with my mouth dropped open.

The house was originally an old barn, and it was converted into a home sometime in the early 1900s. The magnificent structure in front of me no longer looks dilapidated and run down. It has brand new, sparkly white siding, one of those new, fancy, red metal roofs, and the small rundown front porch has been removed. In its place is a huge, wraparound porch lined with red Adirondack chairs that takes up the entire front of the house and wraps around both sides all the way back to the end of it. Professional landscaping with black mulch lines the base of the porch and it's filled with beautiful flowers and neatly trimmed hedges.

I knew Hastings Farm had grown by leaps and bounds over the years, but I wasn't expecting *this*. Old Man Hastings must have finally pulled that stick out of his ass and decided to spruce up the place now that they get thousands and thousands of customers each year traipsing all over the farm.

Smoothing my hands down the sides of my emerald green, sleeveless, Donna Karan wrap dress, I make my way across the gravel driveway to the brick walkway that leads up to the porch. My matching green Louboutin heels click against the surface, and I glance nervously around the yard at a bunch of workers milling about, carrying bales of hay out of the big red barn an acre away and working on a few tractors parked next to the barn. They're all dirty and sweaty and wearing jeans and T-shirts, and I feel extremely overdressed for this interview, even though I'll be working in the house and not out in the fields. I know my dad said the job was basically mine, but I still need to make a good impression.

I pause on the top step when my eyes travel over to the horse pasture. A tingle races up my spine when I see a man on a horse, clutching the reins and bent low over the beautiful, black Arabian's neck as he races along the fence line. He's wearing a blue-checkered flannel and a white cowboy hat, and I feel like I just stepped onto a movie set for a western.

"Cut! Let's do that scene again, but this time, jump the fence, race over to the stunning woman in the green dress, grab her arm, and pull her up on the horse behind you."

That's one thing you never see in New York—a real, live cowboy. It's nice to know Stephen didn't kill everything inside of me, and I try not to pant when the man pulls the horse to a stop, expertly swings his leg over the saddle, and dismounts. Even from this distance, I can see how well he fills out that worn pair of jeans, and I have to force myself to stop staring at his ass as he bends over to check one of the horse's hooves.

I curse myself under my breath and force my eyes away from that great ass to move the rest of the way up the steps to the front door. No more men for me. Ever. Maybe when I move back to New York I'll become a nun. I'm not Catholic, but I'm sure they'll make an exception for me. I look great in black. And I know a few prayers that my dad taught me when I was younger. *"Here's to you. Here's to me. Friends for life, we'll always be. But if we find that we disagree, fuck you, here's to me!"*

Actually, I think that's a toast, but whatever. Catholics drink wine at church, right? It's fine.

Taking a few deep breaths to calm my nerves, I run my fingers through my long, dark brown hair, wishing I was able to wash it in something other than White Rain shampoo from the White Timber drug store. I really hope my theory is right and Old Man Hastings isn't a crotchety bastard anymore and hires me. I should probably stop calling him Old Man Hastings, but for the life of me, I can't remember his first name. Even Ember would call her dad Old Man Hastings when he wasn't around. I'll just go with Mr. Hastings. It's professional, and I am nothing if not professional.

As I lift my hand to knock on the door, it flies open before my fist can connect with the wood.

"Mrs. Sherwood?" I ask in surprise when I see the older woman standing in front of me.

Her short salt-and-pepper hair is all askew, and what looks like a mixture of flour and red paint is splattered all over the front of her white blouse. At least I hope it's paint. If it's blood, I will continue ruining my hair with White Rain shampoo and asking my dad for money to buy tampons until the day I leave.

"Brooklyn Manning! My, oh my, didn't you grow up into a beautiful young woman!" she exclaims, making me smile brightly at her compliment.

Arlene Sherwood has been the Hastings' house-keeper for as long as I can remember. She always had some kind of delicious baked good waiting for Ember and me after school, and she made doing homework and studying for tests fun by doling out Skittles to us every time we got an answer right. We never bitched and moaned when she forced us to go outside and play instead of staying inside, because she always put together exciting little treasure hunts for us around the farm, complete with hand-drawn maps and a pot of gold (box of penny candy from the White Timber drug store) for us to find at the end.

I'm surprised to see she still works here. She's got to be around the same age as my dad, and I figured she would have left years ago. Not just because of her age, but because I assumed she would have been in prison for killing Old Man Hastings. Er, *Mr.* Hastings.

"Come in, come in! You just look so gorgeous, and here I am looking like something the cat dragged in," she complains with a laugh as she holds the door open for me.

I preen like a peacock walking through the door, considering I haven't been able to have my hair colored in three months. My hair is no longer a silky, shiny shade of Dark Chocolate Mahogany from the expensive salon I went to in Manhattan. It's more like "I'm Too Poor to Dye It, Gross Brown."

As soon as Mrs. Sherwood closes the door behind me, I feel like I've walked into a time warp. The outside of the farmhouse got a makeover, but the inside is exactly how I last saw it twelve years ago, complete with the smell of Pine Sol she uses on every wood surface in the place. I take a deep breath, and I'm instantly transported back to warm summer nights catching lightning bugs in mason jars, when all of New York City didn't know what color underwear I wore, or accuse me of being a homewrecker. There's no sixty-year-old man emptying his catheter in front of me, or pouting because I won't let him eat bacon wrapped in bacon, deep fried in bacon fat, stuffed inside a Twinkie.

It's peaceful and it's calming, and I want to stay here forever.

"Sorry I'm such a mess. It's been a rough morning," Mrs. Sherwood explains as she leads me into the kitchen right off the entryway, my eyes widening in shock when I step into the large room.

The kitchen *definitely* got an upgrade. No more stained and faded yellow linoleum tile. No more plastic, laminate countertops in the same awful yellow color. No more cheap oak cabinets. And no more appliances that dated back to the 70s.

My eyes take in the white subway tiles that line the walls, my heels clicking against dark gray wood flooring. I run my hand along the beautiful white and dark gray marble countertop as I move into the room, and I practically drool over all the white cabinets and shining, stainless steel appliances.

I smile when I see a pan of monkey balls sitting on the butcher block island in the middle of the room. It's a funny name for a dessert, but it's the most delicious thing I've ever tasted, and I'm immediately nostalgic. Mrs. Sherwood used to let us help her dip the little balls of dough in melted butter, roll them in cinnamon and sugar, and then stick them all together in a loaf pan. It was messy, but the end result was definitely worth it. My had quickly darts out to pull one of the dough balls away from the gooey pile in the pan.

"No!" Mrs. Sherwood shouts, causing me to snap my hand back in alarm. "Sorry, those are for—"

"Oh, no. *I'm* sorry! They're probably for the employees, right? My dad said I'd be managing a few of them or something. It's wonderful you have help inside the house. How many other employees are there?"

She looks at me funny, and as she starts to open her mouth, a loud screeching sound followed by a crash comes from another room on the far side of the house. There's more screeching that almost sounds like a cat dying, followed by another crash and a loud thump, and then silence. The silence is almost worse than whatever the hell *that* was.

Shit. Maybe that really is *blood on her shirt.*

"Is everything—"

"Shhh! Don't make a sound. If we're really, really

quiet, maybe they won't know we're here," Mrs. Sherwood whispers, her eyes wide with fear as she nervously glances out the kitchen doorway.

What the fuck kind of people do they have employed here?

All of a sudden, the silence disappears and all hell breaks loose. The pounding of footsteps down the hall sounds like a herd of elephants is on its way toward us, and ear-piercing screams echo through the house, making me want to cover my ears before they start bleeding.

"Sweet, merciful Jesus, take me now," Mrs. Sherwood mutters as I take a few steps back and hide behind the woman, bracing myself for whatever is about to crash into the room and devour our souls.

I know, I know! I shouldn't be using the poor woman as a shield, but she's in her sixties. She's had a good, long life. I'm only thirty, for fuck's sake! I still have a lot of living left to do. I have a reputation to fix, and for the love of all that is holy, I can't die with hair like this! My tombstone would say **Here lies Brooklyn Manning. Would you just look at her hair? Such a travesty. No wonder she was such a hussy.**

As the thundering of footsteps and the screams get louder and closer, I slowly peek my head around Mrs. Sherwood's shoulder, and my worst nightmare comes flying around the corner and into the room.

"She pulled my hair!"

"She took Rabbit Foo-Foo and put him in the toilet!"

"Did not!"

"Did too!"

"You're such a baby!"

"Stop calling me a baby!"

"*Girls*!" Mrs. Sherwood bellows at the top of her lungs, holding her hands up in the air to quiet the two demons standing in front of her. "That's enough! If I hear one more word out of either of you, no monkey balls!"

The two monsters straight from the pits of hell immediately clamp their mouths closed.

To say I'm not much of a kid lover is putting it mildly. They're loud, and messy, and you can't take them in public without packing up your entire house with all the shit they need. And don't even get me started on parents. I don't need to know how many months old your little darling is. She's *two*, Karen, not twenty-four months. When she goes to college, are you going to tell people your 216-month-old got accepted to Stanford?

Mrs. Sherwood turns around to face me and gives me an encouraging smile that makes my blood run cold.

"Brooklyn, meet your … *employees,* Mia and Grace. You'll be their nanny this summer."

What. In. The. Actual. Fuck?

Chapter 3
Sticky Life

WHEN I WAS a teenager, my dad had this friend from his construction job named Rodney Johnson. Rodney was a single father, just like my dad. Unlike my dad, whose wife left him—and me—because she got tired of being a wife and a mother and living out in Bumfuck, Nowhere, Rodney's wife died during childbirth. My dad would invite Rodney over once a week for dinner and a few hands of poker with some of his friends from the Rotary Club, to give him a break from his infant daughter. That break was courtesy of me.

At thirteen, while I was still trying to deal with the misery of having a mother who up and left without a backward glance, and a father who refused to even mention her name again and threw away any photo we had of her, I was stuck learning how to take care of a baby for a few hours every week in my bedroom, while the guys smoked cigars out in the kitchen and drank whiskey. They laughed and played cards and talked about "the good old days," and I paced around my room, wondering how something so small could scream and puke so much.

Rodney would knock on the doorframe of my room at the end of the night, pull a few sweaty, wrinkled dollar bills out of his back pocket, and shove them in my hand as I practically tossed his baby at him, thanking me for taking care of his sweet girl before making a hasty exit. His "sweet girl" could practically spin her head all the way around on her neck while spewing puke all over my hair, and I swear if the light hit her face just right, her eyes glowed red. Three dollars covered in ass sweat was not worth that nightmare week after week, but I saved every penny for the next three years, as well as my allowance, and it gave me the ability to buy a piece of shit car on my sixteenth birthday and make sure I was never, ever home again on poker night.

This is most definitely where my abhorrence for all things children stems from. If the air blows just right, I can still smell the puke in my hair. I'm not like those women whose ovaries clench with longing whenever they hear a baby cry. My ovaries shrivel up and die if a baby so much as glances in my general direction.

As I stand here in the Hastings' kitchen, still hiding behind Mrs. Sherwood while I stare at the two little heathens standing in front of me, covered in the same mixture of flour and what I'm just going to assume at this point is the blood of whatever animal or human they were sacrificing in their bedroom, I realize they aren't babies. They can walk and talk and if stupid *Karen* were here right now, she'd probably tell me they were between the ages of sixty and eight-thousand months. Whatever. Math is stupid. I'm assuming Nosferatu is somewhere around that age, and since these are clearly his offspring, my math is probably right.

I have to say, they are kind of adorable when they aren't speaking. They each have a long mess of dirty blonde hair, bright green eyes that match the color of my dress, and the taller one has a spattering of freckles across the bridge of her nose. That bigger one is also looking at me almost the same way as Felicity did that night of the bar opening—like she's wondering what would be the easiest way to kill me and make it look like an accident. The younger one grabs a handful of her long hair and shoves in into her mouth, making me cringe in disgust.

Mrs. Sherwood moves away from me to grab the pan of monkey balls off the counter, and before I can scramble after her and cling to her body for protection, the shorter one spits the hair out of her mouth, races across the room, and plows into me, wrapping her tiny arms around my legs and squeezing the hell out of me.

"Oh, God. Why are you sticky?" I mutter, holding my hands up in the air like I'm at a 7-11 and some guy just pulled out a gun.

Take whatever you want! Just get this kid off me!

Her wet and mysteriously sticky hands cling to the backs of my knees as she stares up at me, and I have to swallow back the vomit that is creeping up my throat. Who knows what the hell is on her hands? She's a kid. It could be any number of things. Gum, chocolate, the entrails of her former nanny....

"You're pretty," she tells me with a toothy smile, a giant gap in her bottom row of teeth where one of them is missing.

It's almost adorable until she sticks the tip of her tongue through that hole and wiggles it at me, like some sort of creepy worm.

"Mia, let go of Miss Manning. You'll get her pretty dress all dirty," Mrs. Sherwood scolds.

Mia doesn't listen. She just clings to me tighter, and a shiver of revulsion travels through my body when I feel stickiness dripping down the back of my leg.

"I don't need a babysitter. Especially one like *her*. Who dresses like that to come to a farm?"

Since Mia is the one getting her germs all over me and is still waving her tongue at me through the hole in her teeth, the charming angel glaring at me with her arms folded across her chest must be Grace.

"This dress is a Donna Karan," I scoff.

"Well, Donna sucks and it's ugly," she fires back.

Oh, no she did not!

I wonder if she's the one responsible for Mia's missing tooth. She looks like she has a great right hook and wouldn't hesitate to punch her sister in the face.

Maybe *she* could teach me how to dodge a punch. I let out a hysterical giggle at just how much my life has fallen apart.

"Grace, behave," Mrs. Sherwood admonishes, giving her a stern look that just makes the girl roll her eyes and huff.

Mrs. Sherwood holds out the pan of monkey balls to Grace, and when the girl turns her nose up at them, Mrs. Sherwood just sighs and puts the pan back on the counter. What kind of a person turns down freshly made monkey balls? Does she not understand the deliciousness that is dough covered in melted butter, cinnamon, and sugar? This kid definitely isn't human.

I can't be a *nanny*. I don't even *like* kids. How in the hell am I supposed to nanny them? What does nannying even entail? Don't they like, change diapers and feed them bottles and put them down for naps? Grace looks like she'd slit my throat if I even suggested a nap. I could probably take her. I'm twice her size. But putting a kid in a choke hold would do nothing for my reputation. I don't need to be known as the hussy, home wrecking, kid wrestler.

All of a sudden, it occurs to me that these are probably Ember's daughters. I knew she got married and had a kid or seven, but I'm Facebook friends with pretty much everyone from high school. They all have kids.

Kids all look the same. They're always dirty and usually have a finger in their nose. I scroll past those pictures faster than the random dick pics that creepers send me.

Shit. Shit, shit, shit.

I can't just say no to being a nanny to Ember's kids. Not only do I need the money, I can't exactly rekindle an old friendship by telling her that her kids gross me out.

"Are they housetrained?" I ask Mrs. Sherwood.

She just shakes her head and laughs at me.

Seriously, answer the question! Why is that funny?

"We're not puppies. God, you're an idiot," Grace mutters.

The sound of the front door opening and slamming closed saves me from telling Grace to suck it.

I should probably google how to behave around kids when I get back to Dad's house later.

"Daddy!" Mia screams, finally taking her sticky hands off of me and racing out of the kitchen.

A few seconds later, the man I saw riding the horse out front walks into the room with his cowboy hat-covered head tipped down low so I can't see his face, carrying Mia in his arms.

Oh, screw you, ovaries!

No, I still don't like children, but come on! Seeing a hot, manly cowboy wearing tight jeans, with his cowboy boots thumping across the floor, and carrying a kid in his arms would make anyone weak. Too bad he's

Ember's husband. Damn. I should have paid better attention to her Facebook photos. Lucky, lucky girl.

And then he lifts his head and our eyes meet.

Wait just one damn minute. This isn't possible. There's no fucking way.

"You!" I shout, my eyes bugging out of my head.

"What the hell is *she* doing here?" he growls, setting Mia down on the ground.

My only source of happiness right now is that Mia presses her face to his jean clad leg and wipes her nose back and forth against the material, leaving a trail of snot behind.

Clint Hastings. Ember's older brother and my arch nemesis growing up.

Whatever. I know I'm not a superhero in a comic book, but this guy has been the bane of my existence since the day I met him when I was in kindergarten, he was in second grade, and he threw a rock at my head. I kicked him in his tiny nuggets first, since he told me I couldn't play baseball with him and his friends because I was a girl, but that's not the point. If this *were* a comic book and we were meeting in a dark alley, I'd be holding my fists above my head next to a talk bubble that says **So, we meet again. Tonight I will get my revenge and you will die by my iron fists!** *WHAM! BAM! KAPOW!*

I cannot *believe* I was checking out his ass when I got here. There's got to be a bottle of bleach somewhere in

43

this kitchen I can pour into my eyes.

"What am *I* doing here? What are *you* doing here? Aren't you supposed to be off in Silicon Valley becoming the next Mark Zuckerberg?" I ask, making sure my eyes stay above his neck and aren't tempted to head south and see if those tiny nuggets hugged in his tight jeans grew in size since the last time I threw my foot into them.

Which would have been his senior year of high school, right here in this very kitchen, at his graduation party when he asked me if I bought the dress I was wearing in the toddler section.

It was a LBD! It was supposed to be tight and tiny, god-dammit!

And seriously, what is he doing here? Last I heard through the high school grapevine, after he graduated from UCLA, he became a hotshot software developer at some huge company in Los Angeles and hadn't been back home in years. Not that I ever asked. Or cared. You know, just idle chitchat after one too many glasses of wine and a friend request on Facebook from someone we went to high school with.

"Awww, have you been keeping tabs on me all these years, fancy pants? I knew you always had a thing for me." Clint smirks.

"In your dreams. You smell like horse shit."

"You *look* like horse shit," he fires back, that stupid grin never leaving his face.

"Horse shit!" Mia shouts with a smile, throwing her tiny, sticky fists in the air.

"Girls, why don't you go up to your rooms and find something to do," Mrs. Sherwood wisely suggests.

I'm guessing you aren't supposed to swear in front of kids. Maybe Clint needs a few Google lessons on child rearing as well.

Surprisingly, Mia and Grace turn without a word and march out of the room. When they're out of earshot, Mrs. Sherwood puts her hands on her hips and gives us each a reproaching look.

"You two haven't seen each other in twelve years. Isn't it about time you bury the hatchet and end this ridiculous hatred for each other?" she questions.

"She told the entire high school I lost my virginity to my computer and set it on fire," Clint complains.

"Oh, come on! It was a joke. Like anyone believed that. Besides, your penis was entirely too tiny to start any fires by thrusting it in the USB port." I snicker, remembering the day I started that rumor and the beauty of Clint's face when he heard it after lunch.

"Aren't you supposed to be living the high life in New York? I thought you swore you'd never come back to this one-horse town. Have a nice *trip*? See you next *fall*." He grins.

"I knew it!" I shout, pointing my finger at him. "I knew you tripped me during that homecoming game my freshman year, you rat bastard!"

That trumpet player in the band who pointed and laughed at me? That was Clint.

Yes, I'm still holding a grudge about that shit. Grudges and I are old friends. We have wine together every Thursday and talk about old times and all the people we hate. It's a very therapeutic relationship.

"All right, that's enough!" Mrs. Sherwood scolds. "My goodness, you two are worse than the girls."

Your honor, I object!

"Clint," she continues. "Brooklyn is going to be the girl's nanny this summer, so stop acting like a toddler and use your manners."

I stick my tongue out at him behind Mrs. Sherwood's back, pulling it in quickly when she turns to face me, which gives Clint the opportunity to give me the finger when she's no longer looking at him.

"Brooklyn, we really need you. I'm getting too old to handle the girls full-time now that they're out of school for the summer."

She looks me up and down and gives me a sheepish smile.

"You might want to wear something… a little less fancy when you come over tomorrow. You look wonderful," she quickly adds. "But, you know. The girls can be a little messy."

I notice Clint is now staring down at my legs right along with Mrs. Sherwood, and he has a gleam in his eyes that I don't like one bit.

"See you tomorrow, fancy pants. Make sure you

wash the shit off your legs before you go to bed tonight." He winks, touching the brim of his cowboy hat before sauntering out of the room.

I quickly look down at my legs, and my eyes widen in horror when I see something brown and gooey dripping down the left one, clearly the mysterious sticky substance Mia wiped all over me when she came in the room.

"It's not shit! It's chocolate from your messy, sticky kid!" I shout after him.

Oh, God. Please let it be chocolate and not actual shit.

My hair damn well better appreciate the hell I'm going to endure in the name of good conditioning.

Chapter 4
Pouting Life

For at least nine months, I've been having this same dream almost every night. I'm driving my car down a road, listening to music and perfectly happy, and then all of a sudden, my car swerves off the road and there's nothing I can do to stop it. I hit mailboxes, I run over garbage cans, I frighten small children who run screaming out of my way, and I turf every lawn I drive through. I always wake up right before I crash into something, like a house or a brick wall. I had that damn dream again last night after I finally managed to fall asleep, and decided to google it. All this time, I thought maybe that dream meant I should start obeying speed limit signs, and stop joking that those numbers are just a suggestion. It turns out, that dream means I'm being irresponsible with my choices. Which makes sense now, considering those stupid dreams started right around the time I met Stephen. And of *course* I had another one on the day I saw Clint Hastings again for the first time in years and took a job being a nanny to his kids.

Clint fucking Hastings.

I still can't believe I was ogling his ass yesterday. I had to take two scalding hot showers when I got home just to try and scrub the ickyness from my skin. I will never admit this out loud to anyone, but I always thought Clint was cute, in a nerdy, boy next door kind of way. When I spread the rumor that he lost his virginity to his computer, it really wasn't that outlandish of a lie. He'd converted the entire basement of the farmhouse into a computer workshop, with computer pieces and parts sitting on every available surface, which he tinkered with whenever he was home. At school, he spent every free period in the computer lab. When most teenage boys were stealing their dad's *Playboy* and *Penthouse* magazines and hiding out in a barn to drool over the pictures of naked women, Clint would be locked in his bedroom orgasming over the newest edition of *PC World*.

Great. Now I'm thinking about Clint and his orgasm face.

I don't even understand the Clint Hastings I saw yesterday. He was wearing *jeans*. Well-worn jeans that hugged his thighs and ass. I could actually see the muscle definition in his thighs when he bent to set Mia down. In high school, Clint wouldn't have been caught dead in a pair of jeans. He always looked like he was heading off to an IT meeting, in his freshly pressed khakis and crisp button down that never failed to be neatly tucked into his dress pants.

And the fact that he was on a horse, clearly doing work around the farm, just blows my mind. Old Man Hastings used to yell at Clint on a daily basis to stop tinkering with his stupid electronics and help out in the fields. I also started a rumor back then that he was a vampire since he rarely left that dark basement, and I assumed it was because the sunlight would burn his skin. His pale, teenage face has been replaced with a five o'clock shadow of scruff, and the bronzed color of his skin from working outside makes his green eyes even brighter.

It's not fair that he got hotter with age, has two beautiful—albeit satanic—daughters, and probably has the perfect life, when I'm standing at the threshold of hell and my life is in shambles. The only bright spot is that I'm sure his kids will be in prison before they turn eighteen.

"If you keep pouting like that, a bird is gonna come along and shit on your lip."

I angrily shovel another mouthful of yogurt and granola into my mouth and glare at my dad. "I'm not pouting. I don't pout."

"You're pouting. You're two seconds away from throwing yourself on the floor and having yourself a good, old-fashioned temper tantrum." He chuckles with a shake of his head, picking up a piece of turkey bacon, curling his lip at it, and then tossing it back on his plate.

"This shit tastes like the bottom of my shoe."

Pushing my chair away from the table, I grab his plate and stomp over to the sink, dumping everything down the drain.

"Hey, I wasn't finished," he complains as I turn on the garbage disposal to drown out the sound of his voice for a few seconds.

Flipping the switch to shut it off, I turn around and cross my arms as I lean back against the counter.

"You're not getting real bacon, so get used to it."

"Just because you're in a pissy mood doesn't mean you need to take it out on bacon. What did bacon ever do to you?" he questions.

"It gave you three ninety-percent blockages in your arteries, that's what it did to me," I remind him.

"Listen, it took me sixty years to do that much damage. Now that they've fixed me, I have at least another sixty years of good eating left in me." He shrugs.

"That's not how this works."

I shake my head at him, turning back around to rinse off the dishes in the sink from breakfast, and the ones I left here last night after dinner. I was too grumpy to do anything after I made dinner, other than make sure my dad was comfortable in his chair and lock myself in my bedroom to think about what happened out at the Hastings' Farm. My mood didn't get any better when Stephen sent me a text, begging me to call him for the hundredth time, which I ignored, just like the other text messages he's sent and voice mails he's left since I fled from New York. Even lying on my bed, staring up at a poster of Joshua Jackson from his days on *Dawson's Creek* still taped to my ceiling didn't help my mood.

Oh, Pacey, why hath you forsaken me?

"I can't believe you lied to me about what the job was at Hastings Farm, or clue me in on the fact that Clint works there," I mutter over my shoulder, as I load the dishes into the dishwasher.

"I didn't lie. I fudged the truth a little bit. And Clint doesn't just work there, he runs the place. His dad got the cancer right after Clint graduated from college and couldn't handle running the place anymore. He told Clint he could either have the farm or they were gonna sell it. Clint already had Grace at that point and decided he'd like to raise her here instead of in California, and he didn't want the farm leaving the family," my dad replies, meeting me at the sink with our coffee cups.

Interesting.

I knew Old Man Hastings got cancer. I saw a Facebook post about it and sent Ember my condolences via Facebook Messenger. She never said a word about Clint moving back home, though.

I snatch the coffee cups out of my dad's hand and rinse them out.

"You know I'm not a fan of kids. Especially kids that belong to Clint. No wonder Mrs. Sherwood can't handle them. He passed his sparkling personality on to them," I mutter, thinking about the death stare Grace aimed at me the entire time I was in the kitchen, and her insult of Donna Karan.

"Those girls haven't had an easy go of it, and neither has Clint. He's a good, hardworking man. He gave up everything to come back home and take over the family business. You two might actually get along and realize you have more in common than you think if you'd take that stick out of your ass and give him a chance," my dad chastises.

"I've grown fond of the stick up my ass. It's a built-in jerk repellant."

My dad shakes his head at me and walks away from the sink.

"Hey!" I shout, drying my hands on a towel and turning around as he pauses in the doorway. "What about the girls' mother? Why isn't she around to watch her own kids? Does he have her chained up in the basement or something? Oooh, she was a mail order bride, wasn't she? Did her visa expire and she got shipped back to whatever country he bought her from?"

My dad sighs heavily and pinches the bridge of his nose.

"There's this thing we do here in Montana that you might not be familiar with after living in New York for so long. It's called *polite conversation*, otherwise known as *talking*. You should try it with Clint, instead of always throwing insults at him. You catch more flies with honey," he reminds me before turning and walking out of the room.

"Yeah, well, flies are annoying and pesky, and I don't really *want* to catch them!" I yell after him.

Polite conversation with Clint Hastings? Nope. Never gonna happen. It's fine. I'm a resourceful woman. I'm sure I can find out everything I want to know about the guy just by spending five minutes in town and asking the right questions. Not that I really *care* about Clint, or feel bad that he hasn't had an easy go of it. Just simple curiosity. I'm going to be taking care of the guy's kids for the summer. It'll be like doing research on a new employer, which is always the most important part of any job.

Unfortunately, my research will have to wait. With a look at the clock hanging on the wall next to the kitchen doorway, I realize I have less than an hour to get ready for my first day of being a nanny. I wonder if my dad still has all his old hockey gear from when I was younger and he used to play on a league with some of his friends from work. I'm thinking a face mask, heavy duty padding, and a nice, hard stick will help me handle those two little spawns of Clint Satan.

Chapter 5
Bullshit Life

"BROOKLYN! OH MY God, you're really here!"

As soon as I step down out of my dad's truck in front of the Hastings' farmhouse, all the trepidation about dealing with Mia and Grace today, as well as dealing with their equally annoying father, disappear in an instant when I hear Ember's voice.

I have just enough time to close the truck door and brace myself before she slams into me, wraps her arms around my waist, and hugs me tightly to her. We stand in the driveway hugging and laughing, and it feels like no time at all has passed since the last time I saw her. She still smells like Beautiful from Este Lauder, and I don't even try to hide the fact that I'm sniffing her hair, which makes her laugh even harder as we continue squeezing the life out of each other. She started buying that shit with the money she earned on the farm when we were teenagers, because it was the fanciest perfume they sold at the White Timber drug store, and I love that nothing has changed in that aspect.

I also love that my chin can still rest comfortably on top of her head. Since she's just barely five feet tall, I always used to call her my little wood sprite and tease her about how I could put her in my pocket and take her everywhere with me. People in town used to joke and call us twins, even though it was glaringly obvious we weren't. Ember is a tiny midget, and I'm 5'8". She has light blonde hair with natural caramel highlights, and I have dark brown hair that's almost closer to black. She has chocolate brown eyes, and I have light blue eyes that are so pale they're more gray than blue.

When we finally pull apart, she holds tightly to my hands and gives them a squeeze as we continue staring at each other. I'm not really an emotional person, but right now, standing here with Ember on her family's farm, I have to swallow back the tears. I never realized until just this moment how much I missed her hugs. Or hugging people in general. New Yorkers air kiss each other's cheeks or give firm handshakes. They don't hug. Not even people who have known each other for years. I had a friend in college named Stephanie. We roomed together all four years and even shared an apartment together for three years after we graduated. I considered her one of my closest friends in my entire life, second to Ember. When she got married and moved to Staten Island, it was like she moved to another country. We spoke on the phone every once in a while, but the next time I actually saw her in person was a few years ago at a grand opening for a restaurant. It was the first time we'd seen each other in three years, and when I leaned in to give her a hug, she put her arm out between us and awkwardly patted my shoulder.

That memory makes me quickly let go of Ember's hands, wrap my arms around her, and give her another big hug.

"I missed you so much. Quick, tell me how shitty of a friend I am and how much you hate me before I start crying," I tell her, taking another big sniff of her hair before finally letting her go.

"You're a shitty friend and I hate you. Especially because your boobs are still nice and perky and I could bounce a quarter off your ass," she complains.

I laugh and shake my head at her.

"You're not supposed to compliment me. You're supposed to make me feel like crap. You suck at this."

"Fine. I can see your roots, and holy shit! Is that a gray hair?" she asks with wide eyes as she stands up on her toes and reaches her hand out toward the top of my head.

I quickly smack her hand away, but I still can't wipe the smile off my face, even though she insulted my hair.

"Sorry, that's the best I can do. I think you've had enough things going on in your life to make you feel like crap. You don't need my help." She shrugs.

That's all it takes for the smile to slowly disappear

from my face.

"Fuck. You know," I moan.

"If it makes you feel any better, I'm pretty sure I'm the only person in White Timber with Wi-Fi and a smartphone. I got the Google alert as soon as the first person uploaded that punch to SnapChat," she explains.

If Ember knows, that means Clint knows. I'm really not all that upset about Ember knowing about my pathetic drama, but the fact that Clint has one more weapon in his arsenal to use against me makes me want to run to the nearest bushes and throw up. I can't let that guy have the upper hand, or I'll never survive the rest of this summer.

Sensing my mounting panic, Ember quickly grabs my arm and squeezes it reassuringly.

"I didn't tell anyone. I know we haven't really kept in touch very well all these years, but I still love you. I wouldn't do that to you. Besides, you've always kept all of my secrets," she reminds me with a smile.

"Like the first time you gave a blow job freshman year, and then immediately threw up in the guy's lap after he finished." I laugh.

"Oh, God. Danny Meyers. It tasted like onions. I still can't even *smell* onions without wanting to barf." She winces.

"Or how you lost your virginity sophomore year to Ryan Andrews, in the back of Clint's car that you borrowed, and we told him we washed the interior for him because Stacy St. Peter got drunk and peed all over the back seat."

"Poor Stacy. He always called her Stacy St. Pee-Pee after that," Ember says with a shake of her head.

"And that time after prom junior year, when you told your parents you were staying at my house, and you spent the night at a hotel with Carson Jameson. You called me at two in the morning to come get you because you had to take Carson to the emergency room." I cackle.

"I tried to be all cool and sexy and roll us over in bed without breaking our *love connection*, and the poor guy fell off the bed and cracked his head wide open on the nightstand. Jesus, why do all my deep, dark secrets involve sex?" she complains.

"Because you were very generous. With your vagina," I joke. "And look at you now. You're a married woman with… kids, and shit."

She rolls her eyes and lets out a quiet chuckle.

"I have *a* kid. He's seven and his name is Lincoln. I see you still have a deep love of children. Are you sure you want to watch my nieces all summer? They're adorable and I love them, but they scare the shit out of me."

"Speaking of the little angels, where are they this morning?" I ask, glancing nervously around, expecting one of them to pop out from behind a tree and stab me, or smear something disgusting all over me.

I smartly took Mrs. Sherwood's advice and picked out my least fancy outfit to wear today, which was a struggle. Living in New York for so long and attending so many events, I didn't exactly keep any farm appropriate clothing in my closet. Until I got my first paycheck and could run to the general store in town and stock up on cheap jeans, T-shirts, and a pair of cowboy boots, my black, cropped Nike yoga pants, and the white Gucci tee I'd managed to get all the coffee stains out of, along with my black, sparkly Gucci flip flops would have to do. I seriously considered showing up wearing an apron over my clothes, with elbow-length rubber gloves, a hairnet, and a hospital mask over my face, but thought that might be overkill.

"They're probably out doing their morning chores. We'll have some time for me to give you a quick tour of all the new stuff on the farm, and give you a few tips on how to stay alive while you're with them, before I have to pick up Lincoln from daycare," she jokes with a smile as she slips her arm through mine, and we start to head toward the big red barn an acre away from the house.

Sadly, it's not all that funny. I'm really afraid I might die within an hour of being alone with them.

"Auntie Cole! Auntie Cole!"

We both pause and look up when we hear Mia shouting for Ember, and I try not to groan when I see her running toward us, with Clint following right behind.

Today, he's wearing a green Henley with the long sleeves pushed up to his elbows, and sweet Jesus, can we all say *arm porn*? Where in the hell did those forearms come from? And with the way that cotton shirt molds to his body, he's got some nice chest porn going on too. He's wearing the white cowboy hat again, and he's shaved the scruff from his face, which gives him chiseled jaw porn. As Mia throws herself at Ember and she scoops her up into her arms, I watch all my porn fantasies saunter toward me and hope to God I don't have drool dripping down my chin.

Think about that time he tripped you at the homecoming game. Or that time he made fun of your little black dress. Or that time he asked you if you wanted a shovel when you got your second helping of mashed potatoes at dinner. Or that time he told Bobby Chapman you had herpes, and Bobby conveniently "forgot" about your date to the movies. Or that time you almost kissed the day you graduated from high school.

Shit! No! Don't think about that!

"Well, would you look at that. Fancy pants came back." Clint smirks, sliding his hands in the back pockets of his jeans when he stops in front of us.

Stop looking at his lips, stop looking at his lips!

"How's it going, Cunty Clint?" I ask with a sassy smile, crossing my arms in front of me, using the nickname I gave him when I was in seventh grade, making sure to whisper the nickname so Mia can't hear me.

See? I'm already excelling as a nanny.

Sure, seventh grade might be a little young to learn about that word, but when his mother got him a birthday cake and the bakery smushed all the letters of *Clint* together until it very obviously looked like it said "Happy Birthday, Cunt" in sparkly blue frosting, and his mother called the bakery and screamed at them for fifteen minutes, I considered it a very educational day.

I know, it's a dumb nickname, but it always pissed him off.

Unfortunately, that smirk just grows bigger until it's a full-blown smile, and since he shaved his stupid face, now I can see both of his stupid dimples.

"I do know my way around one, so thank you for the compliment," he tells me with a wink.

Nope, nope, nope. Do not think about Cunty Clint knowing his way around any of your parts.

"It's always nice to see you, Cookie Brookie," he adds, making me grind my teeth and glare at him.

Leave it to Clint to use a nickname that's even worse than the one I gave him. Sure, it sounds all cute and sweet, but Clint knows damn well it's not. Let's just say, that picture of me passed out with my underwear showing wasn't the first time my goods were on display for everyone to see.

Every year, the Rotary Club in town puts on a dinner at the end of the summer. It's a big event, and everyone in town goes. They set up a huge tent outside on the town square, and after dinner, all the different high school groups get up in front of everyone and perform for the first time after practicing all summer. The band plays a few melodies, the choir sings a few songs, the cheerleaders perform a dance routine, and so on and so forth. After that, they let a few of the seniors play DJ for the rest of the night, and everyone dances and generally has a good time.

As a cheerleader who'd made the varsity squad for my upcoming tenth grade year, I was extremely excited to show off the dance routine we'd been working our asses off on all summer. So excited, that I forgot to put on my spanky pants. In case you don't know what spanky pants are, they're basically a polyester pair of underwear the same color as your cheerleading uniform that you wear over your real underwear so you're not flashing everyone when you do a leg kick or a toe touch. I was so into that damn dance routine, and was nailing every single move, that I had no clue until it was over that everyone in the crowd was pointing and laughing at me the entire time. Not only did I continuously flash the audience every time I moved, but I did it wearing a pair of bright blue Cookie Monster underwear, with Cookie Monster's face shoveling in a mouthful of chocolate chip cookies right over my crotch.

"Hope you're ready for your first day of work, *Cookie Brookie*," Clint laughs, repeating that stupid nickname again, like he just *wants* to get punched in the face.

"We heard you the first time, moron. Still not funny," Ember tells him, sticking up for me as she sets Mia back on the ground.

"Do you like cookies? I love cookies! Can I call you Cookie Brookie?" Mia asks excitedly as she throws herself against my leg and wraps her arms around it.

Clint just laughs as I awkwardly pat the top of Mia's head, which is, of course, sticky. I quickly pull my hand away and try to discreetly wipe whatever that shit is off my palm by rubbing it against the back of Mia's shirt.

Whatever. Don't judge me. The kid is already filthy; it's not like it even matters. She's covered in dirt, and there's hay sticking out of her hair like she spent her morning rolling around in the horse barn. Which she probably did. The first item on my nanny agenda is going to be giving her a bath every day. Possibly every hour. Maybe even every time she walks out of a room.

Ember grabs Mia's hand and starts pulling her toward the house.

"I'm just gonna hose her off before I leave," she tells me, which makes me want to get down on my knees and kiss the ground she walks on. "I'll stop back and give you the grand tour later."

I realize as she walks away that she's leaving me alone with Clint, and my need to worship her dies a quick, painful death. I'd rather roll around in the horse barn with Mia and whatever the fuck got in her hair than be alone with him.

As soon as Ember and Mia disappear into the

house, Clint steps right up into my personal space until the toes of his cowboy boots are up against my bare toes sticking out of my flip-flips. He's standing so close that if I take a deep breath, my boobs will bump into his chest. I'd like to insult him like I did yesterday and tell him he smells like shit, but my brain has suddenly gone to mush. He doesn't smell like horse shit. Not even close. I know he's been working all around the farm this morning and he should stink to high heaven, but of course he doesn't. He smells like soap and a hint of woodsy cologne that makes me want to hump the nearest tree and become one with nature, thanking the good Lord for inventing cedar and sandalwood and making it smell so delicious.

I'm tall, but Clint is at least five inches taller than me. I make the mistake of looking up at him and those damn green eyes of his. They practically twinkle as I stare right into them when he bends his face down closer to mine, until I can feel his warm breath tickling my cheek as he whispers close to my ear.

"I promised Mia that her new nanny was looking forward to getting her makeup done by her. We took a trip to the general store last night, and Mia is very excited to see how you look in electric blue eyeshadow and hot pink lipstick."

When he's finished whispering these rubbish sweet-nothings in my ear, he steps back away from me with a smile, turns, and starts heading back toward the barn, whistling as he goes.

And stupid me, instead of coming up with an amazing insult to fire back at him, all I do is stand here in the front yard like an idiot and stare at his ass as he goes.

This is just bullshit.

Chapter 6
Sugar High Life

"*M*IA IS THE *easy one,*" Ember said. "*She won't give you any trouble,*" Ember promised.

Ember is a fucking liar and I'm seriously questioning rekindling our friendship right now.

I should be happy she at least washed the girl down before she fled the scene and left me here alone, but that quick bath Ember gave her was shot to shit less than ten minutes after she left. Seriously, how can one tiny child manage to find anything and everything that will make her dirty as soon as I turn my back? She currently has peanut butter in her hair that I already washed out twice. I even hid the damn peanut butter behind the cereal on the top shelf of the giant walk-in pantry, so I have no idea where she's finding this shit.

In the last several hours, I've learned that Mia is five and Grace is ten. Not that this knowledge gives me any kind of insight on what the hell I'm supposed to be doing with them, but it will give me an idea of where to start in my next Google search later tonight. I've also learned that Mia loves cats, but only orange cats. She wants to work at McDonald's when she grows up so she can eat free french fries forever and ever. She got bit by a mosquito last night and it itches really bad. Her favorite color is anything pink with sparkles. She would just *die* if she ever got to pet a unicorn. She's trying to learn how to whistle and needs to constantly practice by blowing as hard as she can in my face—which never results in a fucking whistle, just kid breath all over me. And she knows all the words to the movie *Frozen*, which she has recited at least six times since I got here.

Let it go, Mia. Let it fucking go.

This kid can talk. Scratch that. This kid never shuts up. Coincidentally, I learned all of these things while sitting on the edge of the tub, watching her poop. I guess that's a thing I'm required to do. A few months ago, I was wearing a designer dress and sharing a glass of champagne with Carrie Underwood at her album release party. Today, I'm covered in peanut butter, electric blue eye shadow, hot pink lipstick, and enough hair spray to make the Leaning Tower of Pisa stand up straight, while watching a kid take a dump and talk about unicorns.

The only good thing about this hot mess is that I figured, since Mia was a talker, it would be the perfect opportunity to grill her about Clint. Sadly, that didn't go according to plan.

*"So, is it just you, Grace, and your dad living on the farm?"
(i.e.: Where the hell is your mother?)*

"I pooped really big! Come look!"

*"Your dad seems comfortable on the farm. Does he like
running the place? (i.e.: When in the hell did he get so hot, and
where are all his khakis, computers, and other nerdy things?)*

*"I have a booger in my nose I can't reach. Can you get it for
me?"*

*"Does your dad ever talk about when he was younger?" (i.e.:
Has he ever even fucking mentioned me before? Has he thought
about me in the last twelve years? Do you think he likes me? Do
you know the name of a good therapist?)*

"Let's play hide-and-seek! Tag, you're it!"

So, yeah. Mia has been missing for about twenty
minutes. In my defense, she's really fucking fast and I
haven't been to a spin class in over three months. I'm
out of shape. I never heard the front door open and
close, so I know she's still in the damn house somewhere. I'm pretty sure at five she's old enough to know
not to stick a knife in a light socket or take a bath with a
toaster, but just in case, on my seventh trip through the
kitchen to look for her in all the cupboards, I hid all the
knives in the pantry with the peanut butter, and put the
toaster out on the front porch.

"Mia!" I shout for the hundredth time as I head
upstairs and start opening doors. "If you come out right
now, I know a unicorn you can pet, we'll go into the
next town to get McDonald's french fries, and I'll let

you put sparkles on anything you want!"

I don't care if bribery with kids is frowned upon. I'll do whatever it takes at this point. I can't lose one of Clint's kids on my first damn day at work. Not only will he probably be a little sad he's minus a kid, but he'll never let me live it down.

"Did you seriously lose Mia?"

Closing the door to a spare bedroom when I've checked every nook and cranny and didn't find a chatty, sticky five-year-old, I slowly turn around in the upstairs hallway and come face-to-face with Grace. As soon as Ember left and Mrs. Sherwood went into town to run some errands, I asked Grace what she wanted to do. She rolled her eyes at me, ran upstairs, and locked herself in her bedroom for the rest of the day. I'm not gonna lie; I breathed a little sigh of relief that she still seemed to hate me. That's one less kid I needed to worry about. Unfortunately, being alone with Mia was like being alone with sixty-five rabid cats who just did a few lines of coke.

"I didn't *lose* her. I just… misplaced her. We were playing hide-and-seek, and that's kind of the point of the game," I reply in annoyance.

I cannot believe I'm letting a ten-year-old judge me and I'm actually getting defensive about it.

"Dad's gonna be pissed."

She smirks at me, clearly full of glee that I did something that will get me in trouble.

"Are you allowed to say *pissed*? I think that language is a little old for you."

Look at me, being all stern and nanny-like!

"Yeah? Well so is that makeup and bad hair-do. It makes you look *thirty*," she fires back.

"I *am* thirty! Thirty is *not* old!" I shout, wondering if they make muzzles for smartass little girls. "And besides, I let your sister do my hair and makeup, so this is all her fault. Can you possibly cut the attitude for two seconds and help me find her?"

All of a sudden, her face softens and she loses the permanent scowl. She really is a beautiful little girl when she shuts her mouth. I have no idea what kind of shit she's had to deal with in her young life, and I sort of feel bad about throwing the attitude right back at her.

"Hey, Brooklyn?" she asks quietly, biting her bottom lip nervously.

Finally! I knew there had to be a nice kid in there somewhere.

Bending over, I rest my hands on my knees so we're at eye level, and I give her a smile.

"What's up?"

She smiles at me for the first time, and I notice she's got the exact same dimples in both of her cheeks as her father. This kid is going to be a heartbreaker when she's a teenager.

Grace leans in closer to me and rests her hand on my shoulder.

"Suck it."

Before I can come up with an appropriate response, Grace whirls around and whips me in the face with her hair, before marching back into her room and slamming her door closed so hard it rattles the hinges.

"You little motherfucker," I mutter under my breath as I stand back up.

I spend the next hour stomping around upstairs, going from room-to-room, screaming Mia's name, bribing her with my first paycheck, promising to buy her her very own McDonald's, and even agreeing to let her do my hair and makeup every single day for the rest of the summer.

Nothing works, and I'm really starting to panic. What if she's hiding somewhere eating peanut butter and silently choked on it? What if she snuck out of a window, fell into some bushes, and broke all her bones? What if she's pooping somewhere and got exhausted talking to herself, fell in the bowl, and drowned?

Not even the prospect of being able to snoop through Clint's bedroom made me feel better. The smell of cedar and sandalwood just distracted me and made me more flustered than I already was. I didn't even care about going through the medicine cabinet in his bathroom to see if he had a prescription for Viagra, or rifle through his nightstand in the hopes of finding gay porn I could use against him. All I could think about was Clint walking through the front door and the look on his face when I had to tell him that his baby got flushed down the toilet.

Racing into the kitchen once again, I start opening all the lower cabinets, pulling every single item out of them, and flinging them around the room, hoping Mia might be hiding behind something and I missed her the first ten times I looked in these damn things. Pots and pans go flying, cutting boards smack against the fridge, a handheld mixer goes skidding across the hardwood floor, and an entire drawer of wooden spoons, plastic spatulas, rolling pins, and rubber scrapers gets upended, just in case she curled into a ball in the bottom of the drawer and piled everything on top of her.

Stepping over the disaster, I swallow back the tears as I go to the opposite side of the kitchen, and slide open the white, double barn doors in front of the pantry.

"You found me!"

"Jesus Christ!" I shout, when Mia throws her arms out in excitement, a bag of sugar falling out of her hands and spilling all over the floor at my feet.

"Jesus Christ!" she screams back, clapping her hands together in glee.

She's sitting cross-legged on the top shelf, and I don't even want to think about how she managed to climb up there without falling. All I know is that there is a jumbo-sized jar of peanut butter and about twenty very sharp knives within her reach.

"I win hide-and-seek!" she singsongs as I walk into the pantry, push up on my toes, grab her under the arms, and gently pull her down from her hiding spot. I hug her tightly to me as she wraps her arms and legs around me like a spider monkey.

Her sticky fingers start playing with my hair that didn't make it up into the very messy ponytail she put on one side of my head, and I don't even care that she's making it look worse and putting more knots into it than it already has.

I should probably be concerned that she has sugar all around her nose and upper lip, and I'm fairly confident she was snorting that shit while she was in the pantry, but I'm not. I don't care. She didn't drown in the toilet, and it looks like none of her bones are broken.

"I was hiding behind the back door over there, and I watched you look in here three times, and I was laughing so hard, but I covered my mouth so you wouldn't hear me, and when you left the room, I climbed up in here and *I win hide-and-seek*!" she rambles, shouting in my face so loudly it makes me wince.

She starts squirming in my arms, and even though I kind of want to hold onto her forever just to reassure myself that she's alive, I have to put her down before I drop her.

"I win, I win, I win, I win! I get to pet a unicorn, and I get McDonald's, and I get to do your makeup again, and I get aaall the sparkles!" she shouts, running around me in circles a few times before she zooms out of the pantry so fast all I see is a blur of dirty blonde hair and a cloud of sugar fluttering to the ground in her wake.

With a sigh, I pick up the half empty bag of sugar from the ground and set it on one of the shelves, shaking my head when I get a better look at the pantry.

There are at least fifty opened and empty packets of Kool-Aid littering the ground, along with two empty boxes of cereal, one empty box of Twinkies along with all the empty clear, plastic wrappers that used to house them, and an open bottle of syrup tipped over on the top shelf that is now dripping down onto the pile of garbage all over the floor.

"What the fuck?"

I jump and let out a scream, turning away from the carnage in the pantry so fast I smack right into Clint. His hands quickly wrap around my upper arms to steady me, and my hands automatically press flatly against his chest.

Holy pectoral muscles, Batman.

Clint is looking down at me, and I'm looking up at him, and we're standing so close I can feel his breath on my face and see the gold flecks in his green eyes. He lost the cowboy hat at some point today, and now I can see his dirty blond hair that's cut really short on the sides and a little longer on top. It's just long enough for it to be messy from him running his fingers through it, and I suddenly have the urge to reach up and run *my* fingers through it to see if it's as soft as it looks.

"The '80s called. They want their hair and makeup back," he laughs softly, breaking me out of my thoughts and the ridiculous *feelings* I was having.

I don't have feelings. Not anymore. I turned them off after Stephen the Shithole. I especially don't have feelings for Cunty Clint. I probably got a secondhand sugar high from Mia. That's the only explanation for what's happening right now.

Jerking my arms out of his hold, I take a step back from him to clear my thoughts. Instead of making it look all defiant and graceful, I slip on the pile of sugar on the floor and slam my back into one of the shelves, managing to grab onto it and steady myself before I fall flat on my ass and look like an even bigger idiot.

Clint crosses his arms over his impressive chest, and the corner of his mouth tips up as he watches me flail around in his pantry. Lifting my chin, I run my fingers through my hair that isn't in a ponytail hanging all askew off the side of my head, and the damn things get stuck in a sugar-peanut-butter-Kool-Aid-who-knows-what-the-fuck-else knot. It takes me a few seconds to extract them, and I lift my chin once again and walk around him, making sure to smack my shoulder against his arm as I go.

"Grace is in her room, and Mia is most likely attempting to fly off the roof. She probably won't be hungry for dinner, since she ate roughly three pounds of sugar today. Have fun with that!" I chirp as I continue moving through the kitchen and out into the hallway.

My hand pauses on the knob to the front door when I hear Clint shout from the kitchen.

"Where the hell are all my knives? And my toaster?"

"Get a mirror and bend over!" I shout back, smiling to myself for the first time since that stupid hide-and-seek game.

I slam the door closed behind me, pausing on the front steps. My smile quickly falls when I realize having the last word wasn't as much fun as I thought it would be. I have to wake up tomorrow and live through this hell all over again.

"In the words of Mrs. Sherwood—sweet, merciful Jesus, take me now," I mutter to myself.

Chapter 7
Past Life

I HID IT really well from everyone around me, but I hated my life when I was a teenager. I hated being in a house where I could still smell my mother's perfume, but was starting to forget what she looked like, since my dad got rid of all her pictures. I hated that every time I tried to talk about her, ask questions about her, or even mention her name, my dad would storm off into his room and not come out until the next morning, pretending like nothing ever happened. A month after she left, I stopped trying to talk to him about her.

I lied to everyone I knew, even Ember, about my relationship with my mother. You would think in a town this small, my lies would have been figured out pretty quickly, but my dad's complete and utter refusal to talk about her helped me out in that way at least. Whenever Ember would ask about her, I'd tell her we talked on the phone all the time, and I'd tell her our relationship was better than ever. Whenever I got something new to wear to school and friends would ask about it, I'd tell them my mother bought it and sent it to me. Every summer, I spent a week at my grandparents' house in Idaho. When I came home, I'd gush about how my mom stayed there with me, how she took me to all the best malls to go shopping, and how we'd stay up until all hours of the night talking.

I made up elaborate tales about my mother, and how she'd always dreamed of moving back to New York one day, the city she grew up in, and where my father met her when he was stationed there in the Navy. I told them she never wanted to move back here to Montana when he left the Navy, but she did it for my dad, and made it work for as long as she could. I told them how she fell out of love with my dad and decided to take the leap and move back to make it easier on him. I explained to everyone that it killed her to leave me, but she didn't want to uproot me and take me away from my friends and the only home I'd ever known during my teenage years. I told them she was waiting for me in New York, and that's why I couldn't wait to get out of here.

The truth was, I have no fucking clue where my mother went when she left us. I came home from school two weeks after I turned thirteen and found my dad sitting at the kitchen table with a note from her in his hand that simply said **I'm sorry. I can't do this anymore.**

I thought it was a joke. I thought I would run into their bedroom and find her sitting on their bed where she'd smile and say, "Gotcha!" When I ran into their bedroom, all I saw were empty drawers still pulled out of the dresser, and her half of the closet completely bare. She never called. She never sent a postcard or a letter. She disappeared into thin air. The last time I saw her was before I left for school that morning. She tried to get me to eat a piece of toast and an apple. I rolled my eyes and huffed, and told her to stop nagging me, that I'd eat something if I was hungry. To this day, I always eat breakfast, even if I'm not hungry. It's ridiculous, and I'm thirty years old and *know* it's ridiculous, but I still wonder every day—if I would have sat down at the kitchen table with her and eaten that stupid toast and that dumb apple, smiled at her instead of rolling my eyes, maybe she wouldn't have left.

The only true fact in all the bullshit I spewed to everyone was that my mother was indeed from New York, and that's where she met my father. I always wanted to go to New York, even before she left, but after she was gone, it turned into an obsession. I imagined walking down the street and bumping into her. I pictured her crying, throwing her arms around me, and telling me she never should have left me. Obviously, that never happened, but I spent the last twelve years constantly aware of my surroundings whenever I walked through the city, always searching for her among the crowds of people.

The last time I saw Clint before I moved to New York was the day I graduated from high school. He was a sophomore at UCLA and he'd only been able to come home twice since he left White Timber, both of those times at Christmas. Since my dad and I traveled a few hours away to see his side of the family on holidays, I never got to see Clint when he came home those two times. When I was at the farm and Clint would call from college to check in, Mrs. Hastings would pass the phone around so he could talk to everyone. When it was my turn, he would ask me how many guys I turned gay with my shrill, annoying voice, and I would ask him how many chicks he gave herpes to.

I told Ember and anyone who would listen that it was a good thing he never came home and we couldn't be in the same room with each other, or one of us would have died. Namely, him.

I only told my diary and the Joshua Jackson poster on my ceiling that I kind of missed him. I missed the way he would run his hands through his shaggy hair whenever he was frustrated. I missed how his dorky eyes would light up whenever he talked about computers. I even missed fighting with the big nerd. Fighting with him made me forget about the fact that my mother never loved me and didn't give a shit about me. Coming up with new barbs to lob at him, and new rumors to spread, gave me something else to think about other than all the things I did that made her leave. Clint was the only person in town who never asked me about my mother. Not that we ever had any kind of meaningful conversations or anything like that, but he also never once used her against me in our arguments or insults. I thought about her so much on a daily basis that he made me forget I was unlovable and easy to leave.

The last time I saw him before a few days ago, Ember's parents threw us a joint graduation party at the farm for all our family and friends, and it started off as one of the best days I'd ever had. Ember's parents told me they were surprising her by flying Clint in for the party, and it killed me to keep it a secret from her. Especially since I'd spent a week writing down every good, new insult I'd come up with since the last time he called home, and it was hard not to share them with her and gauge her level of amusement to know whether they were good or not. I had a few doozies about syphilis and some research I'd done on that I was dying to use on him about how many computer nerds had to go to the emergency room on a yearly basis from jerking off too much because they couldn't get laid.

I spent twice as long on my hair and makeup, and squeezed my ass into that damn little black dress he'd made fun of a few years prior, even though my boobs had grown in size, and I knew he'd definitely make another comment about me shopping in the toddler section. I was eighteen, and finally legal, and I thought maybe a few years in college hanging out with dorks all the time would make him desperate enough to maybe make a move on me.

Much to my surprise, Clint spent the entire party completely ignoring me. Not one comment about my dress, and not one insult about my annoying voice. Nothing. He never even glanced in my direction. I was always known as the girl who didn't drink in high school. My dad, as distant as he was, was also kind of a cool dad in his own way. I was always allowed to drink, as long as I did it at home, or stayed wherever I was, and I let him know what was going on. Because of that freedom, getting drunk out in a cornfield with the rest of my classmates who paid an older brother or sister to buy them booze never appealed to me. I was always everyone's designated driver, which—let me tell you—is as annoying as you would think. I don't know how many times I had to clean up puke out of the back of my car, or help sneak someone through their bedroom window so their parents wouldn't know they were hammered.

On the night of our graduation party, I snuck out into the horse barn with half the football team and a handful of cheerleaders, and proceeded to drink myself silly after I'd had enough of being ignored by Clint. And since I'd never had much more than a sip of alcohol before that point, four Bartles and Jaymes strawberry daiquiri wine coolers was all it took before I was giggling like an idiot and tripping over everything.

Before I knew it, I was all alone in the barn, lying on my back in a pile of hay, making snow angels and singing *The Brady Bunch* theme song at the top of my lungs.

"How much have you had to drink?"

I jerked upright in the hay when I heard Clint's voice, immediately regretting that decision when everything started to spin. I smacked my hand against my forehead and closed my eyes, groaning loudly when it felt like there were a million tiny elves in my head, pounding their tiny hammers against my skull.

"I don't know. How much do I have to drink to make you go away?" I asked, dropping my hand from my head and squinting up at him out of one eye.

Aside from myself and Ember, who were the guests of honor, everyone else at this party was dressed in jeans and cowboy boots and other casual attire. Of course Clint had to be the only one who showed up in black dress pants, a white button-down, and a black tie. And of course he didn't look like an idiot. He looked hot. He looked older and more mature than all the other idiots my age, who were probably puking in the fields right now, or out finding some cows to tip. He looked like he was getting ready to conduct a board meeting. He looked like a hot CEO of a company, ready to pound some skulls and demand to know why stocks were down the last quarter, and the only thing that would put him in a good mood was when the meeting was adjourned and he got to bend his secretary—who happened to look just like me—over the conference room table.

Ember and I may or may not have gotten access to an online porn site recently where we'd watched an office-themed porn. We made fun of the whole thing, but I'd had a lot of dirty dreams since we watched it that all involved Clint.

If I squinted harder, I could almost pretend like we were in a conference room and he was pounding his fist on the table, demanding a cup of coffee. And then the smell of horse shit permeated the air and completely ruined that fantasy. Along with Clint opening his mouth again.

"Are you having a stroke? What's wrong with your eyes?"

"Shut up and let me die in peace," I muttered, dropping my head to stare down at my hands in my lap.

He flopped down on the hay next to me and gently bumped his shoulder into mine. I let out a sigh and turned my head to look at him, suddenly aware of how close our faces were.

He stared into my eyes and didn't say a word. Goose bumps broke out all over my bare arms, but I didn't want to move to rub them away and ruin whatever was happening.

"Aren't you going to say something insulting about my dress?" I whispered.

His eyes trailed down to my lips and I licked them nervously. I watched Clint's Adam's apple bob as he swallowed a few times, never taking his eyes off my mouth.

"Maybe I'm tired of the insults," he muttered softly.

His eyes came back up to meet mine, and I don't even know who started moving first. All of a sudden, our noses were touching and his mouth was a centimeter away from mine. My heart was pounding in my chest, and I hoped to God he couldn't hear it. I'd been fantasizing about this moment for far too long. I briefly wondered if I was so drunk that I was imagining things. But I could feel his breath against my lips, and when his hand came up between us to rest against the side of my cheek, I could feel the warmth of his palm.

"I must be an idiot," Clint whispered so softly that I almost didn't hear him.

I closed my eyes and held my breath, waiting for his lips to press against mine.

"Brooklyn! Let's go! We got a huge cardboard cutout of the Statue of Liberty for everyone to take a picture in front of! New York or bust, motherfucker!"

Clint's hand suddenly dropped from my cheek when fucking Danny Meyers shouted into the barn. When I opened my eyes, Clint was already standing up and moving away from me.

He didn't even look back at me when he walked away. He shoved his hands into the pockets of those stupid black dress pants and just left me there.

I curse at myself and wipe a tear off my cheek as I turn onto the road that will take me to my dad's house. Why in the hell am I even taking this stupid trip down memory lane right now? It's gotta be because of exhaustion after dealing with Mia all day. I'm tired and sticky, and I just want to wash all this shit off my face and go to bed. I spent a lot of years thinking about that almost-kiss, but I thought I'd blocked it from my memory. Of course it came back in high definition and now won't stop playing on a loop in my head since I'm forced to be around Clint again after all this time. At first, I used to analyze that whole "I must be an idiot" thing he said to me, and thought for sure he meant he was an idiot for not trying to kiss me sooner. Since we never spoke again after that night and I moved away, I came to realize that he was most likely calling himself an idiot for his momentary lapse in judgement, trying to kiss a drunk girl he couldn't stand.

I'm so annoyed with myself for thinking about this crap that I don't realize there's a sheriff behind me, until the flashing blue-and-red lights reflect off my rearview mirror and the blare of the siren makes me jump and almost swerve off the road.

I quickly slow down my dad's truck and pull off onto the berm, shutting off the engine. I groan when I flip down the visor and check my reflection in the mirror.

Why didn't I at least wash this stupid bright blue eye shadow off my eyes that goes from my eyelids all the way up past my eyebrows before I left the farm?

I roll down the truck window just as the man in uniform gets up to my door.

"Care to tell me why you were driving so fast, ma'am?"

The man bends down so he can look into the truck and his eyes widen as he does a double take.

"Brooklyn Manning?"

Jesus. What are the odds that I just had a stupid high school flashback that involved this idiot, and now here he is?

"Danny Meyers," I say, putting on the fakest smile in the world.

"Well, shit! I forgot someone said you were back in town. I saw your dad's truck and I thought maybe someone had stolen it, on account that he's not supposed to be driving and all just yet. You look... great," he says, staring at my hideous makeup and equally hideous hair, his words just as fake as my smile.

A part of me wants to tell him I don't normally look like this, but I don't really give a shit at this point. Danny isn't exactly going to be on the cover of GQ anytime soon with that enormous beer belly threatening to pop the buttons on his uniform, and his receding hairline. Ember will definitely enjoy it when I tell her that his entire body smells like onions now, and not just his jizz.

"How's the Big Apple? You gonna stick around long, or are you heading back soon? We should get together, have some drinks, talk about old times," he tells me, the smell of onions wafting through the car with every word he speaks and making me want to put my hand over my nose.

"New York is great! Can't wait to get back!" I reply, my voice sounding entirely too happy and chipper. "I should probably get—"

"Oh, yeah, yeah. You probably need to get home to your dad. Make sure you give him my best. When he's feeling better, tell him I'll buy him a beer up at the VFW. I'll give you a White Timber High alumni pass tonight and just let you go with a warning, as long as you promise to watch your speed. Go Wildcats!" he shouts, holding his hand up in the open window for a high-five.

I awkwardly smack my hand against his and start to roll my window back up, when Danny presses his hand down on top of the moving window to stop me.

"Hey, remember that time during the homecoming game when you tripped and bit it at the fifty-yard line? God, that was hilarious!" he says, throwing his head back and laughing.

Oh, screw you, Clint Hastings. Screw you and my stupid teenage crush.

Chapter 8
Maple Inn Life

I'M ALREADY SO frazzled after my interaction with Danny and my stupid trip down memory lane that pulling into my dad's driveway and seeing seven cars parked in the yard, as well as a White Timber ambulance in front of the garage, threatens to chuck me right over the edge into full-blown crazy town.

I don't even take the keys out of the ignition; I just fly out of the truck, race up the front porch steps, and start shouting my dad's name as soon as I run through the door. My feet come to an abrupt halt when I get to the doorway of the living room, and my panic quickly morphs into disbelief at what I'm seeing. And smelling.

"Dad, what the hell?" I shout, throwing my hands up in the air and letting them smack back down against my thighs.

His living room has been converted into a poker den of corruption. The furniture has been shoved back against the walls, and there are four card tables set up in the middle of the room, piled high with beer cans and junk food. There's a cloud of cigar smoke hovering above everyone's heads seated at the tables, so thick I can't even see the ceiling.

I didn't really give a shit about seeing Danny Meyers a few minutes ago in my current state of looking like I was an extra in a bad '80s music video, but as I look around the room, I see at least six more of my former classmates. It's like a goddamn White Timber High reunion, where everyone looks great, and has aged well, and has great jobs, and perfect lives, and then I walk in, the music comes to a screeching stop, and everyone tries not to make eye contact with the loser who never amounted to anything.

I was the fucking prom queen! I've been living it up in New York working for the largest fashion magazine in the world! I am not a loser!

Ignoring the shocked stares from my former classmates and a few of my dad's friends, I march over to the table where he's sitting and stand next to him with my hands on my hips.

"What are you eating?"

He doesn't even look up at me. He just takes another huge, messy bite of the sandwich in his hand.

"A BLT," he grumbles, tiny pieces of toast and bacon flying out of his mouth when he speaks.

"Really? Because that just looks like an entire pound of bacon in between two pieces of bread."

He shrugs his shoulders as he finishes off the last bite, wiping his hands on the front of his shirt.

"Fine, so I'm eating a BLT, minus the LT."

Picking up the glass next to his plate, I bring it up to my nose and gag a little when I take a whiff.

"Tequila? Seriously? Dad! You just had open heart surgery!"

"I saw an article last month where daily consumption of tequila in moderation can help with your dad's Crohn's disease. It's been doing wonders for—"

I let out a low growl as I glare at Carson Anderson, the guy I went to prom with my senior year, who's sitting at the table behind my dad.

"So, how've you been, Brooklyn? You look… great," he says, his head cocking to the side as he studies my rat's nest of hair.

I am so tired of people telling me I look great with that damn pause in the middle. I'd have much more respect for them if they told me I looked like straight up asshole. At least Clint was honest when he saw me earlier.

Ughh, stop trying to make Clint seem like he isn't a douchebag! He's the king of douchebags!

"Why is there an ambulance outside? Are you okay?" I question my dad, trying not to roll my eyes when he licks his finger and starts picking up all the tiny pieces of bacon on the table that escaped his sandwich, and then sticks his finger back in his mouth.

"Oh, that's mine! I'm off duty. Is that a fancy New York City hairdo? It looks… great on you," Landon Walker, the captain of the football team, whose only claim to fame in high school was being able to belch the alphabet after drinking a case of beer, tells me.

Seriously? This *guy is judging me?*

Yep, this is it. I have officially reached my breaking point.

Without another word, I stomp out of the room and down the hall, escaping into the bathroom. I take five minutes to wash all this shit off my face, pull the ponytail out of my hair, and brush it until there are no more knots, and it's hanging in loose waves down my back. After that, I rush across the hall to my old bedroom, stripping out of my tee and athletic pants as I go. Ripping the first thing I see off of a hanger in my closet—a lavender strapless romper—I step into it and pull it up my body, sliding on a pair of tan, high-heeled wedges I got for a steal at Barneys.

Marching back out of the room, I walk right past the living room without even looking in to see what other stupid choices my dad is making.

"Hey! Where ya going?" my dad shouts as I throw open the front door. "Can you pick up some more tequila while you're out? The top shelf stuff, not that rot gut shit!"

I don't even answer him, slamming the door closed behind me as I go. As soon as I get into his truck, I grab my purse from where I left it on the front seat and pull out my cell phone. Scrolling to the contact I just added earlier this afternoon, I hit the Call button, and Ember picks up on the first ring.

"Question. Do you have an awesome husband who will keep an eye on your kid at a moment's notice, so you can go to a bar and get trashed? Asking for a friend," I add, starting up the truck and backing out of the driveway as I hold the phone between my cheek and shoulder.

"As a matter of fact, I do. On a scale of one to ten, how trashed are we talking?" Ember asks.

"Eighty-seven."

"Shit. That's defcon, emergency level drinking. I'm in. I haven't had a night out in months. I'll meet you at the Maple Inn."

Ember doesn't even say goodbye; she just hangs up on me in the middle of shouting to her husband that she's going out and he's in charge.

God, I missed her.

THE MAPLE INN isn't actually an Inn. I have no idea why it's called this, since it's just a tiny dive bar, and the only bar aside from the VFW in White Timber. Since you have to be a veteran with a VFW membership to drink there, the Maple Inn is our one and only option.

It's located on Main Street along with every other business in town, stuck between the public library and The Timber Diner. It's roughly eight-hundred square feet, with dirty and stained black and white tile on the floor, just enough room for ten barstools along the bar, and a bench seat that runs the entire length of the wall next to the bar, with four tables and two chairs at each one.

There are two guys at the bar who look like they've been sitting there since before I was born, and a couple making out at one of the tables, completely oblivious to everything around them.

Since I left town before I turned twenty-one, this is the first time I've ever stepped foot in this place. I'm severely overdressed, just like I always seem to be, but I don't give a shit. I don't recognize anyone here, so it's perfect. Flopping down on a barstool, a woman who could have given me a run for my money in the bad '80s music video competition, comes over and stands in front of me on the other side of the bar. Her permed, bleach blonde hair has been teased and sprayed so much that a hurricane wouldn't be able to move one single strand. She's wearing stonewashed jeans that look like they've been painted on, a white T-shirt, and a matching stonewashed jean vest. I almost want to look at the calendar on my phone just to double check what year it is.

"What can I getcha?" she asks in a bored voice,

wiping down a section of the bar between us with a dirty, white rag.

"You wouldn't be able to make a lemon drop martini, would you?" I ask hopefully.

She sighs loudly, crossing her arms in front of her as she looks me up at down.

"Let me guess. Allen Manning's kid. The fancy New Yorker with a stick up her ass."

Seriously? I don't need this shit right now.

"Can you make a lemon drop or not? This *stick up my ass* is getting pretty painful, and I could use some liquor to ease the pain," I reply sarcastically.

She glares at me for a few more seconds, and then finally drops her arms, resting her hands on top of the bar.

"I don't know. What's in it?"

"Vodka, Triple Sec, and lemon juice, with sugar on the rim."

My mouth waters as I rattle off the ingredients. Even after high school, I still never became much of a drinker. A glass or two of champagne or a lemon drop was about all I could handle when I was out at events. I didn't want to be a drunk, slurring idiot when I was technically working, and I never really grew to like the taste of alcohol. I just always felt like I fit in more if I had a drink in my hand. But right now, I kind of want to take a bath in vodka and just drink the tub empty with a straw.

The woman lets out another annoyed sigh, tossing her rag onto the bar and turning around to look at the wall of liquor behind her. I don't really feel all that confident when she grabs a bottle from the shelf and has to blow dust off of it before she removes the lid, but I'm committed to getting drunk at this point, and I'm just going to ignore the fact that the bottle of Triple Sec she's pouring into a glass might have been on that shelf long past its expiration date. I also decide not to point out that a lemon drop should be shaken, and the ingredients shouldn't just be dumped into a glass, but I don't want this woman to kick me out of the only bar in town, so I keep my mouth shut.

I have to bite down on my lips when she slides the glass across the bar and then tosses a few sugar packets next to them.

"I don't have time for all that fancy sugar-rim shit," she mutters, before moving down to the other end of the bar to fill up a beer glass from the tap.

Grabbing the glass, I take a huge sip of the drink, immediately regretting that decision. My eyes water, I start coughing uncontrollably, and I have to pound on my chest with my fist before I can breathe again.

I feel a hand smack against my back a few times, and turn my head to find Ember smiling at me.

"Let me guess, you ordered some fancy shit that Sheila didn't know how to make?" she asks, taking the seat next to me and waving at the bartender. "I'll take a beer whenever you get a minute, Sheila."

The woman smiles at her and nods, grabbing another glass and filling it with beer from the tap.

"It tastes like pure gasoline," I reply in a hoarse, choking voice.

Ember laughs as Shelia sets her beer down in front of her, and I listen as they make small talk for a few minutes, taking tiny sips of my drink that won't kill me. When Sheila walks away again, Ember turns on her stool to face me, holding her glass in the air between us.

"Here's to old friends, getting trashed together just like old times." She smiles, as I lift my glass and clink it against hers.

"We never got trashed together. I was always the one to hold your hair back when you puked, remember?"

"Good times, good times," Ember muses. "I guess it's my turn to return the favor. But if you puke in the bathroom here, try to avoid going anywhere near the sink. The plumbing is bad at Jack's Auto Repair, and Jack uses the sink here as a urinal, since he's a husky guy and can't fit in the stalls."

I plug my nose and quickly down the rest of my drink, not even caring that it feels like lava going down my throat. I'll do anything at this point to erase the memory of everything that happened today, and the knowledge that since I'm a lightweight, I will most likely become intimately acquainted with Jack's urine.

Chapter 9
Drunk Life

"HOW DRUNK ARE you right now?" Ember asks, getting into my personal space to look deeply into my eyes.

Her bar stool tips forward, and I have to quickly grab onto her before she lands in my lap. I push her back upright, and she signals for Sheila to bring us another round of drinks. I just finished my third lemon drop, and I'm happy to report it no longer tastes like gasoline.

"I'm buzzed, but I can still feel my teeth and do basic math problems," I inform her as Shelia sets another beer in front of Ember and starts making my drink.

"You can't do basic math problems when you're sober." Ember snorts.

We clink our glasses together again after Sheila sets mine down in front of me, and I guzzle half of it before setting it back down on the bar.

"Okay, so you seem to be drunk enough to give me the deets on this dude who ruined your life in New York. Please tell me you didn't know he was married," she begs.

I'm a little offended that she has to even ask me that question. I know she hasn't seen me in twelve years, and I've changed a little, but not that much. Does she really think I turned into some awful person who would sleep with a guy if I knew he was married?

"Jesus, no! Of course not!" I tell her.

Knowing I'm going to need more than a few lemon drops to get through this, I flag Sheila down again. This woman seems to be incredibly busy and annoyed whenever I ask her for something, even though the couple still making out hasn't ordered anything to drink since I got here, and the two guys at the other end of the bar started getting up and helping themselves to the beer.

"What kind of top shelf bourbon do you have?" I ask Sheila.

"We got Wild Turkey, and it's on the top shelf. Will that work?" she asks in a bored voice.

"Absolutely!" I nod with a big smile, just so she doesn't spit in my drink.

Sheila grabs the Wild Turkey from the top shelf, slams two shot glasses down in front of me, and fills them to the brim until the dark amber liquid spills out onto the top of the bar.

I throw them back one right after another, and press my fist against my mouth to keep the vomit down. As soon as I'm sure this nasty liquor will stay in my stomach, I turn to face Ember.

"I'm sorry for asking if you knew he was married. I shouldn't have done that," Ember apologizes.

"It's okay. We haven't talked in a while. I get it. I had no clue who he was or that he was married. We were together for six months, and I thought he was perfect. Looking back on it now, I can see it all so clearly and it pisses me off. He always made up excuses why he couldn't meet my friends. He always took me as far outside of the city as possible when we went out, to these little dive restaurants. I thought it was sweet and charming that he had all this money and didn't care about flaunting it, but he just didn't want to run into his wife or anyone who was in on their secret marriage. His penthouse was beautiful, but had literally nothing but furniture in it. No personal photos, no personal touches, nothing but the bare essentials. And he said he'd lived there for ten years. I thought it was refreshing that he didn't need to clutter the place and it didn't look like a bachelor pad. God, I suck." I sigh.

"You don't suck. He was an asshole," Ember says with a shake of her head, getting Sheila's attention and silently pointing to my two empty shot glasses, and then at herself. "How did you meet him?"

At this point, Sheila should just pull up a stool right in front of us and never walk away.

"I met him at my favorite Chinese takeout place a few blocks from my apartment," I tell her, remembering that night and how giddy I was and how perfect he seemed. "We both ordered General Tso, and when they called out the first order, we both went up and tried to grab the container at the same time. He insisted I take it, and we stood there talking while he waited for the next one. We wound up sitting at one of the tables to eat and talked for the next three hours. Jesus, it seemed so romantic and like fate. Now, it's just pathetic. I was attracted to the guy because we shared a love of General Tso."

"It's not pathetic! General Tso is delicious, man. And it's hard to meet people. Cut yourself a break. I couldn't even imagine dating again. I'd require a blood sample, a full background check, a minimum of ten references, and a face-to-face interview with the guy's mother *and* grandmother," she says.

"How did you meet your husband?" I ask, as Ember quickly does both of her shots, fanning her wide-open mouth for a few seconds afterward.

"You know Jessup Rudd, the pharmacist for the White Timber drug store? That's Brandon's uncle. Jessup retired ten years ago, and since he never married or had any kids, and Brandon is his only nephew, he kind of always knew he'd take over the business, so that's what he went to school for," she explains.

"Oh my God. Tall guy, brown hair, totally adorable, and wears glasses? I met him getting a bunch of my dad's prescriptions filled," I tell her, remembering how nice the guy was when he patiently explained everything to me each time I had to go in there.

"Yep. That's him. Brandon moved here from Washington, and I basically started dating him because he was the only fresh meat in town." She laughs.

"And he has access to good drugs," I remind her.

"That too. Yeah, drugs!"

"You went from boning nothing but athletes who excelled in keg stands in school, to marrying a straight-laced pharmacist. Who are you and what have you done with my best friend?" I ask in feigned shock.

"I know, right? He's good in bed, so I can forgive him for the starched, white lab coat and pocket protector." She shrugs.

I can't even say Stephen was good in bed. He was mediocre, at best. I figured our chemistry would develop in time, like an idiot.

Thankfully, Sheila sets down two more drinks each in front of Ember and me, without us even having to ask her.

"I kind of love you right now," I tell Sheila, lifting my glass toward her in a toast.

"Yeah, yeah. Just don't puke on my bar," she mutters before walking away.

"I will make you love me, Sheila!" I shout after her,

taking a sip and setting my glass down before turning back to Ember. "I'm gonna go to the bathroom. I'll be right back."

The alcohol I've consumed doesn't really hit me until I stand up and the room tips sideways. I shuffle my feet along the bar, grabbing onto every stool as I go so I don't fall flat on my face. When I get to the last stool and realize there's at least a five-foot space between it and the bathroom door, I decide the best option is to take a giant leap instead of trying to walk. One jump is better than five steps, according to booze.

I fling my body toward the bathroom, grabbing onto the handle as I slam into the door and stumble inside the small room. Quickly righting myself and smoothing down my hair, I continue walking inside like nothing unusual just happened.

"Hey, Jack."

I wave to the guy currently standing in front of the sink in the bathroom as I walk on unsteady feet toward the first stall.

"Hey, Brooklyn! Heard you were back in town," Jack replies, his smile reflecting back at me in the mirror as he continues peeing in the sink.

Locking myself in the stall, I curse at myself when I realize I never should have worn a romper to go out drinking. There's nothing more awkward than having to get completely naked just to go to the bathroom.

"You here for good this time? Heard from Margie

down at the bank that you're watching Clint's kids out at the farm," Jack shouts, as I release at least seven gallons of pee.

Thank God I'm drunk and this isn't weird in the least.

"Nope! Just temporary. Can't wait to get back to New York. It's the absolute best!" I yell back, kind of hating myself for lying to the guy when he's being so nice and friendly while he pisses in the sink five feet away from me.

"Well, good luck with that. Those girls are adorable, but they sure are a handful. Clint's a good guy though. He's been through a lot," he tells me.

"Yeah, yeah. He's been through so much. Such a shame the… *things* he's been through. We should discuss that."

"You two still at each other's throats?" he asks with a chuckle, totally not taking the bait.

I finish up and almost trip over my feet as I pull the romper back up into place.

"Does a wombat shit in the woods?"

"I… I don't actually know the answer to that," Jack replies, as I flush the toilet and exit the stall to find him zipping up his jeans.

"I don't either, Jack. Nice talk."

I give him another wave as he starts washing his hands, and I make a hasty exit out of the bathroom, only tripping twice because of the spinning room as I go. Ember is holding out a bottle of hand sanitizer for me as soon as I sit down, and she squirts a generous portion into my hands before shoving it back in her purse.

I'm so mesmerized by staring at my hands as I rub them together that I realize I might be a little drunker than I thought. I also realize that Ember has my cellphone in her hand, and she's typing away on it.

"What are you doing?"

"Stephen sent you a text while you were in the bathroom. Did you know he's sent you thirteen texts in the last week?" she asks, handing my phone back to me when she's done.

"Yes. I've been thoroughly enjoying ignoring all of them," I tell her, grabbing my drink and finishing it off so I can erase every memory of Stephen from my mind.

I squint down at the screen, unable to make any of the teeny, tiny little letters come into focus.

"Did you break my phone? Why do these letters look so weird?" I complain, shaking my cell, because that should fix the problem.

Ember reaches over, grabs the phone from my hand, and flips it around so it's no longer upside down.

"Ohhh, that's much better." I giggle.

Sure enough, Stephen sent another stupid text telling me we needed to talk.

"Fuck off, leave me alone, and go sniff a dick, you steaming pile of donkey shit," I state, reading Ember's response to him out loud. "That was beautiful. I particularly like the dick sniffing part."

"My son got in trouble at school last month for calling someone a dick sniffer. I tried to yell at him, but holy hell it's just so funny to say!" She laughs, swaying a little in her seat.

"I think we're drunk."

"I don't think we're drunk enough," Ember states.

"You're really smart and pretty, so I'll defer to you," I tell her with a nod.

"Dick sniffer!" we both shout at the top of our lungs.

"Dick sniffer!" a guy at the end of the bar echoes, before falling backward off of his stool.

☆

"JESUS. YOU TWO were annoying as teenagers. You're even worse as adults."

I lift my head from the bar when the smell of cedar and sandalwood tickles my nose, and the deep voice with a slight raspy sound to it makes me want to clench my thighs together.

Looking to my left, I see three Clints standing next to me. As if one wasn't bad enough, now I've got three hot cowboys who hate me, shaking their heads at me.

"You're a snick differ!" Ember shouts at him from behind me. "I mean snick differ. Sick dicker! Dicker dicker!"

I snort when I laugh, quickly clamping my mouth closed when all of the Clints morph into one. He grabs my hips, slowly turning my bar stool to face him, and then moves in between my legs. My bare thighs rub up against his jeans, and I wonder what he would do if I hooked my legs around his waist and pulled him against me.

Tipping my head back to stare up at him, I take a minute to study his face while he's busy talking to Sheila. His big, warm hands are still holding securely onto my hips, and combined with all the alcohol I've consumed, I don't know how I can focus on anything right now, but focus on him I do. His hair is damp, and I'm guessing he just took a shower. He's wearing a green tee the same color as his eyes, with the Hastings Farm logo on the front of it, the material stretched tight over his muscular chest. His tongue darts out to lick his bottom lip after he thanks Sheila for calling him, and I swear I have a mini orgasm.

"You got my sister?" Clint asks, looking over my shoulder.

I turn away from Clint before I do something stupid like lean forward on my stool and lick his face, to see a familiar guy with brown hair and brown eyes behind his glasses, helping Ember walk around us.

"Hey, Brandon! Remember me?" I shout, wishing I knew where the hell my inside voice went. "Ember said you're really good in bed."

Brandon laughs and kisses the top of Ember's head, which kind of makes me want to cry because it's so sweet.

"You're not a sniffer dicker, baby. Not at all," Ember reassures him, wrapping her arms around his waist and snuggling into his side as they move past us, her voice fading the farther away they walk. "Where's our kid? Did he drive you here? He can't drive yet, can he? Oh my God, how long have I been gone?"

Once they're out the door, I attempt to get off my stool, but Clint is still standing between my legs, blocking my way.

He's staring down at me, not saying a word, and I can't handle the quiet or the way he's studying me. After a few seconds, he finally shakes his head, moves his hands off my hips, and grabs my arm, helping me slide down off the stool.

As soon as he's sure I'm not going to topple over when I'm standing, he grabs my hand and laces his fingers through mine, pulling me toward the door like it's totally natural and we do this shit all the time. I try not to freak out, but I know my hand is sweaty and gross, and I try really hard to come up with a good insult to say to him so I can feel like I have the upper hand, but all I can think about is how good it feels to have my hand in his.

The cool night air feels amazing on my flushed skin as soon as we walk outside, and I close my eyes and take a bunch of deep breaths, letting Clint guide me toward his truck. He helps me get in the passenger seat, and I'm so annoyed with myself for getting all flustered around him that I smack his hands away when he leans over me and tries to help me buckle my seatbelt.

He just chuckles, closing the door and walking around the front of the truck to the driver side. I lean my head against the window and close my eyes as he starts it up and pulls out of the parking lot, the sway of the vehicle making me really, really tired all of a sudden.

We drive in complete silence for a while, and I try one more time to say something insulting, but all this damn booze is like a truth serum. I can't stop the words that come out of my mouth, even though I know I'm going to regret them.

"Why didn't you ever call me after my graduation party?" I whisper, squeezing my eyes closed and refusing to look over at him.

He's quiet for so long that I start to think he didn't hear me. Right before I feel myself being pulled under into sweet, sweet oblivion, I finally hear him whisper back, and it's probably the alcohol muddling everything in my brain, but he almost sounds kind of sad.

"You never called me either, fancy pants."

Chapter 10
Chump Life

YOU WANT TO know what the sign of a good nanny is? The fact that the kids you are in charge of are still alive after two weeks in your care. I should really get a gold star, a pat on the back, or maybe even a monument in my honor on the town square. As long as I keep Mia away from sharp objects and anything with high fructose corn syrup, she's actually not that bad. I've learned that if you just smile and nod every couple of minutes, she totally thinks you've heard every word she's said. That only bit me in the ass once, three days ago, when she asked me if she could draw a picture on her bedroom wall. Her purple unicorn she drew with markers I found out were not washable looks like a dick with eyes, but it's fine. I'm fostering her creativity and all that shit.

Grace and I have come to an agreement that helps us keep the peace. She stays locked in her room the entire time I'm here, and if I knock to make sure she's still alive, she's required to open the door long enough to show me proof of life. The first day of this arrangement, she told me twice to suck it, and called me an idiot three times. Since then, she just opens the door for two seconds then slams it in my face without saying a word. I'd call that progress.

Thank God for Mrs. Sherwood. She pretty much works the same hours as I do, nine to five during the week and off on weekends. It gives me a little bit of adult interaction in between chasing Mia all over the damn place, and she always helps me pick up the messes Mia makes when I make the mistake of turning my back on her for a few seconds. It's honestly astounding that a five-year-old can dump an entire tote of Legos down the stairs, squirt a bottle of toothpaste all over her bed, and shove ten slices of bread into the DVD player in her room in the time it takes me to pee. Mia now sits on the tub talking to me while I go to the bathroom, so that's super fun.

Ember is here almost every day as well for a few hours to work around the farm, which has been just as wonderful. She finally took me on a tour the day after our night at the Maple Inn, both of us wearing dark sunglasses and cursing at every loud noise as we both held one of Mia's hands between us and walked around the place.

When we were younger, all the pumpkins for sale were placed in neat rows right in front of the big red horse barn, along with a wooden crate of gourds in every color and bundles of corn stalks leaning all along the barn that customers could purchase. There was just a small wooden stand off to the side where a calculator and a money box was kept. One of my favorite memories was being able to help out at the stand with Ember. Mrs. Hastings would have a bunch of strands of those big white bulbs hanging from the trees above the stand, and Old Man Hastings would set up a small fire pit to keep us warm at night. Ember and I were in charge of handing out candy to all of the kids that came with their parents to shop for pumpkins and other fall decorations, while Mrs. Hastings handled the money. The only candy they ever had were these things called Sixlets. If you aren't familiar with them, they're like the poor man's version of M&M's, but just as delicious. They're little balls of candy-coated chocolate, and they come in a small, clear tube of plastic wrapping, with ten Sixlets in a single file.

Now, that little pumpkin stand has its own huge wooden building. All the pumpkins and gourds and corn stalks are still outside for people to peruse, but there are easily ten times as many of everything. They also let people go out into one of the fields closest to the building and pick their own pumpkins if they don't see something they like that's already been picked. Inside the building, you'll find everything you can possibly imagine that's made with pumpkin. Pumpkin pies, pumpkin jelly, pumpkin donuts, pumpkin butter, pumpkin-scented candles, ceramic and wooden pumpkin decorations for your home, and a million other things I'm sure I'm forgetting. Ember is in charge of the store. She makes a lot of the items herself, and orders the things she doesn't.

Where Hastings Farm used to only cater to the fall decoration needs of the locals, they now ship their pumpkins and gourds and corn stalks to stores all over the united states. People also come from all over Montana to shop here, whether they drive here by car, or come in a huge bus. Additionally, the farm books tours for elementary schools from all the surrounding cities, so classes can come out and learn about farm life.

It's seriously amazing how this little family farm that only catered to the people of White Timber, has turned into a huge business, and according to Ember, it's all because of Clint. Once he took over the business from his dad, he worked his ass off making sure it would be sustainable for a long time to come.

I don't remember much from my night out with Ember two weeks ago, aside from a really weird memory of watching a guy pee in the bathroom, and Ember yelling something about dicks. The only thing I *do* remember with perfect clarity was the fact that Ember's husband and Clint had to come rescue us. Sheila will no longer be getting one half of a broken heart, BFF necklace from me now that I know she's the one who called Clint and told him he needed to come get us. It's just my luck that he continues to see me at my absolute worst. I'm also pretty sure I said something really stupid to him during the ride back to my dad's house. Something honest and pathetic that vodka and bourbon made me do, which had something to do with me whining about why he never got in touch with me after my graduation party. It's a good thing I can't remember what he said back to me, because I'm sure it was insulting, and probably included a good laugh at my expense.

If I were a bigger person, I'd seek him out and ask him about it, but I'm not. I'm small and pitiful and much happier not really remembering how that conversation went. Besides, it's not like I've really had the opportunity to chat with him since I'm busy being a nanny, and he's busy running a farm. I've caught plenty of glimpses of him here and there in the last two weeks when I'm outside with Mia, and every day at lunch, he'll come inside to grab something to eat or say hello to the girls. He only pauses long enough to insult me, never once bringing up that night in his truck, before racing back outside so quickly you would have thought there was a bomb in the room seconds from exploding.

In his defense, there was. It's *me*. I am the fucking bomb, and I'm about ready to explode all over his ass if he keeps pretending like I didn't say something so mortifyingly honest. This isn't like him at all. He enjoys making fun of me and pointing out my faults. He should be having a field day, listing all of the poor choices I made at the Maple Inn. He has the upper hand here and he's not even using it to his advantage. What a chump.

"What's a chump?" Mia asks.

Shit. Did I say that out loud?

She's lying on her stomach on the end of her bed, brushing a Barbie doll's hair, while I'm leaning with my back against the headboard, a pile of notecards strewn all around me, and a bucket of markers in between my legs. Luckily, I got my first paycheck last week, and the first stop I made on my way home from the farm was the general store in town. I bought three pairs of jeans, which I cut off into ratty jean shorts, and a pair of awesome red cowboy boots. Trying to be frugal with my money, I asked Ember if I could have a few Hastings Farm T-shirts when she took me on the tour, and I'm wearing the fitted, pale blue one right now. Mia decided to take a break from Barbie a half hour ago, and proceeded to draw smiley faces on my jean shorts.

Have at it, kid. This entire outfit only cost me ten dollars.

"A chump is Brooklyn."

Mia and I both turn our heads to find Grace standing in the doorway of Mia's room, leaning against the doorframe with her arms crossed in front of her.

"Well, look who decided to *grace* us with her presence."

I snort at my own joke, and Grace just rolls her eyes at me.

"Ha, ha, you're hilarious."

This is the most amount of words she's said to me in two weeks. I should probably keep my mouth closed and not spook her, since she's like a crazed animal in the wild who will attack at any moment, but that's never been my style. In all of my nanny research on how to deal with a difficult child, every article said you should make sure to establish who's in charge, and not let the child walk all over you. Grace has not only been walking all over me; she's been kicking the shit out of me, and it's getting a little old. Clearly scolding her and telling her she's being a jerk isn't going to work. She'll just be *more* of a jerk then, because she knows it annoys me. It also said you should try putting the child in timeout if they're being insolent, but Grace has pretty much been timing herself out for two entire weeks, and it hasn't seemed to make a difference in her attitude toward me.

Time for plan B.

"I'm almost done, Mia. Are you ready to have some fun?" I ask her, coloring in the picture I just drew on the notecard and setting it down with the others.

"I'm *so* ready! This is the best day *ever*!" she chirps excitedly, pushing up to her knees and bouncing up and down on the bed. "I'm gonna be so fast, and I'm gonna win, and I'm gonna get a prize! Is the prize a unicorn with sparkles? I want a unicorn with sparkles for a prize!"

I laugh and shake my head at her, setting the bucket of markers on her nightstand. Out of the corner of my eye, I see Grace slowly move into the room and closer to the bed. I don't look up at her; I just busy myself stacking the notecards into a neat pile and making sure they're in the right order.

"What are you guys doing?" Grace asks quietly.

"Brooklyn made a scavenger hunt for me! I get to read clues, and go find the next clue, and the next clue, and the next clue, and then when I get to the end, I get a prize and it's gonna be a *unicorn*!" Mia screams, almost falling off the bed with her bouncing excitement.

"You can't read," Grace informs her.

My eyes widen in mock surprise, and I press one of my hands against my chest, criss-crossing my legs and leaning forward closer to Mia.

"Shoot! I think I might have made this scavenger hunt too hard. Now what are we going to do?"

"Grace can read! Grace can read real good! She reads me stories all the time! Can Grace come with us? *Grace*! You have to come with us! I'll share my prize with you when I win!" Mia begs, folding her little hands together under her chin and batting her eyelashes at Grace.

Damn, this kid is good.

"Oh, I'm sure Grace has better things to do and wouldn't want to participate in a silly little scavenger hunt that has the best prize *ever* at the end of it," I tell Mia, grabbing my sheet of notebook paper that lists the order of the cards and where I should put them, double-checking everything, and not looking up to see if Grace is even close to falling for this.

"Please, Grace! Please, please, please! I'll do all your chores for the next week!" Mia promises.

Grace lets out a huge sigh right next to me, and I finally take a peek at her out the corner of my eye without lifting my head.

She's still glaring at me, but the corner of her mouth is twitching, and if I'm not mistaken, I do believe she's trying really hard not to smile.

"Uggghhh, *fine*! I'll help you with this stupid scavenger hunt. But you have to do my chores for *two* weeks," she tells Mia.

Mia screams so loudly that Grace and I both wince as we watch her jump off the bed and start running in circles around the room.

"I really hope the prize isn't a box of things made with sugar," Grace mutters to me as Mia goes racing out of the room, and the two of us walk side by side, following her out.

"Shit. Yeah, I didn't really think this through all the way," I reply.

Grace laughs as we go down the stairs, and I try not to pass out from the sound that isn't at all condescending and just filled with pure joy. Sure, it's kind of at my expense considering I'll be the one that has to deal with Mia's sugar high when she finds the box at the end of the scavenger hunt that's pretty much filled with giant handfuls of every kind of penny candy I found at the general store yesterday, but whatever.

Yep, I'm officially a chump. But this is what I like to call a win, ladies and gentleman. Now, when's that monument going to be ready for the town square?

Chapter 11
Jerk Life

"SHOULD WE MOVE her? That can't be comfortable."

Grace and I stand next to the coffee table in the living room with our hands on our hips, staring down at a sleeping Mia. She's sprawled across the top of the table on her stomach, her arms and legs spread-eagle, with her cheek resting on a pile of pink and white candy corn, and a half-eaten pink Laffy Taffy clutched in one of her fists. Various other pieces of pink candy—since pink is her favorite—and empty wrappers litter the table all around her body. If we could lift her up without disturbing anything, the top of the table would look like a pink chalk outline of a body at a crime scene. Death by too much candy.

"Do you really want her to wake up right now?" Grace asks.

"I won. Caaandy," Mia mumbles in her sleep without opening her eyes, shoving the Laffy Taffy in her mouth and sucking on it like a pacifier.

Wrapping my hand around Grace's arm, I start slowly backing away from the table, pulling her along with me. We move backward on our toes, careful not to make a sound until we get to the doorway, letting out the breaths we were holding. I take one last look at Mia to make sure she's still sound asleep, and we turn and head across the hall into the kitchen.

Grace takes a seat at the table and I move to the pantry, sliding open one of the doors and pulling out a small gift bag I put in there earlier while the girls watched TV for a little bit to give me time to set up the scavenger hunt around the farm. Walking back to the table, I sit down next to Grace, putting the bag on top of the table and pushing it over in front of her.

"What's this?"

"It's your prize from the scavenger hunt," I tell her.

"But Mia won. And she already got her prize."

"Oh, please. You and I both know Mia didn't really win. The only reason she found that box of candy in the tractor wheel was because you did all the work. She just kept running up to every tree screaming, *Unicorn! Where are you, unicorn?*' She's not the smartest tool in the shed, is she?"

Good God. I've been in this town less than a month and already using one of my dad's famous quotes.

Grace smiles and starts to reach for the bag, pausing with her hand hovering over it, and her smile quickly disappears.

"Let me guess. A bunch of girly, pink candy, and stupid plastic jewelry," she mutters, dropping her hand back to the table.

Not only did I fill the scavenger hunt prize box with every pink piece of candy I could find at the general store, I also filled it with enough plastic, sparkly bangle bracelets and necklaces that added at least five pounds to Mia's tiny body.

"Guess you won't know until you look inside." I shrug.

With a sigh, Grace grabs the bag and pulls it down onto her lap. I smile when her eyes grow wide as soon as she looks inside, her hand diving into the gift bag and quickly pulling everything out one-by-one, setting the items on the table in front of her.

Four packs of MLB trading cards, a bag of chocolates wrapped in foil that look like little baseballs, a pen shaped like a baseball bat with a matching baseball notepad, two packets of grape Big League Chew gum, and a New York Yankees baseball cap I got years ago when I went to a game and never wore it again.

Today might be the first day I've spent any time with Grace, but I've been pretty observant during the handful of seconds before she would slam her bedroom door in my face. Where Mia's room is all pink and sparkly and filled with Barbie dolls, stuffed animals, dresses, play jewelry, makeup, and every other typical little girl thing you can think of, Grace's room is the exact opposite. In the brief flashes I'd get of Grace's room, I saw New York Yankees posters all over her walls, a couple baseball bats leaning against the wall by her window, and a shelf filled with a bunch of MLB baseball hats, where I was pretty certain I never saw one for the Yankees.

"Holy crap!" Grace exclaims.

"You probably shouldn't say that."

"Oh my crap!" she amends with a cheeky smile.

"Sure. Much better. You don't already have a Yankees hat, do you?"

She shakes her head, picking up the hat and putting it on, looking over at me for approval. Without giving it a second thought, I reach over with both my hands and tuck her hair behind her ears to get it out of her face.

"Now it's perfect. I can see your pretty face."

She rolls her eyes at me, but when she quickly ducks her head to grab a pack of the gum and tear it open, I can see the corner of her mouth tip up into a smile.

"Did your dad ever tell you the story about the day we met?" I ask as Grace shoves a handful of the stringy gum into her mouth, holding the open packet out to me and offering me some.

She shakes her head as I dip my hand inside and pinch some of it between my fingers, tipping my head back and dropping it into my mouth. I chew it for a few seconds before continuing.

"I was in kindergarten, and he was in second grade. I came over to play with your aunt Ember, and your dad had a bunch of friends over. They were playing baseball in the front yard, and I asked if I could play with them. He told me no, because I was a girl."

"Really? What did you do? Did you cry? Did you tell on him and get him in trouble?" Grace asks.

"Hell no! I did the mature thing. I kicked him in the nuts, told him he was a jerk, and that he just didn't want me to play because he knew I'd mop the field with him."

Grace smacks her hand over her mouth, her shoulders shaking with laughter.

"I think it's kind of cool he grew out of that nonsense and doesn't think girls can't play baseball anymore. I'm sure you guys must have some awesome games out here at the farm."

Her laughter fades away and her hand drops from her mouth. She busies herself taking the cap off the baseball pen, flipping open the notebook, and doodling on one of the pages.

"We used to. He's too busy now for stuff like that." She shrugs, keeping her head down and focusing really hard on her doodles.

I can actually feel my heart breaking in half when I hear the sadness in her voice. I want to say something to make her feel better, but I have no clue what that would be. I see both sides here. This is a huge farm and it takes a lot of work to keep it running smoothly, and all of that responsibility falls on Clint's shoulders. But at the same time, he's missing out on so much by working so hard.

"My mom always got annoyed whenever we'd go out and play baseball," Grace says quietly.

My ears perk up and I lean forward, trying not to make it too obvious that I'm hanging on her every word.

The mysterious mother. Finally.

"She thought it was dumb that I liked baseball more than girl stuff, like Mia. She was always arguing with my dad about how he shouldn't encourage me to do boy stuff. They fought all the time. Maybe if I didn't like boy stuff so much, she wouldn't have left and never come back."

Nope. Never mind. Now *my heart is officially breaking.*

Now I understand why my dad said Clint and I might have something in common, and why everyone in this town said he's been through a lot. He didn't lose his mother, but he lost the mother of his kids, and I can only imagine how hard that's been on him, having to raise these girls all by himself.

"Oh, sweetie," I whisper, reaching over and placing my hand on top of hers to get her to stop scribbling in the notebook.

I don't know what in the hell the right thing is to do here. Something tells me I should be racing out of the house to find Clint so he can deal with this. Not because

I don't want to, but because it should be *him* comforting his daughter over something like this, not me. I know it's probably what I *should* do, but I can't walk away from her, not right now. Not when I know exactly how she's feeling, and all the guilt she's carrying inside of her.

"Let me tell you something right now, and you better listen to me. Nothing, and I mean *nothing* you did made her leave. Do you hear me? Sometimes, moms just leave. Sometimes, they're just not cut out to be moms. It has absolutely nothing to do with you."

She finally looks up at me with tears in her eyes and her chin quivering.

"Do you have a mom?" she asks softly.

"I guess I do. Somewhere. She left a long time ago."

"She wasn't cut out to be a mom either?" Grace prompts.

I shake my head. "No. She wasn't. It kind of sucks."

"Yeah. It really sucks," Grace agrees.

"Have you talked to your dad about any of this?"

I'm pretty sure I already know the answer to this one, but I'm asking it anyway.

She quickly whips her head back and forth. "He doesn't like to talk about her. It makes him mad."

Son of a bitch. It's like I'm reliving my childhood all over again.

"Well, I know we don't know each other very well yet, but I'm pretty cool. If you ever want to talk about her, I'll always listen, okay?"

She nods silently, and I move my hand off of hers to let her continue doodling.

A few minutes later, Mrs. Sherwood comes into the room with a basket of laundry in her hands, setting it down on the table next to us.

"Looks like you can punch out now, Brooklyn. I got it from here until Clint finishes up for dinner," she tells me with a smile, as she starts pulling towels out of the basket and folding them.

Pushing my chair back from the table and standing up, I give Grace a pat on the head as I walk around her, letting Mrs. Sherwood know that Mia is currently in a coma on the coffee table in the living room.

"You'll be back tomorrow, right?" Grace asks, as I pause in the doorway.

Looking back over my shoulder, I smile at her.

"Tomorrow's Saturday, and you guys are on your own for the weekend. But I'll be back first thing Monday. Maybe we can play some baseball or something."

A smile lights up Grace's face, and I silently pat myself on the back as I walk out into the hallway. As soon as I turn the corner and head toward the front door, I let out a squeak of surprise when I run right smack into Clint, leaning against the wall with his hands in the front pockets of his jeans.

Nervous excitement courses through me at being so close to him again, and I curse myself for being so pathetic.

"Hey, loser. You're actually not going to run away from me this time, like a scared little girl?" I joke.

Clint doesn't even crack a smile. He just turns away from me and heads toward the door.

"I'll walk you out."

Well, alrighty then.

As I grab my purse from the side table by the door and walk outside behind him, I don't even bother trying not to look at his ass. It's a thing of beauty, and I'm going to appreciate it if I want to, dammit. Maybe he's walking me out here so he can apologize for acting so nervous around me since the Maple Inn. Of course I'll have to insult him a little bit just because of the torture he put me through. Maybe something along the lines of, *"I'm sure it's not the first time you made a woman pass out from boredom in your presence."* Then, things can go back to normal. We can go back to picking on each other constantly without him acting all weird and trying to get away from me as fast as he can. He can go back to not being able to stand me, and I can go back to fantasizing about him in secret, knowing nothing will ever come of it. Of course I'll try and go a little easier on him now that I understand all the shit he's been through. I'm a giver like that.

When we get to the driver side of my dad's truck, I lean against it while Clint starts pacing back and forth in front of me, sliding his hand through his hair as I watch him.

"Let me just make this easy on you," I speak up after a few quiet minutes. "I accept your apology."

He finally stops pacing and looks at me like horns have suddenly started growing out of my head.

"Why in the hell would I apologize to you?" he asks through clenched teeth.

Under normal circumstances, an angry Clint would make me very pleased. Something tells me these aren't exactly normal circumstances, and I have no clue why he seems to be incredibly pissed at me.

"Um, maybe for acting all weird and nervous around me? I mean, I don't know what all I did on the ride home from the bar last week, but I'm pretty sure at some point I apologized, and I even thanked you for picking us up. It's not like we made out or anything disgusting like that," I tell him.

Shit! We didn't make out and I forgot, right? Right?

He laughs, but it's definitely not one filled with humor.

"I don't have time to deal with that bullshit right now, because it doesn't even matter. What matters, is you giving *my* daughter advice about something you don't know a fucking thing about."

I swallow past the lump in my throat and keep my back plastered to the side of the truck when he takes a step closer to me until we're toe-to-toe.

"Her mother left two years ago, and we haven't

heard a word from her since. She just packed up her shit and left her two girls behind, without so much as a phone call since then. Don't you dare sit in *my* kitchen, trying to suck up to *my* kid, by pretending like you two have something in common. Your mother might not have lived here, but at least she still gave a shit. At least she still loved you, at least she still called you, and at least she still made an effort to see you. You don't know anything about what Grace is going through, and you sure as hell aren't going to be sticking around when the summer is over. You'll leave, and then I'll have to pick up the fucking pieces. You can go back to your happy little life in New York, trolling for married men, and forget all about us."

I can't stop the gasp that flies out of my mouth, or the tears that fall from my eyes. So much for Clint possibly not knowing about what happened in New York. And so much for me thinking there might actually be a decent human being in there somewhere that I still maybe had a thing for.

Swiping angrily at the tears on my cheeks, I step to the side and start digging through my purse for the keys.

"Good job," I whisper, my voice cracking with emotion. "You officially win the insult war. You definitely secured the title of Biggest Fucking Jerk in the World."

Turning my back on him when I finally find the keys, I don't bother trying to stop the tears from falling as I fling open the door, get inside, and start up the engine.

As I back up and turn the truck around, it doesn't even make me feel a little bit better to see a whole shit ton of regret on Clint's face when I glance at him in the rearview mirror as I drive away.

Chapter 12

CLINT
Regretful Life

"SON OF A bitch. Fuck!"

I kick the dirt at my feet with the toe of my boot, scrubbing my hands down my face as I watch the cloud of dust floating above the driveway from Brooklyn's truck slowly disappear.

"You forgot pigheaded, dumbass, and shit for brains."

Quickly whirling around, I find Mrs. Sherwood standing on the top step of the porch with her hands on her hips, looking like she's two seconds away from marching over to me and smacking me upside the head.

"Don't start," I mutter, taking a few steps in the direction of the stables.

"You take one more step, Clint Alexander Hastings, and I will paddle your ass just like I did when you were eight and that smart mouth of yours got you in trouble," she warns.

Of course she has to bring up the one and only time

she ever spanked me, and *of course* it had to do with the woman who just peeled out of my driveway. Brooklyn kicked me in the balls and *I* got in trouble for it. Mrs. Sherwood always did have a soft spot for Brooklyn, and it looks like nothing has changed.

Okay, there, shit for brains. Like you haven't always had a soft spot for her as well?

I angrily run my hand through my hair, tugging as hard as I can on it, hoping it will erase the memory of her standing in front of me with tears streaming down her cheeks.

Brooklyn Manning doesn't cry. Ever. No matter how many times I picked on her, no matter what kind of embarrassing situations she always got herself into growing up, no matter what life threw at her, she never, ever shed a tear. She was always so fucking strong and defiant, and it was always a goddamn turn-on to see her all fired up and pissed off. There shouldn't be a sharp pain in my chest that I'm itching to rub away just because I was the one to break her. I thought she'd give it right back to me. I thought she'd call me every name she could think of, and possibly make up a few creative ones. I thought she'd stomp her foot and pitch the biggest fit known to man. I didn't know how to handle the fact that I was pissed at what I overheard in the kitchen, and when she turned around and looked at me, so hurt and defeated, I wanted to immediately take back every word I said and pull her into my arms.

"What I don't understand, and what I'm gonna need you to explain to me, is how you could have said such awful and hurtful things to a woman you've been half in love with since the day you met her," Mrs. Sherwood continues, making my head slowly turn back to look at her, my eyes wide and my mouth gaping open.

"Oh, please. I'm old, but I ain't dead. My eyes work perfectly fine, thank you very much," she informs me. "You been chasing that girl around since the day she stood up to you and kicked you in the nuts. You came back to this farm, working your ass off to make it good, pretending like you were happy to be here. Yet the first time I saw you smile since Mia was born was the day you walked into the kitchen and saw her standing there."

Jesus. Leave it to Mrs. Sherwood to make me feel like an even bigger idiot than I already do.

I was one of the many guys in this town who had a thing for Brooklyn back in the day. She was fucking gorgeous with her dark hair, pale blue eyes, killer body, and her refusal to ever back down from any challenge. Even after all these years, every single male under the age of sixty has stopped me in town since she's been back, asking how she is, if she's dating anyone, and if I think they'd have a shot with her now.

I was a coward back when we were teenagers. I was a computer nerd who only had friends because my sister was popular, and because I was "friends" with an equally popular Brooklyn. I knew she was out of my league from the moment I met her, and that feeling never went away. She was destined for bigger and better things than this small town, and I knew I'd never have anything to offer her to make her stay.

Sure, I went off to California and did my own thing for a while, but I hated every minute of it. I hated how fake everyone was. I hated how everything moved so fast, and people were always trying to one-up each other with better cars, bigger houses, and who could make more money. I wasn't forced to come back here because my dad got sick. I came back here, because I couldn't breathe in the big city. I needed wide-open spaces, familiar faces, and peace and quiet.

I thought I was doing fine. I thought I was handling everything okay. Running the farm, raising the girls on my own, and doing my best to make sure they forgot about their worthless mother and moved on with their lives, doing whatever I could to try and be happy. And then Brooklyn walked back into my life, and it felt like I'd just woken up from a coma. Everything was louder, more colorful, brighter, newer, and more exciting. I couldn't wait to wake up every day just to catch a glimpse of her. I couldn't wait to walk into the house and see what kind of mess she'd gotten into with Mia, my little troublemaker. I counted down the seconds until I finished up with work in the afternoons so I could take my lunch break, race inside, and fire an insult at her, just to watch her eyes sparkle and her brain work overtime to lob one right back at me. She made me feel alive again for the first time in years.

And then I walked into the house a little bit ago and overheard her talking with Grace. I went through such a wide range of emotions I thought my head would implode.

Sadness—that my girl was so tied up about her mother and never said anything to me about it, and I'd been too much of an idiot to notice.

Jealousy—that she opened up to Brooklyn instead of me.

Hurt—that all of my faults where my daughters were concerned, and how much I'd been neglecting them, were being thrown right in my face.

And white hot rage—when Brooklyn tried to make it sound like they had everything in common, making promises to her I know she wouldn't be able to keep. Just like twelve years ago, when I lost my head and almost kissed her, the reality that she wouldn't be sticking around here hit me like a two-by-four across the face. White Timber isn't her home anymore. It's just a temporary stop. Soon enough, she'll be leaving us behind, taking her color and brightness and happiness right along with her.

"It doesn't matter. She overstepped, plain and simple," I tell Mrs. Sherwood, completely avoiding the whole "half in love with her" comment.

"Boy, your mother would be turning over in her grave if she heard the bullshit coming out of your mouth right now," she says with a shake of her head.

"Um, Mom's not dead. She's living it up in Florida in a condo with Dad. I just talked to her yesterday. They joined a bowling league."

"Don't sass me! If she heard the things you yelled at Brooklyn, she'd keel over, and then start flailing around six feet under."

She steps down off the porch, walks right up to me, and pokes her finger in my chest.

"Listen up, buddy boy. You better pull your head out of your ass, and you better pull it out of there fast. You don't know everything you think you do about that girl. She put on a brave face for a lot of years, but I know for a fact she has *everything* in common with your girls. Every. Thing. Do you honestly think she would have said those things to Grace if she didn't know *exactly* what that little girl was going through? If she didn't know about the pain and the guilt and the torture of being left behind and never thought of again? Of having to live with thinking for all these years that she's easy to leave and unlovable?" she asks, making my stomach roll with nausea.

It can't be true; there's no way. I listened to Brooklyn brag about her mother and their relationship for years. She'd tell anyone who asked, and even those who didn't, how close they were and how their bond was even stronger after she left town.

Son of a bitch. Son of a mother fucking bitch!

She talked about that woman incessantly, and there was always something a little forced about it, but I was too busy fantasizing about getting in her pants and didn't pay that close of attention. No one talks about how amazing their mother is that much, especially a teenage girl. How in the fuck didn't I see that?

"Ahhh, I see the lightbulb is finally turning on," Mrs. Sherwood muses, patting me on the arm.

"I'm going to assume you know this inside information because of all the extra time you've been spending with Mr. Manning?"

It's Mrs. Sherwood's turn to look at me with wide eyes and her mouth dropped open in shock.

"I ain't dead yet. And my eyes work perfectly fine." I smirk, repeating the words she said to me a little bit ago.

"I have no idea what you're talking about." She huffs, crossing her arms in front of her.

"Oh, really? Like how you always seem to make too much for dinner, even though you've been cooking for the same number of people for years, and those leftovers always somehow make their way over to Mr. Manning's house? And I'm guessing you're just being a good neighbor when you stop over there a few times a week to clean his house. I have to say, it was awfully suspicious that on the day he was being released from the hospital, when he called a few days ahead of time to see if you could pick him up, I overheard you telling him you had to work. When you'd already requested that day off," I muse, tapping my finger against my chin. "Awfully suspicious."

"You can just wipe that smirk right off your face," she scolds. "Allen Manning and I are friends. Friends do nice things for each other. It's not that out of the ordinary for a friend to strongly suggest that he should call his only daughter and ask her to come home. And besides, this isn't about me. This is about *you*. You've got some groveling to do, and it damn well better be good."

"It doesn't matter, does it? She's still not sticking around. She still has a life in New York to go back to," I remind her.

"Says who? I haven't heard her mention New York since she got here. Not once. And according to her father, she hasn't said diddly about it to him either. I'm thinking all she needs is a little incentive to stay. I know for a fact that there's a little girl sitting at the table inside, who would really enjoy some one-on-one time with her daddy and help him come up with a plan."

As soon as those words leave her mouth, the front screen door opens and slams shut, and Grace walks out onto the porch, holding Mia's hand.

Jesus, I'm such an asshole. In more ways than one.

I wanted to raise my girls here in White Timber,

because I wanted them to have the best life I could possibly give them. Even though I was more interested in electronics than farm life when I was younger, I could never deny this was the best place to grow up. Busting my ass to make sure they had a legacy in this farm for when they're older, a roof over their heads they could be proud of, and anything their hearts desired didn't do jack shit toward giving them a good life. My undivided attention, making sure they know I'll always be here for them, and helping them make happy memories that will last a lifetime is all they really need, and I've fucking failed at that.

Moving around Mrs. Sherwood, I take the steps two at a time until I can squat down in front of them. Reaching my hands up, I run my palms down both of their heads, cupping their cheeks, and try not to break down like a fucking baby that Grace looks shocked as shit that I'm touching her. My strong girl quickly clears her throat and wipes the shock off of her face, as I drop my hands down to rest on top of my knees.

"Dad, I think we have a problem," she informs me.

"What's that, ba—"

The word *baby* gets immediately cut off when Mia opens her mouth and a stream of chunky, hot pink puke comes flying at me, hitting my neck and my chest. It proceeds to drip down the front of my shirt and pool in the crotch of my jeans.

"Mia doesn't feel well," Grace adds, pressing her

hand over her mouth and trying her hardest to cover up her laugh.

"Thanks for the notice," I mutter, staring down at the explosion of pink vomit all down the front of me.

I hear a clicking sound, followed by a giggle, and look up to find Mrs. Sherwood standing behind the girls, holding up her phone and snapping a shit ton of pictures of me.

"Oh, yes. This is perfect." She laughs, dropping her arms and pressing a few buttons on the damn thing.

"What are you doing?"

"Giving you a head start on that whole groveling thing. Grace, come over here and show me how to send a text to Miss Brooklyn."

Chapter 13
Twilight Zone Life

How MANY DAYS in a row can you use dry shampoo in your hair before you officially become a disgusting human being who gives zero fucks?

I should probably also poll the audience and see how many days one can live on a box of Cheez-Its and a two liter of Mountain Dew before your stomach starts eating itself, in desperate need of real sustenance.

I've spent the entire weekend lying on my bed, hugging my box of crackers under one arm, and my Mountain Dew under the other, talking to the Joshua Jackson poster on my ceiling. I thought what happened in New York was rock-bottom, but I was sorely mistaken. *This* is it. I'm am officially in the pits of hell.

Not even the handful of photos Mrs. Sherwood sent me Friday night of Clint covered in pink puke could lift my bad mood. Mostly because that asshole still looked hot, even covered in chunks of vomit.

I hate that I didn't stand up for myself out in his

driveway two days ago. I should have shouted, and cursed, and called him every name I could think of, defending myself and making him feel like shit for the things he said to me that couldn't have been farther from the truth. Instead, I stood there and took his verbal lashing, and I fucking *cried*. I let him see how much he hurt me, and I think that's the worst part in all of this. Probably because I never thought he would do something like that to me. Sure, we have a very unhealthy relationship that revolves around picking on each other, but it's always been in good fun. I've never said anything overly cruel, and the things he's said to me were always more annoying than mean. I can't get past the fact that he took every insecurity I have and threw it in my face. He reminded me what a liar and a loser I am in regards to my mother. And he reminded me I'm a home wrecking hussy, even if I didn't set out to intentionally ruin a marriage. The fact that he thinks I did hurts more than anything.

Fifteen minutes ago, I got a text from Mrs. Sherwood asking if my dad and I were home, because she had something she needed to drop off. I know I should get up and do *something* to attempt to look human, but it's just Mrs. Sherwood. If she's put off by me wearing a pair of my dad's gray sweatpants with the waistband rolled down twice, and the same pale blue Hastings Farm shirt I was wearing Friday, with my hair in a messy bun on top of my head, so be it.

There's a knock on my bedroom door, and my dad pops his head in when I tell him it's unlocked. He hasn't bothered me all weekend, so at least I have that to be thankful for. When I walked through the front door Friday night and he took one look at me with my tear-stained cheeks, he turned the volume up louder on the television after letting me know there was a gallon of double chocolate chunk ice cream in the freezer. At that moment, I kind of felt bad for how much I'd been nagging him since I got here.

"Someone's at the door for you," he tells me.

With a sigh, I sit up in bed and swing my legs off the side, brushing some of the orange crumbs off my shirt as I stand.

"You want some fatherly advice?" he asks, as I walk across the room and pause in front of him.

"Not really."

"Good. Because I don't know how to do that," he mutters.

For the first time all weekend, I have to fight back a smile.

"Listen. Clint has—"

"Blah, blah, blah, Clint has had a hard time," I cut him off, with a roll of my eyes. "I don't give a shit. So have I."

"Can I finish what I was gonna say?" he asks in annoyance.

I glare at him, keeping my mouth shut for him to

continue, getting ready to cover my ears like a toddler.

"As I was saying, Clint has behaved like a goddamn asshole. He's a good man for the most part, and I like him, but if he makes you cry again, I'm gonna load up my shotgun and pump his ass full of lead," he informs me, my mouth dropping open in shock. "If you don't wanna work out at the farm anymore, I wouldn't blame you. Don't worry about money. I got plenty of money for whatever you need. But just saying, I didn't raise you to back down from a challenge, or to let someone walk all over you."

What in the shit is happening right now?

"How do you even—"

"It's rude to let company wait around on the front porch," he cuts me off, when I start to ask him how even knows what the hell happened on Friday.

With that, he turns and walks down the hallway, disappearing into his room.

Shaking my head in complete confusion, I quickly head in the opposite direction as my dad. I have no clue why he didn't just invite Mrs. Sherwood in. Sometimes he can be such a pain in the ass. A sweet pain in the ass who offered to shoot Clint for me, but a pain in the ass nonetheless. Flinging the door open, I can't help but smile when I see Mia and Grace standing on the front porch.

Who knew that after only a few weeks, a couple of kids would actually make me happy, instead of making me want to run in the opposite direction, screaming my head off to get away from them?

"Hey, girls! Mrs. Sherwood brought you with her?" I ask, confused when I look over their heads and don't see her standing behind them on the porch.

I squint, trying to see if she's somewhere out in the yard, but it's too dark to see much farther than the bottom of the porch steps.

Before they can respond, I hear a few thumping footsteps, and Clint suddenly appears from the shadows to the right of the door. He moves to stand behind the girls, all three of them spotlighted by the bright porch light.

My smile instantly falls when I see him, even though my traitorous heart starts pounding in my chest. At first glance, I want to stomp my foot that he has to look so good in his typical uniform of well-worn jeans, a flannel tucked into them, and cowboy boots, while I look like complete asshole. But then I take a second to study him, and I see stubble on his face, dark circles under his eyes, and his hair is all askew from where I'm sure he's been incessantly running his hand through it.

My first instinct is to slam the door in his face, but I can't do that. Not with the girls smiling up at me. I'm pretty sure that's exactly why he's standing behind them, with his arms around them and his hands tightly gripping their shoulders. The look in his eyes is one full of sadness, with a touch of nervous fear as he uses them as a shield, like I might try to kick him in the nuts.

*Which sounds like a fabulous idea, but again, the girls.
Damn him!*

I force myself to look away from him, since it hurts too much to look into his eyes and see any kind of worry or pain there. He doesn't get the right to feel any of that shit after what he said to me.

"What are you girls doing here?" I ask softly, forcing myself to keep my eyes on them and not let them stray back up to Clint.

I don't realize they've been standing here with both of their arms behind their backs until they pull them around in front of them, clutching tightly to huge bouquets of flowers that they hold out toward me.

"Dad said these used to be your favorite flowers, and they're mine too, because they're pink and I love pink and Grace hates them because they're pink, but I don't care because they're so pretty, so here you go!" Mia rambles, as I take her bouquet with a soft laugh.

Shooting Star flowers have always been my favorite; it's true. They're wildflowers that grow at the far edge of the Hastings fifty-acre farm. They can grow to be around sixteen inches tall, and the bright magenta petals flare rearward around the pointed, yellow center, resembling the tail of a shooting star. I not only love them because they look like a shooting star, but because I'm probably the only person in the world who hates the smell of flowers. They always make me think of being at a funeral. The Shooting Star doesn't have a floral smell at all.

When Clint was old enough to drive one of the tractors, Ember and I would beg him to give us a ride out there at least once a week, so we could pick them and put them in vases all over the house. Clint would tell me my ugly face would make them wilt and die within an hour, and I would tell him his dragon breath would kill them long before my face could.

Dammit. Stop thinking of things that make you smile. This is not the time to smile.

"Dad also wants you to know he's sorry for being a big dummy," Mia chirps with a huge smile on her face.

"And for being a jerk, an idiot, and… what was the last one?" Grace asks, turning to look back over her shoulder and up at Clint.

"A jackass. But don't say that one," he tells her in a quiet voice.

The sound of his voice sends shivers up my spine, and once again, I'm cursing myself for being such an idiot when it comes to him. And for the tears that pool in my eyes and the lump in my throat that won't seem to go away, as Grace looks back at me and hands me her bouquet of flowers.

Clutching the stems of at least two dozen flowers tightly in my hands and hugging them to my chest, I finally lift my eyes and look at Clint again. He looks as miserable as I feel, and that almost makes things a tiny bit better.

"That's really low, using your kids, Hastings. Really low," I whisper.

"Gotta pull out the big guns when necessary, Manning," he replies with a crooked smile.

"Do I hear my girls out there?"

My dad's voice echoes from behind me, and as soon as the girls hear it, their eyes light up and they practically shove me out of the way to go racing into the house.

"Papa M! Papa M!" Mia yells, as my dad squats down in the hallway, and both girls throw themselves at him.

He wraps his arms around both of them, and I start to wonder if I'm hallucinating. Maybe Shooting Star flowers are poisonous and I never knew. Maybe touching them is the equivalent of having a really bad acid trip, and I'm high as fuck right now.

Speaking of flowers and acid trips, there was this flower that grew all around White Timber High called a Moonflower. They were called that because they only bloomed at night. Senior year, someone dared Joey Phillips to eat one during the last home football game of the season. In the final play of the game, Joey came running out onto the field, bare-ass naked, screaming that there was a kangaroo chasing him.

Please don't let me start stripping and running around the house screaming about kangaroos.

"What in the hell is happening? Did I accidentally

take drugs?" I mutter, watching my dad throw his head back and laugh… *laugh* at something Mia whispers in his ear.

All of a sudden, I feel the heat from Clint's body when he steps forward on the porch, the front of him pressing up against my back as we both stand in the doorway looking down the hallway. He bends his head down close to my ear and—

Seriously, fuck you, body! Stop losing your shit, just because you can feel his warm breath against your ear. We hate him, remember? Just because he's sorry, and looks all sad and pathetic, and picked your favorite flowers for Mia and Grace to give you, doesn't mean we forgive him.

"Yeah, so I guess the girls have been here a bunch before with Mrs. Sherwood. As soon as I pulled into the driveway, they got all excited when they realized you live here too. Apparently, Mrs. Sherwood and your dad have a thing," Clint explains softly.

"A thing?" I reply in shock.

"It could be a sexual thing, or it could be a friend-ship thing. I haven't really put my finger on it yet."

"Never, ever say *sexual thing* again when talking about my dad," I warn him, which makes him chuckle.

Which makes goose bumps break out on my arms.

Which makes me want to claw my skin off and throw it in his face for doing this shit to me.

"Did they seriously call him Papa M?" I ask, still watching my dad laugh and carry on with the girls.

"I've been told he asked them to call him that," Clint responds, and I can feel his chest slide up and down against my back as he shrugs.

"Can we go in the garage and play with the Barbies?" Mia asks my dad.

Uh, what?

My dad finally looks up at me with a sheepish look on his face.

"I got a box of all your old toys out there. Keeps them occupied when Mrs. Sherwood stops by."

"Please, for the love of God, don't tell me my dad and Mrs. Sherwood have sex in here while the girls play with my old toys," I groan under my breath, making Clint laugh softly again.

Dammit! I need to keep my mouth shut and stop saying things that bring him joy. Clint does not deserve joy. He deserves a swift kick to the crotch. Which, coincidentally, I also feel pressed up against my ass and—son of a bitch! Now I wish I really were on drugs!

"I don't think Grace wants to play with Barbies. Grace doesn't like Barbies. Barbies are dumb," I say in annoyance.

I don't know why I said this. I sound like an idiot. What is wrong with me?

"Well, obviously," my dad scoffs. "Grace and I usually shoot some hoops with your old basketball and hoop that's still hanging up over the garage door. Her free throws are getting pretty good."

I have officially entered the Twilight Zone. My dad likes kids just as much as I do. Or, used to. He didn't even pay this much attention to *me* when I was younger, and I was his flesh and blood. I should be jealous right now, but for some reason, I'm not. It's kind of cute, in a weird-as-fuck way.

"Sorry, guys. We gotta get back to the farm so the girls can take their baths and get to bed," Clint announces.

The girls groan, and my dad starts telling them some stupid dad jokes to make them feel better. Something about how he can see potatoes growing out of their ears because they're so dirty.

Honestly, who is *this guy, and what has he done with my dad?*

While they're preoccupied, I finally turn around to face Clint.

"You coming to work tomorrow?" he asks, running one of his hands nervously through his hair, which of course I find just the tiniest bit endearing.

"Of course I'm coming to work tomorrow," I scoff. "I'm not a quitter, even if my boss is a jackass."

"Good. That's good. That's great. The girls really, really like having you there. They like seeing you every day. It makes them really happy, even if they don't act like it sometimes," he tells me, making me wonder if he's talking about the girls, or him.

Which is all so fucking confusing.

I don't bother replying, because anything I say or do right now will be complete horse shit. I'll either scream at him, punch him in the face, or drop down to the ground, rocking back and forth as I cry like a baby.

Clint's eyes never leave mine, and no matter how hard I try, I can't make myself look away. I hear the pounding of the girls' footsteps down the hall behind me, and don't even look away when they shove past me and back outside onto the porch, scrambling quickly down the stairs and over to the driveway.

"See you tomorrow, fancy pants," Clint says with a wink, before turning away and jogging down the steps.

Instead of standing in the doorway watching him walk away like an idiot, my brain finally wakes up. I quickly move back inside and slam the door closed, turning around and slumping against it as my dad comes down the hallway and joins me.

"Don't give me that look. Those girls keep me young. And they're not as annoying as most of the kids in this town," he grumbles.

"Do you want some daughterly advice?" I ask.

"Nope."

"Good. Because I don't know how to do that. You still got any of that good tequila left?" I ask.

My dad pats me on the arm before turning and heading toward the kitchen. I push off of the door and follow behind him.

"It's times like these I'm really glad I didn't sell you to a traveling circus when you were little," he says over his shoulder.

Chapter 14

CLINT
Cotton Candy Life

"U M, A LITTLE help here?"

I glance over my shoulder when no one answers me, to find Brooklyn and Grace still sitting in the middle of a blanket a few feet away, organizing all of Grace's baseball trading cards into a binder with plastic page inserts Brooklyn brought with her this morning.

"You're doing just fine. Try bribing her with sugar," Brooklyn tells me, not even looking up from the binder in her lap as Grace hands her another card to stick inside.

With a sigh, I turn back to the huge oak tree in front of me, looking up at Mia perched on a branch that is out of my reach and entirely too high off the ground. How she even got up there is beyond me. One of the farmhands came over and asked me a question about a tractor we were having a problem with, and the next thing I knew, Mia was scrambling up the tree like a cat. A cat wearing four dresses, a whole shit-ton of plastic costume jewelry, a tiara, and a pair of pink plastic dress-up shoes with two-inch heels.

I hear Brooklyn whisper something to Grace, which causes Grace to let out a full-blown belly laugh. It momentarily distracts me from trying to get Mia down from the tree. I can't even remember the last time I heard Grace laugh, and that knowledge is like a knife right through my heart. Which is why I've taken as many breaks as possible from work over the last week, and have been hanging out with them as often as I could, much to Brooklyn's annoyance.

Every morning when the girls and I are sitting on the front porch steps waiting for her to arrive, I watch her put a fake smile on her face as soon as she sees me when she gets out of her dad's truck. Every time I ask her what's next on the agenda throughout the day, I can tell it takes a lot of willpower for her not to roll her eyes, tell me to go the hell away, or insult me for being so annoying. This shit also makes me feel like someone is shoving a sharp object right through my chest. I did that to her. I made her feel like she couldn't be herself around me, and I ruined everything fun and good about our twisted relationship. Gone are the snide comments and sarcastic put-downs. In their place is a subdued, nervous woman who will barely look at me and is completely uncomfortable with me, and I fucking hate it.

I want the firecracker back who keeps me on my

toes and makes me laugh. I want the woman back from her first few weeks here, who I swore I caught staring at me more than once with something other than annoyance in her eyes. I want the woman in the car on the way home from the Maple Inn, who gave me an inkling of hope that there might be something more between us, when she asked me why I never got in touch with her after she graduated, and she sounded so upset about it.

"I bet you Princess Truffle Butter is in the mood for a sugar cube right about now," I shout up to Mia, taking Brooklyn's advice by mentioning her two favorite things: her horse, and sugar.

I hear Brooklyn snort when I say the name of Mia's horse, and it gives me even more motivation to put my next plan in motion. I've turned into a desperate sack of shit who will do anything to hear the sound of that woman's laughter again.

And yes, Mia's horse is named Princess Truffle Butter. When we got her a year ago, I made the mistake of letting her name the stallion anything she wanted. Mrs. Sherwood had just experimented with a truffle butter sauce for steak at dinner the previous week, and Mia seemed to think it was the funniest thing to say, walking around the house shouting it for seven days straight. Hence the reason we now have a horse named Princess Truffle Butter, and why I will never, ever let the girls look up *truffle butter* on Urban Dictionary.

"Sugar!" Mia suddenly shouts at the top of her lungs.

I have just enough time to brace myself and put my arms out before she flings herself off of the branch, my heart flying up into my throat as I watch her plummet down. I catch her easily and take a few minutes to hug her tightly to my chest, shaking my head when she squirms in my arms, and I set her down on the ground.

This child is going to give me a full head of gray hair before I'm forty.

"Come on, Mia. Let's put my cards away in my room and I'll help you give Princess Truffle Butter some sugar cubes," Grace announces, grabbing the binder from Brooklyn and walking over to us, holding her hand out for Mia to take.

Well, this turned out better than I expected. I thought for sure I'd have to bribe Grace to go do something with Mia so I could be alone with Brooklyn for a little while. I've spent almost every minute with Brooklyn while she's here at the farm over the last week, doing everything with her and the girls from watching movies, baking the most delicious thing I've ever eaten called a pumpkin dump cake, playing board games, doing craft projects, and one horrifying, rainy afternoon during which I let Mia put makeup on me. It was the perfect opportunity for Brooklyn to insult me and tell me I looked like a drag queen reject, but she didn't say one word when she walked into Mia's bedroom and saw me with a face full of blue eye shadow, hot pink lipstick, and some glittery shit on my cheeks that took three showers to wash off.

I can't take it anymore. I need the old Brooklyn back, not this polite, nervous one who isn't comfortable being around me.

My oldest daughter gives me an over-exaggerated wink as soon as she pauses in front of me and grabs her sister's hand.

"Try apologizing *yourself* this time, instead of making us do it. Tell her how pretty she looks and stuff like that," Grace whispers, making me have to fight back a smile.

Jesus. This kid is too smart for her own good.

"Got it," I whisper back with a serious nod. "Apologize, compliment."

"Don't screw it up," she mutters, tugging Mia's hand and pulling her toward the house.

"Don't let Mia have more than one sugar cube!" I shout after her when they're a few yards away.

"Duh! Do you think I'm an idiot?" she yells back.

I hear Brooklyn let out another little snort, and I turn around to see her folding up the blanket she and Grace were sitting on. Thank God the girls are far away now, because watching Brooklyn bend over in those tiny jean shorts makes me have to shift my legs and discretely rearrange my dick before it tries to rip right through the zipper in my jeans.

"Go ahead. I know you're dying to say something about how those two are going to age me long before my time," I tell her, finally getting my dick situation under control so I can walk over and stand next to her.

"Nope. You're doing good. They're really happy being able to spend more time with you," she says softly, tucking the blanket under her arm as she turns and starts to head in the same direction as the girls.

Fuck, I hate this.

When she moves past me, I quickly reach out and wrap my hand around her upper arm, pulling her to a stop as the blanket falls out from under her arm to the ground. I start rubbing my thumb back and forth over the smooth skin of her arm, and I smile to myself when she breaks out in goose bumps at my touch. Taking a step toward her until I'm right up against her side, I dip my head down and press my forehead to her temple, closing my eyes and taking a deep breath. Her skin smells like rainbows and sunshine and—*Jesus Christ*, someone needs to take my man card away. She actually smells just like cotton candy, and the scent instantly transports me back to eleventh grade and the first time Brooklyn Manning ever gave me a fucking hard-on in public.

"I don't have you on my list. Just have a seat at that first table right there and let me check with the office."

I looked up from the Steve Jobs article I was reading in Fortune Magazine when I heard the study hall teacher speak, unable to concentrate on it any more when I watched Brooklyn walk over to my table and flop herself down in the only available chair, which was right next to me.

"Um, this is a junior and senior study hall. The loser freshman study hall is during seventh period," I muttered, trying my best to look annoyed that she was sitting next to me, even though I just wanted to stare at her legs in that short skirt she was wearing.

"Oh, shut up, nerd. I'm having a shitty first day of high school as it is. I completely missed Algebra and Biology, and went to World History twice," she complained.

"Let me see your schedule," I told her, dropping my magazine onto the table and holding my hand out toward her.

With a sigh, she pulled a piece of folded up paper out of the front pocket of her backpack resting on her lap and handed it over.

I laughed as soon as I looked at the top of it.

"This is the schedule you got at orientation last week. Didn't you get a new one in first period?"

"Of course I got a new one in first period. Why does it matter which one I use?"

"Because they specifically told you at orientation to double-check the schedule you'd get on the first day, because it might have changed. Obviously, your schedule changed. Don't you get straight As? How are you so clueless? Wait. I know. You sleep with all the smart guys and they do your homework for you," I teased, the words making me want to throw up in my mouth as soon as I said them.

Fucking hell, please don't let her say she sleeps with all the smart guys or I will throw myself off a bridge, because I'm a goddamn smart guy and she hasn't slept with me!

"Oh, piss off! I don't sleep with all the smart guys, jackass!"

Thank you, Jesus, thank you, Jesus, thank you, Jesus…

"Ah, so you're one of those frigid girls. Good to know." I smirked.

I watched as she lifted her backpack off her legs and set it on the table in front of her before she turned her body to the side to face me. She rested one arm on the table and one on the back of my chair, and then leaned in close until her face was right next to mine.

"I'm not frigid. If you weren't so busy jerking off to pictures of Steve Jobs, maybe you'd finally be able to experience what it's like to touch a real, live girl," she said quietly, the corner of her mouth tipping up into a smirk.

All of a sudden, the sweet smell of her skin completely overwhelmed me, and before I could stop it, my goddamn traitorous dick decided to wake up and swell in my khaki pants.

The loud clang of the bell that signaled the end of this class period rang through the cafeteria where study hall was held, and Brooklyn quickly jumped up from her seat and flung her backpack over her shoulder.

"Are you just gonna sit there all day diddling yourself under the table, or are you gonna go to your next class?" she asked, having no idea just how fucking true that burn was and how much I wished it was socially acceptable to tug one out in the middle of the school day.

"I've got another study hall next period, because I'm brilliant *and already had too many credits this year, unlike you, who can't walk and chew gum at the same time," I told her.*

"You're such a dick," she said with a roll of her eyes as she turned and walked away, making the damn crotch of my dress pants swell even more hearing her say the word dick and watching the sway of her ass until she left the room.

"I am so fucking sorry," I whisper in Brooklyn's ear, pushing the memory from high school out of my head before my dick starts nudging against her hip and she doesn't take my apology seriously.

I hear her let out a shaky breath, and I open my eyes when her head moves away from mine. Her chin is dropped and her eyes are squeezed tightly closed.

"I never should have said those things to you. I was out of line, and I didn't mean a single word of it. I was pissed at myself, and I took that out on you. You made Grace smile again, and I don't know how to thank you for that. I really wish you would punch me in the face or something, so I don't have to keep feeling like shit all the time," I finish.

She blows a huge breath of air past her lips, finally opening her eyes and turning her head to look up at me.

"You also look like shit, just an FYI. They make these things called razors. You should try one."

I smile so hard at her I almost get a cramp in my cheeks.

"There she is. There's my abusive little firecracker." I chuckle. "It's okay. You can admit how irresistibly attracted you are to me. There's no shame in that."

Brooklyn scoffs and rolls her eyes, jerking her arm out of the hold I still have on it, and then crossing her arms over her chest.

"Bite me, Hastings."

"Just name the time and place, Manning," I fire back, getting a whole hell of a lot of satisfaction out of watching the way her cheeks get a little pink and her eyes glaze over.

"Just because you're no longer a dorky computer nerd, doesn't make you hot shit or anything."

It's so adorable watching her lie through her teeth, especially when her eyes trail down my body and she doesn't even realize she's doing it.

Grabbing one of her arms, I have to tug a few times to get her to drop them from being stubbornly crossed in front of her. Sliding my palm down her arm, I lace my fingers through hers and tug her in the direction of the building next to the stables we use as a store on the farm.

"Come on. I wanna show you something."

When her feet refuse to move, I give her hand a squeeze.

"It will show you just how much of a dorky computer nerd I still am, and give you plenty of opportunity to make fun of me," I offer.

"Well, why didn't you lead with that? Let's go, loser."

She quickly walks past me with our hands still connected, reversing our roles so *she's* the one tugging *me* this time. The smell of cotton candy is left in her wake, and I jog to keep up with her so it doesn't disappear.

Just fucking burn my man card at this point.

Chapter 15
Stalker Life

I AM A disgrace.

Am I honestly going to accept Clint's apology just because he got all up in my business, pressed his head against mine, and made my skin tingle and my heart flutter with his quietly whispered words?

Goddammit, I am.

"Blah, blah, blah, a POS system, which stands for blah, blah, blah, which means all of the orders made online go through the blah, blah, blah, then immediately print out so they can be filled," Clint explains, as I nod my head.

He didn't actually say *blah, blah, blah*. There was a lot of technical, nerd jargon in there I didn't understand, but just like with Mia, as long as I smile and nod my head, he thinks I'm paying attention. And I sort of *am* paying attention, but it's just really hard to follow everything he's saying when he keeps standing so damn close to me. In the last half hour, he's brushed his body against mine seven times when he needed to lean over and point to something on the computer, held my hand three times when he needed to pull me to another area in the store, and pressed his hand against the small of my back twice while he was explaining something.

Not that I'm counting or anything.

And seriously, how is it possible that this guy gets even more adorable with each dorky word out of his mouth? He's just so damn cute with how excited he gets, telling me about how he completely computerized the farm when he took over, writing special code to calculate shipping, automating payroll, and even developing an app for the companies who have large accounts with the farm, like all the big chain grocery stores, to make ordering easier for them.

My head and my heart are all tied up in knots right now, and I don't know what the hell is happening. It's almost like he's been… flirting with me since that damn apology. Which is just absurd. I'm sure a therapist would have a field day with me right now, telling me Clint picking on me all these years was his way of flirting, but I mean, come on! He would have said something long before now. He's definitely not shy when it comes to the shit that flies out of his mouth. Aside from that almost-kiss twelve years ago, which he clearly regretted, he's never done something like this. He's never done whatever he could to touch me, or stand so close to me. If anything, he would say something sarcastic and move as far away from me as possible.

It's likely the poor guy is so lonely out here in Bumfuck, Nowhere, with only horses, cows, goats, and chickens for company, that he's decided I might actually look good to him. I'm probably the only single woman in White Timber under the age of seventy. I bet he said to himself, *"Clint, you can't fuck a goat. Might as well fuck Brooklyn."*

"Brooklyn, do you want to fuck?"

Yes, yes, yes, Jesus God, yes!

"I'm sorry, what?" I ask, my head whipping around to look at him over my shoulder.

"I said, Brooklyn, do you want to see the truck?" he replies. "The one I was just telling you about, with the computer system I installed for orders. I just heard it pull up out back to get a load ready to go to Ohio."

Yes, truck. That makes much more sense. Like he'd really ask if I wanted to have sex with him. Good God, stop thinking about having sex with him!

We're standing in his office at the back of the store, and the small room suddenly got a million times smaller. The store out front is empty and quiet since it's still the off-season, and I'm suddenly hyperaware that we're the only two people in this building right now. I'm sure it's just so damn hot in this room all of a sudden because we're standing right in front of the four computers he's got lining a table against the wall next to his desk, and all that equipment must be letting off some serious heat. It definitely has nothing to do with the fact that he's still standing right behind me, with his chest pressed against my back. The same spot he's been for the last half hour as he explained everything on the computers to me, and now I can't get the image of Clint naked and thrusting into me out of my head.

"You should show me the website for the farm," I quickly announce, moving away from him and rushing over to the front of the big wooden desk behind him with papers strewn all over it, and a laptop sitting closed amongst the piles.

"No, don't—"

"Awww, is there porn on here?" I tease, cutting him off when he runs his hand nervously through his hair as he watches me walk up to the desk and lift the lid to the laptop. "It's okay to admit you have a thing for farm animal porn. I won't tell any—"

The rest of my comment gets cuts off when my heart flies right out of my chest and gets lodged in my throat as I look down at the screen of his laptop.

"What...? Where did this...? Oh my God," I whisper, staring in shock at the lock screen photo.

I don't think I could be more surprised right now if there was a picture of Clint *actually* fucking a goat. Instead, taking up the entire screen is a picture of Clint and me from high school. I remember the day it was taken. It was a few days before he left for college. The first crop of pumpkins had been picked, and Mrs. Hastings made Ember, Clint, and me sit on the top step of the front porch, each of us holding a pumpkin in our laps. We bitched and moaned about it for at least twenty minutes, until we finally gave in. And then I bitched and moaned for another five minutes, because Ember made me squeeze in between her and Clint. I made some comment under my breath about how he needed to shower and wrinkled my nose at him, just so I wouldn't be tempted to tell him I wanted to lick him because he smelled so good. I managed to look away from him and smile brightly for Mrs. Hastings a second later.

I never saw the picture, and I always just assumed Mrs. Hastings forgot to get it developed. I also assumed that in the photo, Clint would be giving me a dirty look, or rolling his eyes at me, or flipping me off instead of looking at the camera.

Ember has been cut out of the photo on his screen, so it's just the two of us. And instead of Clint looking at me like he wants to strangle me, he's staring at my profile with a soft smile on his face. He's looking at me the way I look at tacos, and chocolate chunk ice cream, and Louboutin shoes, and everything else I love in this world.

What the hell?

"Why is this on here? Why is Ember cut out? *Why is this on here?*" I ask, my voice getting so loud and squeaky that I'm surprised the window in the room doesn't shatter.

"Press any key. When the password box comes up, type in *Brooklyn18*," he instructs.

I rapidly do what he says, fully prepared to scoff at him when it doesn't work, because why in the hell would he use my name as a password?

As soon as I type it in and hit enter, the lock screen goes away. And once again, I'm staring at the same picture of the two of us, because it's also his wallpaper on the main screen.

"What the hell, Clint?"

I look up from the laptop to find him standing with his hands shoved in the front pockets of his jeans, with the same soft smile on his face as the one in the picture.

His eyes stay glued to mine as he slowly withdraws his hands from his pockets and takes one step closer to me.

"You've been my password since I got my first computer. I always change it to the current year. And that photo has been my background picture on every laptop I've ever owned." He shrugs.

Fucking *shrugs*. Like this is no big deal and I hear this kind of shit from him all the time.

He takes another step, and I start breathing a little faster.

"Why?" I whisper, my throat clogging with emotion.

Another step, and I have to wipe my palms against my jean shorts because they're sweating so badly.

"Come on, Brooklyn. I know you're smarter than that," he says with a damn sparkle in his eyes, taking another step.

You're damn right I'm smarter than that. But my brain is not computing what is happening, and I think I smell smoke. My brain has lit itself on fire.

"Fine. Why *that* picture?" I ask stubbornly, not exactly ready to delve into all the reasons why he uses my name as his password and a picture of us on every computer he's owned.

"It's a good picture."

Yet another step, and I have to press my palm against my chest, because my heart is beating so fast I'm afraid it will explode.

"One of my favorites, actually."

Two more steps, and he's only a foot away now, and I'm pretty sure I might be having a heart attack.

"Do you forgive me for acting like the biggest asshole in the world?" he asks quietly.

"I believe the exact title was biggest jerk in the world," I reply like an idiot.

"Is that a yes?" He smiles, making butterflies flap around in my stomach.

"Sure. Why not? I mean, you obviously have stalker tendencies, so I don't want to do anything to set you off," I tell him nonchalantly, even though teenage Brooklyn is screaming inside.

Oh, who am I kidding? Adult Brooklyn is about to have an

orgasm if he keeps looking at her like that.

"Brooklyn?" he mutters, his face completely serious and not even hinting at a smile over my stalker joke.

"Yeah?"

"Shut up."

I should be offended by that and tell him off, but there's no time. Before I can take my next breath, he closes the distance between us, wrapping his hand around the back of my neck, and yanks me toward him.

It all happens so quickly and so fluidly, in one flawless movement that feels like it was choreographed right out of a Hallmark movie. A really, really dirty Hallmark movie. He moves forward, he jerks me against his body, his hand clutches tightly to the back of my neck, his other arm wraps around my waist, and his mouth crashes down against mine. My mouth opens with a gasp against his lips, and he takes that opportunity to push his tongue inside.

Now, let's get something straight here. I've fantasized about kissing Clint Hastings ever since I first realized that kissing a boy wouldn't give me cooties. In those fantasies, it was always a little awkward. A lot of teeth clacking against each other, confusion about which way we should tilt our heads, plenty of drool, and Clint moaning into my mouth about gigabytes and hard drives, which would ultimately force me to punch him in the nuts and ruin the moment. But you know, it was still a daydream about Clint's mouth on mine, so it worked for me.

This is *nothing* like my fantasies. I have been mastur-bating to all the wrong things for *years*.

There is no clacking of teeth, there is no drool I'll have to wipe away later, our heads automatically know which way to tilt, and he doesn't moan about computer bullshit. When his tongue swirls around mine, he just fucking *groans* into my mouth. The sound makes it feel like someone just sent a shock of electricity right between my legs.

My hands that are pressed against his chest, clutch onto handfuls of his flannel shirt and I tug him closer to me. Clint deepens the kiss, pushing his tongue more firmly against mine as he starts walking us backward until my back bumps into the wall behind us. His arm tightens around my waist and his hand moves from the back of my neck to smack against the wall above my head. I wrap one of my legs around the back of his, using my thigh muscles to pull him closer. He bends his knees and pushes his hips up between my thighs, making my toes leave the ground, and it's my turn to groan around his tongue when I feel the bulge in his jeans rub against me.

His hips anchor me in place against the wall as he continues to slowly thrust his hips between my legs, his tongue moving through my mouth in the same languid rhythm. The combination makes everything between my thighs pulse and tingle, until I tilt my hips up, rubbing myself against him with each of his thrusts, wanting more, more, more. My hands let go of his shirt, and I move them out from between us to wrap them around the back of his head, clutching as much of his short hair in my fingers as I can, to keep his mouth firmly sealed against mine.

I'm so lost in this moment, and what Clint is doing to me, and how he's making me feel so damn desired and wanted, and the fact that *oh my God, Clint Hastings is kissing me and it doesn't feel awkward. It just feels so perfect and hot!* that it doesn't register someone is shouting his name until he suddenly breaks the kiss, drops his arm from its tight hold around my waist, and quickly takes a few steps away from me.

My back stays pressed up against the wall, and I try to remember how to breathe normally again as I watch Clint adjust himself in his jeans before moving over to the doorway and shouting out into the store to one of the farmhands.

How am I supposed to breathe normally when my lips feel raw and bruised from that kiss, my legs are like jelly, and I'm so wet I might have to wring out my underwear *and* my jean shorts when I get home?

I vaguely register Clint telling the guy something about the truck out back and how many orders are going to Ohio, before I finally manage to get my breathing under control. The guy out in the store shouts a thank-you to Clint, and I can hear his boots thumping against the cement floor until they completely fade away.

Clint turns back around to face me, and I really wish I was doing something other than becoming one with the wall. Like, striking a sexy pose, or giving him a wink, or figuring out how to make my fucking legs work so I could saunter right past him and out the door, race back to my dad's house, and analyze the hell out of what just happened with a nice, big bottle of tequila.

He just stands there staring at me, and after a few minutes, I can't handle the silence any longer.

"What in the hell was that?" I whisper.

He just smirks at me, bringing his hand up and using the pad of his thumb to wipe my lip gloss off of his bottom lip. All I can think about is walking over there, smacking his hand away, sucking that full lip into my mouth, and getting that glossy shit off myself.

"That was a long time coming, fancy pants."

Chapter 16
CLINT
Honest Life

"CLINT. EARTH TO Clint."

My body jolts at the sound of my lead farmhand, Jake Masterson's voice, hoping he doesn't notice I wasn't paying a damn bit of attention to what he was just saying. What's a man supposed to do when the hottest woman he's ever known is standing a few hundred yards away, in another pair of those tiny fucking jean shorts, and red cowboy boots that make her long, toned legs look even longer?

When she first got here, it was easy to ignore my old feelings for her, with her fancy ass dresses and expensive shoes, because she looked completely out of place at the farm. It was easy to remember that she was a New Yorker now, and still completely out of my league, especially when she looked so damn uncomfortable and out of her element no matter what she was doing. Whenever Mia would touch her, Brooklyn would hold her hands in the air like she had a gun pointed at her, with a squeamish look on her face, freaking out over whatever sticky mess my youngest would be wiping on her. Mrs. Sherwood told me she let Grace stay locked in her room for two weeks because she was scared shitless of her.

Now that she's started wearing clothes more fit for farm life, and she's relaxed around my girls, she just *fits*. I see her walking around the farm and can't help but smile when she bends down and scoops Mia up without giving a second thought as to what might be on that girl's hands. I watch the three of them sitting on a blanket, with Grace and Brooklyn's backs resting against a tree, and Mia curled up in Brooklyn's lap, with Brooklyn's chin resting on Mia's head, and I want to drop to the ground and cry like a baby at how beautiful the sight is. My girls never even had that when their mother was around. She never sat out in the yard with them and just talked. She never set up scavenger hunts around the farm like I've seen Brooklyn do a few times in the last few weeks. And she never played catch with Grace in the front yard, giving her pointers on how to stand and how to follow through with her pitch. Their mother lived here on the farm for six years, and never relaxed or even tried to fit in and be happy.

Brooklyn has been here a month, and she looks like she never left all those years ago. It makes me equal parts happy and scared shitless. Now more than ever, I don't want her to go. Not just for my sake and all these fucking *feelings* I'm having for her again, but for my girls.

I don't want them to lose something that makes them so happy. I don't want them to lose *her*.

"Seriously, are you going to keep staring at the nanny's ass all day, or are you gonna tell me what I should do for these orders that are going to Idaho?" Jake asks, making me realize my eyes wandered right back over to Brooklyn when she bent over to scoop up a baseball from one of Grace's wild pitches.

"I'm not staring at the nanny's ass," I grumble, forcing my head to turn back to him.

Jake just laughs at me and glances over to where I was looking.

"She does have a great ass," he muses.

"Stop looking at her ass before I rip your limbs from your body and beat you with them."

Jake looks away from Brooklyn and nods with a knowing smile on his face.

"It's about fucking time. You and that girl have been circling around each other since you were kids. Did you make your move yet? I got fifty bucks riding on the night you drove her home from the Maple Inn. Shannon down at the Timber Diner picked this weekend at the opening celebration for the farm. I swear to Christ, if I lose to her, I'll never hear the end of it, so you better have already made your move," he complains.

"You have got to be kidding me," I mutter.

Closing my eyes, I bring my hand up to my face and

pinch the bridge of my nose.

Jake has been our lead farmhand since my dad ran the place. He's in his sixties and still does more work than the men on this farm half his age. He's a good man and like a father figure to me, since my parents moved to Florida, but Jesus Christ he's the worst town gossip I've ever seen.

"In case you're forgetting, White Timber is a small town. Nothing exciting ever happens here. Brooklyn Manning coming back home and taking care of your girls is the most thrilling thing that's happened here since the time she flashed the entire town her Cookie Monster underwear at the Rotary Club dinner. Actually, that time Beth Ann Marcum got drunk on homemade moonshine her sister brought her from Tennessee, and went streaking through the town square is a close second," he tells me with a chuckle. "So, seriously. Did you give her the business yet?"

"For fuck's sake, I'm not answering that question," I growl, dropping my hand from my face.

"Just tell me whether or not I've got a shot at the over/under. If it happened after the Maple Inn, and before this weekend, I get four hundred dollars. I get two hundred if you guys did some necking during that time."

Part of me wants to scream, *"Two hundred dollars is yours, my man!"* and then make him give me a high-five. But the more mature part of me knows it wouldn't be right to give Jake even more gossip he can spread around town. Also, it's not 1963. People don't say *necking* anymore.

I kissed Brooklyn Manning.

I. Fucking. Kissed. Brooklyn. Manning.

My inner teenaged nerd has been patting me on the back since it happened two days ago, saying, *"It's about bloody time, good chap! Cheerio, good on you!"*

Don't fucking judge me. My inner teenaged nerd has a British accent and looks like Alan Turing, a British computer scientist who was known as the father of modern computing and is one of my heroes.

Adult Clint, who is still kind of a nerd, but more of a badass cowboy now, has been giving me fist bumps and saying, *"Shit yeah, brother! Let's celebrate this with some beer after we round up the cattle, and then you can go fuck her up against the barn door!"*

Goddammit, that kiss….

It's all I've been able to think about since it happened. Every time I walk in my fucking office, my dick gets hard. Every time I see Brooklyn somewhere on the farm, my dick gets hard. Every time someone says her name, my goddamn dick gets hard. My dick is semi-hard right now thinking about the way she moaned into my mouth, how wet and soft her lips were, how her hips moved, sliding herself over the bulge in my pants, and how her tits felt smashed against my chest. If I don't start thinking about something awful like puppies dying,

Jake is going to spread *that* shit around the town.

To say I've been a little frustrated the last two days since I haven't been able to spend time with her is putting it mildly. I've had a million and one fires to put out around here that I couldn't push off onto someone else. I thought for sure her seeing the picture of the two of us on my laptop, and her now knowing that I've had a thing for her for a long time, as well as that mind-blowing kiss, would have had Brooklyn running for the hills and doing everything she could to avoid me.

Thankfully, the few times we've seen each other in passing, she's given me that adorable smirk and made a smart-ass comment. My particular favorite was when she was out in the stables helping Grace with her morning chore of feeding the horses, and I had to run in there to grab something out of the tool box in the tack room. Brooklyn was sitting on a bale of hay a few feet away from Grace as she was finishing up and giving some love to one of the horses. When I walked by her, she was flipping through a medical book about horses we keep out there. She never looked up when I passed her, but in a low voice just for my ears, she said, "Taking a break from jerking off? Don't forget to hydrate."

Fuck. I need to kiss her again. I need to do more than kiss her. I need to strip her naked and find out what kind of noises she makes when she comes.

I also need to remember to hydrate. I've lost a lot of fluids in the last two days because of her.

"So, yeah. I'll just figure out this Idaho problem myself. You are of no use to me right now," Jake says with a sigh, patting me on the shoulder before turning and heading off toward the store.

I should probably apologize to the guy, but I'm too happy that this now frees up some time for me. Turning in the opposite direction of Jake, I head over toward the front yard, smiling to myself when I see that Brooklyn is now alone. The girls must have gone inside, and she's busy picking up the baseballs strewn all over the place and tossing them into the bucket she's carrying. Once again, my dick starts swelling in my jeans as I walk and watch Brooklyn bend over, stand up, bend over, stand up. By the time I get to her, she's turned around and sees me coming. She sets the bucket down next to the white fence that runs from the middle of the yard down to the road, rests her hands on the top of the fence behind her, and lifts herself up to sit on it.

Without any hesitation, I walk right up to her, set my hands on her knees, and gently push them open. Taking a step forward, I move to stand between her legs, running my palms up the bare skin of the top of her thighs as I go.

"Well, aren't you a pushy bastard," she quips, with a raised eyebrow as she looks up at me.

Yes. Yes, I am. I don't really see any point in pretending like what happened in my office was a mistake or a one-time thing. There's a saying that fits perfectly for this, considering where I live and what I do. Something about how there's no point in closing the barn door when the horse has already bolted. Basically, what's done is done. She knows about my favorite picture of the two of us, and my passwords. And after that kiss, she damn well better know how much I still want her after all these years. I can't magically erase that memory from her mind, nor do I want to. It's about fucking time I stopped being a pussy where she's concerned and strap on some balls.

Brooklyn's hands are still resting on top of the fence on either side of her hips, and even though she's being a smartass, her chest starts moving up and down faster with our close proximity, making my eyes trail down to her tits, straining against the tight cotton material of her fitted, dark green Hastings Farm T-shirt.

Note to self: Tell Ember to design V-neck shirts. Ones that are indecently low cut so I can get a better look at Brooklyn's cleavage.

"I don't remember you complaining the other day when I was between your thighs," I reply, my thumbs tracing tiny, soft circles over the tops of her legs.

"Well, I am a homewrecker. So clearly I'm all about that shit."

She tries to make a joke, and even smirks at me, but I can hear the hurt in her voice, and I curse myself a thousand times for saying such stupid shit to her. But I like the fact that she isn't going to let this go with one apology and a make-out session. I like that she's going to make me work for it. I don't want her to be complacent and just let me get away with it when I'm being an asshole.

"I knew from the minute that story broke it wasn't true, and it took everything in me not to book a flight to New York and beat the shit out of that asshole for putting you through that," I tell her honestly.

It's time to lay all my cards on the table once and for all. If she doesn't fully understand how long I've had a thing for her, and that my feelings are growing stronger by the minute, there's no way in hell I'll ever have a shot at convincing her there could be something more between us than sarcasm and insults.

"Oh, okay. Suuure," she says with a roll of her eyes. "So, you're suddenly a badass cowboy who owns a farm, and you think you're knight in shining armor material?"

"You're picturing me on a horse right now, aren't you? Like that majestic Old Spice commercial, where the buff guy isn't wearing a shirt," I tease.

Her eyes move away from mine to stare off into the distance with a dreamy smile on her face.

"He was pretty hot. He had superb abs." She sighs.

Inching forward between her legs, I don't stop until the fucking bulge that won't quit is pressed right up against the seam of her shorts, sliding my palms over the top of her thighs to the outside of them. Gliding my hands up her legs higher, I continue sliding them up, over the material of her shorts and around her hips until I'm cupping her ass. Clutching that fine thing in my hands, I jerk it forward slightly, just enough for her to bump tightly up against me. She lets out a little whimper, her hands flying off the fence railing to wrap around my upper arms and hold herself steady.

"I'm hotter," I inform her quietly, our mouths just a few centimeters apart.

It is taking all of my willpower right now not to kiss the hell out of her again, but it's broad daylight, and we're in the middle of the front yard where anyone can see us. What we're doing right now would be enough to get tongues wagging in this town for the next century if someone sees us. Plus, I don't want her to think this is the only thing I care about.

After a few quiet minutes of neither one of us moving, I finally remove my hands from her ass. I bring them up between us and rest my palms against the sides of her neck, pressing my thumbs against her cheeks and holding her face in place so she won't look away from me.

"I know you. Better than anyone. Even though we haven't seen each other in a while, I still *know* you," I tell her quietly. "You would never set out to ruin a marriage. That's not who you are."

I watch her eyes cloud with tears as she stares at me,

and she quickly blinks them away.

"Oh yeah, who am I?" she whispers.

"You're a pain in my ass. But fighting with you every day for a month has made me happier than getting along with someone else all my life. You drive me crazy, you turn me on more than any woman I've ever known, and you make me laugh. You're stubborn, and smart, and strong, and independent, and you are *not* a home-wrecker."

I finally see a small smile tugging at the corner of her mouth.

"So, this is what we're doing now? We're being nice to each other? That's gonna grow old really fast," she teases.

"Fuck no. Let me amend that previous statement. You are, in fact, a wrecker of homes. Have you seen my kitchen from this morning? It looks like a tornado went through there, only blowing around flour, sugar, eggs, and some kind of bright orange and yellow batter all over the counters and kitchen cabinets. I found candy corn stuck to the ceiling."

"That is *not* my fault!" she argues. "Mia wanted candy corn cupcakes. I didn't know five-year-olds didn't have the dexterity to use a handheld mixer. Honestly, what have you been teaching that kid all these years? She is an *awful* baker."

I laugh and shake my head at her.

"Go on a date with me tomorrow night."

She can't hide the happiness on her face, even though she tries as hard as possible.

"Oh my. A date with Clint Hastings. What should I wear?" she asks with feigned, wide-eyed excitement. "Eh, it probably doesn't matter. He'll just talk my ear off about nerdy computer stuff and put me to sleep."

Shifting my hips between her thighs, she lets out a little gasp, her fingers clutching tighter to my arms.

"Wear something sexy that shows off your killer fucking legs. And don't worry, there won't be any sleeping involved."

Chapter 17
Fishing Boat Life

I AM SUCH a coward.

Every word Clint said to me at the farm yesterday has been echoing around in my head continuously for the last twenty-four hours.

"Fighting with you every day for a month has made me happier than getting along with someone else all my life."

Goddamn him for making me swoon.

He never even tried to brush off that whole thing about my name being his password and our picture being his wallpaper as no big deal. I probably would have lied and told him I'd been hacked and he should call the computer police. And even though he never came right out and said he's had a thing for me all these years, that whole, *"Come on, Brooklyn, you're smarter than that,"* comment he made when I asked him why, was pretty much his way of shouting it at the top of his lungs.

And I just stood there, like a tool, and never told

him I felt the same way all this time. Why didn't I tell him?

My phone chimes with an incoming text, the sound making me want to smash it with a hammer. I've been getting nonstop texts ever since I walked through the door last night, and I don't know why I haven't silenced the damn thing. With a sigh, I turn away from the mirror above my old dresser where I was finishing with my makeup, and walk over to my bed where I tossed my phone before I got in the shower.

Just as I suspected, another so-called "friend" from New York, who sent me a link to the article that ran in the *New York Times* yesterday. This is probably the main reason I clammed up with Clint. Not that I had any idea this article was going to happen, but just the fact that even though it crashed and burned, I still kind of have a life back in New York. One that is starting to look a little brighter than it did a few months ago.

Felicity Kennedy finally sat down for an interview. And she finally pulled her head out of her ass and realized I wasn't the one to blame for her marriage going to shit. She uncovered no less than three other women Stephen was having an affair with during their marriage, aside from me. That motherfucking dirtbag. She apologized "to the poor woman I called a home-wrecker, and I greatly regret punching her in the face" and announced that she had filed for divorce.

I don't even know how to feel about this shit. I'm

pissed, I'm hurt, my ego is still bruised from the bashing it took all over New York and social media, and my desire to chop off Stephen's balls and shove them down his throat hasn't lessened. But this news article hasn't made me as happy as I thought it would. I should be ecstatic that the dust is clearing and it's looking like New York just might welcome me back with open arms, instead of pointing and laughing. It doesn't make me happy, though. It just makes me feel *blah*. Clint isn't in New York. Mia and Grace aren't in New York. And my dad, as annoying as he is, isn't there either. I feel closer to him than I ever have before, and the thought of leaving any time soon makes my stomach hurt. But what am I supposed to do *here*? Live happily ever after with Clint and the girls?

Yes, you stupid moron!

If only it were that easy. I can't just live with my dad and… what? Be a nanny for the rest of my life? I adore those girls, and I can't believe I'm saying this, but I really love hanging out with them. Yet that's not who I am. No matter how much I've enjoyed being back home, I'm starting to crawl out of my skin with nothing else to keep me occupied.

With a sigh, I shove my phone into the clutch on my bed and head out of my room. It's not like I need to decide right now. I mean, Clint and I only shared one kiss. One amazing, hot-as-fuck kiss I'd like to repeat as soon as possible, but still. Also, we haven't even had sex. What if he's a dud? What if he's finished in ten seconds, rolls over, and goes to sleep? That type of compatibility needs scientific proof that it will work. Preferably multiple times, in multiple locations, and with multiple orgasms before a decision can be made.

When my goddamn vagina starts tingling just remembering what he felt like between my thighs, with that impressive package rubbing up against me, I know I'm just fooling myself. The test results are in, and they are conclusive. We have a sex match!

And honestly, just because he said all those nice things about me doesn't exactly mean he wants me to stick around forever. This is only our first date, for fuck's sake, and I'm already worrying about what will come next. It will probably be the worst date in history, and then, I won't even have to worry about any of this. And besides, he knows I live in New York. I'm sure he's just assuming this is a temporary thing until summer is over and the girls go back to school.

That thought makes my stomach churn again, and I have to press my hand against it as I make my way out into the living room.

My dad looks up from the crossword puzzle book sitting on the arm of the recliner, giving me a onceover.

"That's what you're wearing?"

I have no clue where Clint is taking me tonight. He left a note for me on the kitchen table this morning, since he would be busy working all day, and it just said he would pick me up at my dad's house at seven. Since the only casual clothes I have are the jean shorts and tees I wear to take care of the girls, I drove an hour away to the closest Target as soon as I got off work and picked up a dress. I could have worn something designer that I brought with me, but that just seemed stupid at this point. White Timber isn't a designer place, and I wanted Clint to be proud to take me out in public, not embarrassed because I looked like I didn't fit in.

"What's wrong with what I'm wearing?" I ask in annoyance, glancing down at myself.

The nights can get a little chilly here this close to the mountains, so I went with something with cuffed, three-quarter-length sleeves just in case I get cold. It's a red and black plaid shirt dress, and it actually looks like one of Clint's flannel shirts, which is what made me buy it without even trying it on. Since Clint requested I show off plenty of my "killer fucking legs," I'm hoping he'll like the fact that the dress comes to right above mid-thigh, and I paired it with my red cowboy boots.

I even treated myself to a box of Rich Mahogany hair color at the general store the other day. I had just enough time after the long drive to and from Target to put the dye in my hair, take a quick shower, shave every body part, rinse out the dye, and get ready. I left my newly colored hair hanging down around my back and shoulders and added a few soft curls to it. I thought I looked pretty damn good, but clearly my father thinks otherwise.

"Nothing's wrong with what you're wearing. But you could have at least shown a little more skin and put some real effort into it for Clint," he informs me.

Jesus Christ.

"What happened to you wanting to fill his ass with lead?" I remind him.

"Eh, we're past that now. He's okay in my book. Especially since you've been walking through that door every night with a disgusting, sappy smile on your face, and you're leaving my good tequila alone," he says nonchalantly.

I call bullshit.

Raising one eyebrow, I put my hands on my hips and tap my booted foot against the hardwood floor. It only takes thirty seconds for him to give in.

"Fine! So I've got fifty bucks riding on Clint making his move tonight, and if I don't win that six grand in the pot, I'll never get the fishing boat I've had my eye on," he complains.

Oh, for fuck's sake!

Clint sent me a text last night informing me that there was currently a bet going around town on when he'd "give me the business." I told him he damn well better put all his money on every day this week. I mean, six thousand dollars is a lot of money. What did you expect me to respond with? I don't feel as pleased with this knowledge now that I know my dad is in on it. I feel like I should take a shower with bleach.

"Dad, you've never gone fishing a day in your life. Or driven a boat. What the hell would you need with a fishing boat?"

He glares at me, smacking his pencil down on top of the crossword puzzle book.

"What if, one day, I decide I *want* to go fishing, on my very own boat? I'm gonna look out the kitchen window into my driveway, and you know what I'll see? Not my own fucking fishing boat, that's for sure!"

Thankfully, there's a knock at the door, and I don't have to worry about giving my dad any more heart problems by strangling him.

Rushing out of the living room, I go the front door, pausing to take a few calming breaths. I wasn't really nervous about going on an actual date with Clint, but now that he's here, butterflies are flapping around my stomach and my heart is about ready to beat out of my chest. Once I calm myself down as much as I can, I open the door.

"Fucking hell, fancy pants," Clint mutters under his breath, his eyes trailing down my body and back up again.

Cue the damn butterflies all over again.

"Yeah, you look all right I guess. At least you took a shower," I muse, not wanting him to know that if my dad weren't a few feet away, I'd be jumping into his arms and wrapping my legs around his hips.

Good God, is he hot. All the scruff has been shaved from his face, leaving his chiseled jaw and adorable dimples in perfect view. It looks like he got a haircut today, the sides cut extra close to his scalp and the longer top pushed back away from his face. He's wearing jeans, but these aren't his normal, faded, well-worn Levis he wears around the farm. He's got on a pair of dark jeans that fit him in all the right places, resting low on his hips. A white Henley that looks like it was tailor made to hug all of his muscles is pushed up to his elbows and tucked into his jeans with a brown belt. The cuffs of his jeans are pulled down over a pair of dark brown, leather work boots, and I can't help but smile that the entire outfit looks brand new and I wasn't the only one who needed to do some shopping and hair upkeep for this date.

"So, where are you taking me? Is it a nerd convention? Am I overdressed?" I ask cheekily.

"Keep it up, smartass, and I'll take you to Best Buy and make you listen to me argue with the Geek Squad about whether a Mac or Windows computer is more superior," he says with a smile, reaching out, grabbing my hand, and tugging me out the door.

"Fishing boat, Brooklyn Marie! Fishing boat!" my dad shouts from the living room as I hurry and pull the door closed behind me.

"What was that all about?" Clint asks with a laugh as we walk over to his truck and he pulls open the passenger side door for me.

"It's best if we just pretend like that never happened," I tell him.

I watch Clint round the front of the truck after he shuts me in, my knee bouncing up and down with nervous excitement for whatever he has planned. A plan that I really hope ends in this dress being on his bedroom floor. Or the stable floor. Or his office floor. Or even draped over Jack from Jack's Auto Repair's shoulder in the Maple Inn bathroom, while he pisses in the sink and we rattle the bathroom stall doors.

My phone chimes with another fucking text from inside my purse as soon as Clint gets behind the wheel, and the skyline of New York at night flashes through my head, killing my pervy thoughts.

Clint glances over at me, and I wave him off as he starts the truck and turns it around to head down the driveway.

"It's fine. Nothing important."

He keeps glancing over at me every few seconds as he drives, and after a few minutes, I have to laugh.

"Go ahead. I know you're dying to tell me whether a Mac or Windows is more superior."

He gives me a sheepish look and shakes his head. It only takes two miles before he breaks.

"I mean, come *on*! The OS X operating system is a clean, refined, easy-to-use interface with…"

I start counting all the trees we drive past and only

half pay attention to what he's saying, but I've suddenly forgotten all about the texts on my phone and the New York City skyline.

Chapter 18

CLINT
Baggage Life

WHITE TIMBER ISN'T big, but what it lacks in size, it makes up for in small town quaintness. Main Street is just as the name suggests—it's the one and only "main" street downtown. And "downtown" consists of just one street, with businesses lining either side for a few blocks, ending at the town square, and a view of the mountains off in the distance behind all the buildings on the right side of the street. The town square is about an acre in size, a grassy area lined with trees on all sides that has a gazebo in the middle, with several picnic tables surrounding it.

We ate dinner on the steps of the gazebo, with a strand of those big bulb lights lining the roof of it to help us see after the sun went down.

Since everything around here closes at five, I ran up to the diner before they closed and picked up dinner to go. Mrs. Sherwood put the food into the oven on a low setting to keep it warm until I was ready to leave, transferred it into insulated containers, and then packed everything up into a bag, along with a bottle of wine and some plastic cups. I took a chance and hoped Brooklyn still had a weakness for the cream cheese stuffed pancakes covered in strawberry sauce that she ordered every time she went to the diner in high school. Thankfully, her eyes lit up and I'm pretty sure I saw some drool dripping down her chin when I opened the container.

I know what you're thinking. What kind of an idiot takes the woman of his dreams to sit in town, eating shitty diner food off their laps?

That idiot would be me. But I'm an evil mastermind idiot, so there's that. She spent the last twelve years living it up in New York, hanging with celebrities, eating at fancy restaurants, drinking expensive champagne, surrounded by the hustle and bustle and noise of a big city. Sure, I could have driven her to the next town over and forked out a shit-ton of money at the French bistro that just opened a few months ago, but why in the hell would I do that? It would completely defeat the purpose of what I'm trying to do.

I want her to remember everything about White Timber that makes it the best place to live. I want her to enjoy the quiet, slow pace of living in a small town. I want her to fall in love with the idea of putting roots down here. I want her to fall in love with the idea of falling in love with *me*.

"God, I forgot how peaceful it is here," Brooklyn

states as we walk hand-in-hand down Main Street. "Every time I've been here since I got to town, I've been in a hurry and never took the time to appreciate it. I'm so used to horns honking, people shouting, music blaring, and trying not to die getting run over by a taxi when you cross the street."

I almost want to rub my hands together like a villain, and whisper, *"Excellent, excellent. My plan is working."*

Tugging on Brooklyn's hand, I bring it around behind me and make her hold onto my waist, and then drape my arm over her shoulders, pulling her tightly against my side as we continue walking. As soon as I start to feel really fucking good about myself, I hear someone call our names.

We pause on the sidewalk in front of the barbershop, and I watch Shannon, the owner of the diner, rush across the street to us.

"Hey, you two! How was dinner? Were the pancakes just as good as you remembered them, Brooklyn?"

Brooklyn rubs her hand over her stomach and smiles at her.

"Too good. I think I gained five pounds eating them."

"You definitely hoovered those things into your mouth pretty fast. Hopefully those five pounds go to your ass and not your thighs," I tell her with a smirk.

Since her arm is still wrapped around my waist, she takes the opportunity to pinch my side as hard as she can, until my eyes start to water from the pain.

"Don't mind him, Shannon. He's still a little gassy from that cheeseburger and fries, and it put him in a bad mood. I almost thought he might shit his pants there for a minute."

The two women share a laugh at my expense, and I tug on a strand of Brooklyn's hair on her shoulder, right by my hand.

"You two are just the cutest. Have a good rest of the night," Shannon tells us.

Before she walks away, she leans in close to me, pushes up on her toes, and whispers in my ear.

"My money's on tonight in the pool, but it has to be after eleven, so don't rush home just yet. I've got my eye on a new industrial stove for the diner. Don't let me down."

With that, she pats me on the arm and crosses back over to the other side of the street.

Brooklyn, of course, laughs since Shannon wasn't all that quiet with her whispering, and we continue walking down the street, back toward the gazebo where I left our stuff on one of the steps.

Removing my arm from her shoulders, I grab her hand and start pulling her across the street to one of the other main reasons I wanted to bring her into town tonight.

"Come on, I want to show you something."

"Is it something in your pants? Because Shannon

will probably slit your throat if she doesn't get that oven," Brooklyn replies with a snort.

I shake my head at her and keep pulling her along until I get to my destination, stopping us right in front of it.

"Remember this place?" I ask, staring up at the building in front of us, with the windows boarded up.

"Wasn't this where they printed the *White Timber Times*?" she asks, looking up for the sign that used to hang over the front window that fell off a year ago during a really bad thunderstorm.

"Yep. Ed Franklin finally retired, and no one wanted to take it over. It's been shut down for about two years now."

"Are you kidding me? There's no *White Timber Times* in everyone's mailboxes on Sunday morning anymore? How in the world does anyone know when the bake sales are, or why Edna Cranston was fighting with Pearl Simmons in front of the hair salon?" she asks with mock horror, pressing her hand against her chest.

The *White Timber Times* was part newspaper, part gossip column. Anything and everything that happened in this town was printed in that paper. News about upcoming events, school functions, scores from all the school sporting events, special sales certain businesses were running, weather forecasts, progress updates on all the crops on the various farms, neighbor disputes, and whose husband had one too many beers at the VFW and passed out in a corn field with his pants around his ankles, were all included in the weekly newspaper.

"I know. It's a travesty. People are just walking around aimlessly, having no idea when they should bake cookies for the church bake sale. Someone really needs to do something about it before the town implodes," I joke.

I'm not really joking though. Brooklyn wrote for a magazine. One of the biggest magazines in the world. Sure, this isn't anywhere near the scale of that, but it's *something*. It's something I know she would love, if she just thought about it for a little while. I know if I want to really convince her that she could be happy here, she needs something more in her life than me and my kids. She needs a purpose, she needs to make her own money and be independent, and she needs to do something that will keep her busy and make her happy.

We stand here quietly staring at the empty building in front of us, and it's killing me not to say something, but I don't want to push her.

"Hey, Mr. Hastings. Hey, Miss Manning."

I drop my arm from around Brooklyn's shoulders and we both turn around to find a teenage girl standing on the edge of the street. I can see from the confused look on Brooklyn's face that she has no idea who this girl is, so I help her out.

"Katie Johnson," I whisper in her ear.

When it still doesn't register, Katie speaks up.

"My dad is Rodney Johnson. You used to babysit me."

"Holy fucking shit!" Brooklyn shouts, quickly clamping her mouth closed and glancing around to make sure she didn't just give one of the old ladies a heart attack who might be out for an evening walk. "You're not a baby! I mean, of course you aren't a baby, but holy shit. Now I feel really old. No offense, but you were a *rotten* baby. But you're like, seriously pretty now, so I kind of have to forgive you for giving me nightmares for most of my life."

Katie laughs and blushes at the same time.

"Katie's in the National Honor Society. She's guaranteed to be the valedictorian of White Timber High, and she already plans on going to Harvard Medical School," I tell Brooklyn.

"Damn, girl. Good for you," she praises.

Sticking my hands in the front pockets of my jeans, I stand next to Brooklyn and listen to her chat with Katie for a few minutes about Rodney, and her plans for the future.

Fucking hell, she's beautiful. And sweet, when she isn't being a smartass. Dammit. She's even sweet then. I'm screwed.

As they wind down their conversation, Brooklyn slides her hand through the crook of my arm to hold onto me, almost like it's a natural reflex and she's not even aware she's doing it. I can't wipe the goddamn smile off my face. That is, until we start to walk away, and Katie reaches out and taps my arm to stop me.

She glances at Brooklyn nervously then crooks her finger at me.

When I lean my head down toward her, she lifts up and whispers in my ear.

"Okay, this is kind of awkward, but whatever. I used my allowance to bet on tomorrow night in the pool. Don't tell my dad. But I really, really need a new wardrobe for senior year. Some new dresses, and new shoes, and new purses that don't come from the general store or Walmart. So…." she trails off.

I hear Brooklyn try and stifle a laugh next to me, and I just give Katie a smile. Turning away from the girl, I walk away as fast as I can, with Brooklyn having to almost jog to keep up with me as she holds tightly to my arm.

"I did that, you know," she informs me with a smile, as we step onto the grass of the square.

"Convinced an underage girl to bet on our sex life?" I ask in shock.

"No!" she laughs, the sound making my heart swell in my fucking chest. "Katie is brilliant. She's going to *Harvard Medical School*. Not to brag or anything, but I practically raised that kid when she was little."

Now it's my turn to laugh.

"You babysat her once a week for a few years."

"Three years, Clint. *Three*. Three of the worst years of my life. She's where she is today because of me," she states with a lift of her chin as we sit down on the steps of the gazebo next to our things.

"I'm not exactly sure you should be patting yourself on the back, fancy pants. I highly doubt you had anything to do with her brilliance."

"Um, hello? I cared for her during her most formative years. She is brilliant, all because I didn't shake her when she was a baby."

Jesus, this woman kills me, in the best possible way.

"Even though you hated it, that was a good thing you did back then. Rodney had it pretty tough there for a while."

"I'm glad he got remarried after I left, and Katie adores her stepmother," Brooklyn adds, mentioning what she and Katie talked about a few minutes ago.

"Tough break, losing her mom so young."

Brooklyn sighs, pulling her legs up onto the step below us, wrapping her arms around her knees.

"We're gonna go there now, are we?" she asks softly.

"It's kind of a big thing, you telling everyone you still had a relationship with your mom all these years," I say gently.

"It's also kind of a big thing Grace and Mia's mom isn't around. Care to talk about that?" she asks in annoyance.

"You first," I challenge.

She rolls her eyes and lets out another big sigh.

"Why didn't you say anything to me? Or even Ember?"

She shrugs, squeezing her arms tighter around her legs. Reaching over, I rest my hand against her back, rubbing soft circles around the center of her spine.

"I didn't tell Ember, because I was embarrassed. And I didn't tell you, because you probably would have used it against me, like you did a few weeks ago," she replies.

"World's biggest jerk, remember? If I could take back all of that shit I said, I would do it in a minute. I hate that you carried that around with you for so long."

She shrugs again, and I turn my body to face her, reaching over with my free hand to tilt her chin up so she'll look me in the eyes.

"You know, it's weird. For so long, I felt like such a loser. What was so bad about me that she left and never came back? Was I that hard to love? That easy to leave?"

I open my mouth to argue with her, tell her she's so easy to love it's almost scary, and so hard to leave it makes me sick to my stomach just thinking about it, but she quickly shakes her head.

"I know, I know. It was stupid to think like that, but how could I not? The weird thing is, I don't feel like that anymore. I think about her, and all I can say is, it's her loss. She has to live with that decision for the rest of her life, not me."

Leaning over, I kiss the top of her head and pull her against my side.

"I have you to thank for that, by the way."

When I look down at her in confusion, she rests her head on my shoulder.

"Well, your girls at least. When I look at them, I don't see losers who are unlovable and easy to leave. I see amazing little human beings who someone would have to be completely batshit crazy to walk away from. If I can feel that way when I look at them, I need to feel the same way when I look in the mirror."

I can barely swallow past the lump in my throat, so I quickly clear it and think about something that doesn't make me so emotional, and just makes me feel numb.

"Her name was Melissa. I met her freshman year of college. She was a computer science major, just like me, and I thought we had a whole hell of a lot in common. We started dating, and before I knew it, I was a father before my junior year," I tell her.

"Can I start calling you teen mom now?" she asks, her body shaking with laughter.

Leave it to Brooklyn to find a way to lighten my mood during this conversation.

"Sure thing, Cookie Brookie."

She elbows me in the gut, and I keep going with this shit-show story.

"Melissa was a born and bred Californian. Her parents hated me when I moved her to Montana after we graduated. She seemed excited at first, but that quickly changed. By the time Grace was four, we weren't even sleeping in the same room, and she was barely speaking to me," I explain, shaking my head at just how stupid I was back then.

"So, you never got married?" she asks softly.

"Hell no. I think I knew before Grace was even born that we shouldn't be together, but I didn't want to quit. I didn't want to do that to Grace. I probably should have tried a whole hell of a lot harder to make things work, but Melissa just didn't give a shit, so neither did I. And of course, during one night of too many drinks at the Maple Inn to celebrate my dad's birthday when they were in town visiting, where we fought for two hours about her not wanting to go before she finally gave in, I thought having another kid would fix everything, because that always works," I say sarcastically. "And that's how I got Mia."

We sit in silence for a few minutes, listening to the quiet sounds of nature all around us, before I suck it up and finish this crap.

"She never made an effort to get to know anyone in town, and she would leave for days, sometimes weeks at a time, never letting me know where the hell she was," I mutter. "I found out after snooping through her phone that she made some friends over in Billings. Friends who liked to party, friends who liked their cocaine, and friends who didn't have two kids at home they should be taking care of."

"Jesus," Brooklyn mutters.

"Yeah. She finally left and went back to California a week after Mia turned three. Haven't heard from her since. I used to send her texts and pictures of the girls to keep her updated after I got over my initial anger, but she never replied. Eventually, I got a message that said my texts were undeliverable, so I'm guessing she changed her number. The shitty thing is, I found out she married some clothing designer, and they now have a son."

Brooklyn lets out an irritated huff, lifting her head from my shoulder to look at me.

"That *bitch*. Give me her full name and social security number. I'll hunt her down and beat the shit out of her."

All I can do is chuckle. I don't know how it's possible for this woman to make me feel so light after talking about such heavy shit.

"Well, well, well. Look who's trying to be the knight in shining armor now."

"Whatever." Brooklyn shrugs. "I've never been in a chick fight, and I've always wanted to. Getting punched in the face by a scorned wife doesn't count. I didn't see that shit coming. I'm better prepared now."

Pushing myself up from the steps, I hold my hand out for Brooklyn and pull her up next to me as I grab the bag of containers and the empty bottle of wine.

"Ready for the rest of our date now?" I ask.

"You mean wining and dining me on the town square isn't all you had planned?"

"Nope."

Her face lights up with excitement, but then her smile quickly falls and a look of worry takes over her features.

"What's wrong?" I ask in a panic, wondering if it's just now hitting her all the fucked up shit that happened with Melissa, and maybe this is too much for her to handle.

Maybe she thinks I have too much baggage.

Maybe she still hates this town and is counting down the minutes until she can leave.

Maybe I completely overshot this and screwed everything up.

"I'm really conflicted right now," she whispers, making my heart drop right down into my stomach. "If you give me the business tonight, Shannon wins. If we wait until tomorrow, Katie wins. Industrial stove, or new wardrobe? Industrial stove, or new wardrobe? Gaaah, this is too much pressure!"

Once the shock wears off at what just came out of her mouth, I throw my head back and laugh harder than I have in years.

"This isn't funny, Clint! I mean, think of all the yummy things Shannon could put on her menu. But… oh my God, I could take Katie shopping! I could introduce her to Nordstrom's, and Louboutin's, and Kate Spade, and Donna Karan, and… fuck. I think I just had an orgasm." She sighs.

Turning away from her, I walk as fast as I can toward the truck, dragging her along behind me.

"Slow down! What the hell?" Brooklyn asks, laughing as I start to jog.

"I'll be damned if I'm gonna let you have an orgasm without me," I inform her.

"Wooohooo! Looks like the industrial stove is in the lead!" she cheers as we get to where I parked, and I fumble trying to pull my keys out of my pocket. "We should stop and tell Shannon the good news."

"Stop talking and get in the truck."

Chapter 19
Cheesy Life

I SHOULDN'T BE this happy.

After the things Clint and I talked about in town, I should be drinking heavily. He has more baggage than the Ambassador Luggage Store in Midtown. But the thing is, he was *honest* with me. I thought Stephen was amazing and our relationship was perfect, and look at the shit he failed to tell me?

And seriously, I don't think I've ever been on a better date. I love that he took me into town and we did something simple and not over-the-top. The idea of driving over an hour away and going to a fancy restaurant or a club with Clint just doesn't feel right. He's a simple guy, and I love that about him.

Shit. I just thought about Clint and the word "love" in the same sentence.

Sure, I was in love with him as a teenager, but that was kid stuff and I had no idea what that word really meant back then. How is it possible I'm falling so fast for a guy that I haven't spoken to in twelve years? All that time apart and being with him again makes it feel like I never left. I never felt like I belonged in White Timber when this was my permanent home. Why in the hell do I feel so comfortable here *now*? Is it because I'm older, and wiser? Or is it because I'm finally letting myself stop thinking there's got to be something better than this small town? I left. I thought I'd found all that "better." I spent twelve years building friendships and a life that, looking back on now, never truly made me happy. I always felt like something was missing. Now I'm starting to realize that maybe everything I was missing was right here where I left it.

"Are your eyes closed? You better not be peeking, Manning," Clint warns me.

After we left town, I was more than a little giddy when he started heading in the direction of the farm. Thoughts of all the different places we could have sex here started flying through my brain, until I was pretty sure it would short circuit. My head was like a twenty-four-hour farm porn channel. You know, minus all the livestock.

"Don't get your panties in a bunch, Hastings. My eyes are closed," I quip.

With his hands resting heavily on my shoulders, he walks behind me, guiding me to wherever we're going. He made me close my eyes as soon as we got out of his truck, and the only thing I know is that we're heading in the direction of the store.

Mmmmm, store sex.

After a few more feet, he finally pulls me to a stop and tells me to open my eyes.

I have to say, I expected to open them and maybe see that he transformed his office into a *Fifty Shades* type set up. Not that I'm into the whole whips and chains thing, but the image of me bent over Clint's desk with a paddle in his hand makes my skin tingle, and all the blood in my body rushes south.

Instead of a secret sex den, I see that a small space behind the store has been converted into an outdoor theater area. Against the back wall of the store, there's a giant, beige outdoor cushion the size of a twin mattress resting against it, covered in different earth-toned pillows, with a chocolate brown throw blanket folded neatly at the bottom of it. Next to the mattress is a small, maple side table, with a huge bowl of popcorn on it, a bottle of wine chilling in a bucket, and two wine glasses. The huge, freestanding movie screen is about fifteen feet away from the end of the cushion. Strands of white Christmas lights have been strung in the branches of all the trees surrounding the area. And there are a handful of lanterns with candles in them sitting in the grass in random places.

"Oh my God," I whisper. "This is amazing."

And it really is. It's sweet, and cozy, and the fact that Clint set this all up for *me* almost makes me want to cry.

"It's not too cheesy? I set up everything before I picked you up earlier, and Mrs. Sherwood brought out the popcorn and wine and lit the candles when I sent her a text that we were on our way."

I turn around and find him sliding one of his hands through his hair, biting his bottom lip, and looking unsure of himself. It's just so fucking adorable I almost can't stand it. He's always so damn cocky that seeing him nervous makes my heart flutter.

"It's totally cheesy. But in the absolute best possible way. What movie are we watching?" I ask excitedly, as he grabs my hand and pulls me over to the cushion.

We both flop down on top of it, propping ourselves up against the pillows and crossing our legs straight out in front of us.

Clint leans over me to reach for something, and when his shoulder slides against the front of my body as he goes, I'm overwhelmed by how good he smells. I want to run my nose against the side of his neck that is right in front of my mouth. I want to lean forward and kiss the spot right behind his ear. Before I can find the courage to do one of those things, he pulls back and gets comfortable against the pillows again, his shoulder pressed right up next to mine.

I realize he leaned over me to turn on the movie projector, when all of a sudden, music starts playing and the screen lights up. I immediately recognize the opening credits song, and I start bouncing up and down in excitement on the cushion.

"Clint Hastings! Did you seriously just put on *Mean Girls*?"

"I'm going to regret this decision of trying to suck up to you with one of your favorite movies from high school, aren't I?" he asks with a deep sigh.

"Boo, you whore! There is nothing to regret about this decision," I inform him, quoting one of my favorite lines from the movie.

This movie came out when Ember and I were in tenth grade, and Clint was a senior. I'm pretty sure we watched it every single time I came over. Which was every day. Back then, the Hastings only had one television and it was in the living room. Clint would lose his shit when we would try to kick him out so we could watch it. He would always refuse to leave the room, which just made quoting the entire moving while it played that much more satisfying.

Sliding his arm around my shoulders, he tugs me back toward him until I'm snuggled into his side. Every part of us is touching from my shoulder tucked under his arm, to our hips pressed together, and my bare legs resting against his jean-covered ones. Once again, I'm completely overwhelmed with how good he smells and the heat from his body that surrounds me.

Clint reaches his free arm out, grabs the bowl of popcorn, and places it in his lap. When the opening scene starts, I dip my hand in the bowl and toss a few pieces in my mouth as he does the same.

As much as we joked about that whole sex betting pool when we were in town, and how much he turned me on when he made the comment about me not having an orgasm without him, he seems pretty relaxed and comfortable now. It's like he's not even thinking about sex. Or me. Or sex with me.

If Cunty Clint doesn't take Cookie Brookie to Pound Town soon, I'm going to lose my fucking mind.

Maybe my breath stinks and it completely turned him off. Turning my head away from him, I discretely cover my hand over my mouth and breathe heavily.

Nope. All good. It just smells like popcorn now. And popcorn is fucking delicious.

Maybe my entire body stinks. That would definitely be a mood killer if I suddenly started smelling like garbage. Stretching my arm that isn't pressed against his side above my head, I quietly smell my armpits.

All good there. I still smell like the cotton candy lotion and body spray I've been using since I was a teenager.

"You okay over there?" Clint asks with a touch of humor in his voice.

"I'm fine. Perfectly fine. Just stretching and getting comfortable. It's a little chilly out here," I ramble.

"You want me to grab the blanket?"

"No!" I shout a little too loudly. "I mean. No, thank you. I'm fine. It's fine. Everything is fine."

Blankets go on beds. People go on beds under the blankets.

People have sex on beds under the blankets. For shit's sake, stop thinking about sex!

Curled up so close to this man, when all I want to do is shove the bowl of popcorn out of the way, climb on his lap, and rub myself against him, I concentrate on the movie and start mouthing the words under my breath, hoping I'll be distracted by this theatrical masterpiece enough to calm the hell down.

"Are you going to be annoying and quote this entire movie?" he asks quietly after a few minutes of my mumbling.

"Is butter a carb?" I respond, quoting the movie, naturally.

"I don't even understand what that means."

"You are a disgrace, Clint. An absolute disgrace." I sigh, resting my head on his chest.

Chapter 20
CLINT
Boner Life

I'M A PRETTY confident guy for the most part. Becoming a father at a young age, being the only responsible and loving parent to my girls for their entire lives, running my family's farm, and having the respect and friendship of everyone in town has made me into a man who doesn't shy away from things and takes charge of situations.

Sitting here next to Brooklyn, with her warm body pressed up next to mine, has reverted me back to the teenage boy who blushed every time he saw a pair of tits on television and got sweaty palms just talking to a girl.

My dick was hard as soon as we sat down on this cushion and I could smell her cotton candy scent. I had to put the bowl of popcorn over my fucking crotch just so it wouldn't be sticking up in the air shouting, *"Touch me! For the love of Christ, touch me!"*

It isn't helping matters that at some point during the first hour of the movie, she shifted more onto her side, draped her arm over my stomach, and her smooth, bare legs became tangled with mine. I'm trying to pretend like I'm completely cool and relaxed. My arm is still wrapped loosely around her, and my other arm is tucked behind my head. I am anything but cool and relaxed. It's taking all my willpower not to flip her over onto her back and push my hips between her thighs.

That God damn sex pool has messed with my head. I don't want Brooklyn to think I don't want her. I want her more than I want my next fucking breath. But I want to take this slow. She's already been pushed enough with her knowing I've always had a thing for her, the whole town placing bets on us, and opening up about our pasts. That's a lot of heavy shit all at one time. I thought sitting outside and watching a stupid teen movie I hate would be a nice, cold bucket of ice water over my head, but it's done the exact opposite.

Every inch of her body is touching me. I can smell her. I can feel her tits pressing against my side with every breath she takes, and I want to rip the buttons all the way down the front of her dress and wrap my mouth around one of her nipples.

Fuck. Don't think about her nipples. Don't think about her nipples!

It's probably a trick of the light, but I swear the goddamn bowl of popcorn twitches a little when my dick swells inside my jeans.

"You want some more wine?" I ask quietly.

I don't really *want* to roll away from her to grab the

bottle and pour her another glass, but at this point, if she breathes again, I'm going to come in my pants like a teenaged boy during puberty.

Brooklyn tilts her face up toward mine, and since I'm looking down at her, our mouths are so close that all I'd have to do is angle my neck the tiniest bit and I could taste her.

"I already finished the bottle," she says with a smile. "I may or may not be a little buzzed."

Fuck. Me.

Her eyes look a little glazed, and they're completely focused on my mouth when she talks.

"I could go inside and get us more popcorn."

Her eyes are still staring at my lips, and she gives her head a slight shake.

"I don't want popcorn," she whispers.

I know she can feel my heart thundering in my chest, since her cheek is pressed right up against it. I should probably be embarrassed by it, but I'm too busy watching her tongue dart out and slowly slide between her lips.

"Do you want popcorn?" she asks, her eyes finally moving up to mine.

"Nope. I'm good. I've had enough popcorn."

Jesus Christ, stop talking about popcorn!

There's an annoying teenaged girl who just got hit by a bus on the screen behind Brooklyn's head, and I should probably be cheering since she was a bitch throughout this entire dumb movie, but Brooklyn is still staring at me, neither one of us saying a word. Her eyes move back and forth between my mouth and my eyes, and right when I decide taking it slow is bullshit, she lifts her chin and presses her lips to mine.

The kiss starts off slow, but as soon as she opens her mouth for me and our tongues slide against each other, it's like someone pressed fast-forward on us.

Brooklyn kicks the popcorn bowl off my lap with her knee, I sit up and drag her over on top of me so she's straddling my lap, and she wraps her arms around my shoulders and pulls me against her. I plunge my tongue deeper into her mouth as her hands grab onto the back of my head, sliding my palms up her bare thighs and under the hem of her dress. When I get to her hips and feel a thin scrap of lace under my hands, knowing she's been wearing a fucking thong under this dress all night, I clutch tightly to her hips and yank her body down to settle right against my cock, straining against the material of my jeans.

She moans into my mouth and rocks her hips against me, and I swear to Christ I see stars behind my eyes. I can feel the heat radiating from between her thighs right against me, and I have never been so super aware of my dick or how goddamn constricting jeans are. My balls are so tight they feel like they're going to explode if she slides against me one more time, and I'm thinking it would be a great way to die.

Moving my hands from her hips, I slide them around under her dress until I'm holding her bare ass in my hands. I squeeze it in my palms and pull her against me harder, helping her rock back and forth.

She's making little whimpering sounds as I suck her tongue into my mouth, and it's like a shot of electricity right to my dick. It pulses inside my pants with each thrust of her hips against me, and I know I'm going to embarrass myself and come in my boxer briefs in no time at all.

I had so many teenaged fantasies about Brooklyn dry humping me that it was probably unhealthy. Every time I was forced to be in the living room when she was over watching a movie, I never paid attention to the movie. I spent the entire time staring at Brooklyn, picturing her getting up from the chair across the room, sauntering over to me, and climbing onto my lap. I jerked off so many times after she went home that I'm surprised my dick didn't fall off.

Not one of those fantasies was *anything* like reality.

Jesus, she feels so perfect on top of me.

Everything about this moment is going to be seared into my brain forever. Her moans of pleasure, the smell of her skin, her hot little mouth kissing the hell out of me, and the wetness I can feel through my jeans with each jerky movement of her against me.

Her thighs tighten against either side of my hips, and she suddenly pulls her mouth away from mine and keeps it hovering close to my lips. I'm breaking out in a sweat, and she's panting against my mouth as I dig my fingers into her ass harder and move her faster.

"Fuck... fucking hell," she whispers.

Hearing her curse like that, knowing this is affecting her as much as me, makes my balls tighten even more, and I know I'm not going to be able to stop my release from happening.

I quickly remove one hand from her ass, clutch a handful of her hair at the back of her neck into my fist, and tug her head back. Moving my head forward, I wrap my lips around the smooth skin of her neck, gently biting down.

As soon as my teeth make contact, she jerks roughly against me, the sound of her moaning my name as she comes like music to my ears, and my dick.

"Clint... fuck... oh my God...!"

With my hand still wrapped tightly around a fistful of her hair, I bite down harder against her neck, thrusting my hips up between her thighs as she continues to rock against me. The pressure in my cock builds and builds, throbbing and pulsing each time she grinds her body down.

I hear her whisper my name again, and that's all it takes for me to come harder than I have in fucking *years*, if ever. It's my turn to moan as my release jets out of me, the pleasure so explosive I'm afraid I might pass out.

A few seconds later, I collapse back against the mound of pillows behind me. With my arms still wrapped tightly around Brooklyn, I bring her down with me until she's sprawled on top of my body, both of us breathing heavily.

Fucking hell. I just gave Brooklyn Manning an orgasm. And she returned the favor.

I'd almost wonder if I were dreaming, but the mess inside my pants tells me otherwise. It needs to be dealt with, but there is no way I'm moving out from under her anytime soon. She tucks her head under my chin and against my neck, burrowing as close to me as she can get, and I tighten my arms around her as I stare up at the stars shining above.

What exactly does one say to the woman he's been hung up on for years, after they dry humped for the first time?

"Was it good for you?"

"Sorry if you can feel my jizz soaking through my jeans. I know, it's disgusting. It can't be helped."

"What are you thinking right now? What are you feeling? Tell me all your hopes and dreams."

Jesus Christ, I'm not a chick! I can't ask her that!

But seriously, what *is* she feeling? Is she weirded out? Is she uncomfortable? Is this awkward for her?

Brooklyn suddenly lifts her head, placing her hands on my chest and resting her chin on top of them.

"You know what this means, right?" she asks with a

smile.

It means you're falling for me and never want to leave?

"Poor Shannon doesn't get her industrial stove."

I can't help but laugh. Not exactly what I was look-ing for, but I wouldn't have it any other way.

Chapter 21
Pantry Life

IT'S THE WEEKEND of the reopening of Hastings Farm to the public, and when I woke up this morning, I couldn't wait to get out there. The Hastings-es have celebrated this weekend for as long as I can remember, but it was always a small affair. Most of the town would stop by, Mrs. Hastings would make a bunch of food and set it up on a tablecloth-covered cafeteria table by the house, and Ember and I were given our usual job of handing out candy to all the kids who came with their parents. Even though the pumpkins aren't quite ready to be harvested yet, the store is open with everything in there available for purchase. The Has-tingses always opened the farm before the pumpkins were ready, because they felt like having everyone here showing love and support helped make the pumpkins grow big and healthy, and would give them luck for a good season.

Before I left to go back to my dad's last night, after

Clint and I snuck into the downstairs guest bathroom for a little making out and some heavy petting that didn't last nearly as long as I would have liked because the girls were still awake, he told me the celebration was a little larger than it used to be. All of the workers stayed late to set everything up, and when I told Clint I wanted to stay and help, he shoved me off and told me he wanted it to be a surprise.

The property that I've always loved, and the celebration I looked forward to every year, has been turned into my worst nightmare, right in front of my eyes.

There are bounce houses of every size and shape littered all over the property, with hundreds of dirty, sticky kids screaming and jumping up and down in them. I'm pretty sure I saw a pile of puke in the middle of the one shaped like a pumpkin, and all those little bastards were just jumping around it, puke flying up into the air and splattering back down on the plastic.

There's a tent set up just for face-painting, filled with screaming and crying kids, getting all sorts of shit painted on their dirty, sticky little cheeks.

There's a pumpkin pie eating contest for kids happening under another tent, and I'm pretty sure any minute now, they're all going to reenact that scene from the movie *Stand by Me,* and instead of blueberry pie hurling out of all their mouths, it will be orange pumpkin pie chunks projectile vomiting out of them. Everywhere I turn, there are kids of every age, running, and screaming, and crying, and throwing temper tantrums.

Okay, fine. They aren't all throwing fits, because this is obviously like a fall-themed amusement park and they are having the time of their lives, but I can't concentrate on anything except the ones acting like little assholes.

"God, I hate kids," I mutter, staring around in horror.

"Um, *we're* kids," Grace points out next to me, with Mia standing on her other side, pouting because I wouldn't let her go anywhere near the puke-covered pumpkin bounce house.

"Yeah, but I've gotten to know you guys, and you aren't complete assholes. I don't know *any* of these monsters. And where the hell are their parents?"

"Where the hell are your parents!" Mia shouts, as a little girl around her age goes racing past her.

"I really need to stop swearing around you guys," I say with a sigh.

"It's fine. Dad swears around us all the time. He just tells us we should never repeat what he says, especially the F-word," Grace responds.

"What's the F-word?" Mia asks with wide eyes, walking around Grace to stand in front of me, holding her arms in the air for me to pick her up.

I scoop her up and rest her against my hip.

"Uh, Fruit Loops," I quickly tell her.

"What? I can't say that anymore? That's my favorite

cereal!"

Thankfully, Ember walks over right then, holding her son Lincoln's hand. I finally met him a few days ago, and he is Ember's twin, with his blonde hair, green eyes, and half the size of all the other seven-year-olds I've seen.

"Hey, girls, you want to take Lincoln over to the face-painting tent for me so I can talk to Brooklyn?"

Oh, no. She's got a serious look on her face. This is not going to end well for me.

I've been avoiding Ember ever since my date with Clint at the beginning of the week. Not really on purpose. I've spent most of my time in between watching the girls, sneaking away and finding places to make out with him. We went to dinner at the Timber Diner twice after that night, had drinks at the Maple Inn another night, and I've had to take my dad to two doctor's appointments and run a bunch of errands for him. I really have been busy, but I'm also not sure I'm ready to tell Ember I've always had a thing for her brother and never told her. She is going to murder me in my sleep. Actually, she won't even be kind and wait until I'm asleep. She'll do it in broad daylight in front of everyone.

When Mia starts to struggle in my arms for me to let her down, I hug her tighter to me.

"Face-painting is dumb. You don't need to get your face painted," I tell her.

"I want a unicorn on my face!" she shouts excitedly, still squirming as hard as she can.

"What's wrong, Brooklyn? Afraid to be alone with me?" Ember asks with an evil smile on her face.

I laugh a little too loudly, and have no other choice but to put Mia down before I drop her. Grace grabs both Mia and Lincoln's hands and starts walking them to the face-painting tent, and I almost call her a traitor, but stop myself when I realize that would be immature.

But seriously, what a traitor.

"I should probably go muck out the horse stalls. Toss some bales of hay that need... tossing. Fire up a tractor or two and make sure they're in working order for the tractor rides later."

I have never in my life done any of these things, and I realize I sound like an idiot, but I don't care. I'd rather shovel horse shit and accidentally run over half the people here with a tractor than have Ember yell at me.

"Don't even think about it, Brooklyn Marie Manning," Ember warns, crossing her arms in front of her.

Shit. My full name. This is it. This is how I die.

"Sooooooo, what's new with you?" I ask in a chipper voice.

"Cut the shit. You've been sleeping with my brother and you didn't tell me?" she shouts.

I quickly turn my head from side-to-side, making sure no one heard her.

"Will you keep it down?" I whisper-yell. "I'm not

sleeping with your brother!"

She stares deep into my eyes for a few seconds, and when she's satisfied with whatever she sees, the pissed off look leaves her face and she nods.

"Good. That's good. I've got fifty bucks on tomorrow night, and six grand would go a long way toward Lincoln's college education," she informs me.

"Are you fucking kidding me right now?" It's my turn to yell, and I don't even care who hears me.

"Seriously, Brooklyn, think of his future. Do you want my son to not go to college? Do you want my sweet, adorable little Lincoln to wind up homeless, living on the streets, sucking dick for cash, because he couldn't afford to go to college?"

"Dude, really? You just said your son's name and *sucking dick* in the same sentence. Even *I* know that's wrong." I cringe.

"Desperate times call for desperate measures. Don't bone my brother until tomorrow night," she states, pointing a warning finger in my face.

I let out a heavy sigh, cocking my head to the side.

"Are you really not mad at me about this?" I ask quietly.

"I was initially. But only because I didn't hear it from either one of you first. I mean, I knew he always had a thing for you. *Everyone* knew he always had a thing for you, but I didn't think you'd come back here and actually want anything to do with him."

"You knew he always had a thing for me? And you didn't tell me? Why didn't you tell me?" I ask in shock.

"Because I thought you hated him! What good would that have done? He's annoying as shit, but he's still my brother. I didn't want you to rip him to shreds and break his heart."

Damn, that stings a little.

"I wouldn't have done that. Because I've always had a thing for him too," I finally admit out loud.

I should probably be saying this to Clint first, but I feel like I owe it to Ember to throw her a bone. And going by the loud, ear-piercing shriek of happiness that flies out of her mouth, I think this makes up for everything.

She throws her arms around my neck, and I laugh as I wrap mine around her waist and she starts jumping up and down excitedly.

"Oh my God, oh my God, oh my God, oh my God! I can't believe this! We're going to be sisters!" she shouts.

"Slow your roll there, short stuff. Did you not hear me before when I said we haven't even had sex yet?"

She pulls out of my arms and beams at me.

"I don't care. It doesn't matter. This is amazing. What did Clint say when you told him?"

"Told me what?"

I jump, and a squeak of surprise comes out of me when I whirl around and find Clint standing next us.

THE SIMPLE LIFE

"Told you that there are way too many annoying kids here and I may or may not have taught Mia some new swear words today and maybe someone should clean the puke out of bounce house number eight," I ramble.

Ember looks at me in confusion, and I subtly shake my head at her. Thankfully, she's a smart woman and immediately catches on to the wide-eyed look of panic I'm giving her.

"Yes. Puke in the bounce house. I should probably go find someone to clean that up. See you two later," she announces, giving me a little thumbs-up as she backs away, pausing for a second and pointing two fingers at her eyes and then at me. "Don't forget. Tomorrow night. Sucking dick for money."

With that, she turns and skips away.

"Do I even want to know what that was about?" Clint asks, flinging his arm over my shoulders.

"Oh, you know. Just your sister planning for your nephew's bright future," I tell him with a smile.

He kisses the top of my head, and I let out a happy sigh.

"Ahhh, just in time," Clint suddenly says.

"What's just in time?"

He points toward the driveway, and I see a caravan of trucks pulling in, kicking up dust and gravel as they go. But these aren't just ordinary trucks, oh no. These trucks suddenly turn the nightmare happening around me into heaven on earth.

"Your surprise," Clint answers.

"You got me taco trucks?" I ask.

"Not *just* taco trucks. There's a pizza truck, cupcake truck, barbecue truck, grilled cheese truck, donut truck, and a pancake truck," he informs me.

"Oh, God. I think I just came," I whisper.

Clint laughs, removing his arm from my shoulder to grab my hand and pull me toward where the trucks are lining up along the driveway.

"Food first, orgasms later."

"Is that a promise? Should we shake on it? I don't know if I trust your dedication to the cause."

He bends his head down as we continue walking, and whispers in my ear, "Believe me, fancy pants, I've been dedicated to that cause since you came on my lap and moaned my name."

☆

"WHY ARE WE walking so fast? I have a stomach full of tacos and pancakes. All this jostling isn't good for me," I complain as Clint drags me through his quiet, empty house.

There is still an entire farm full of people outside, but thankfully, I can't hear any of the annoying screaming of kids now that we're inside. I kind of want to hide in here for the rest of the day.

"Clint? Is that you?"

When Mrs. Sherwood shouts from upstairs, Clint starts dragging me faster, pulling me into the kitchen and across the room.

"Clint?" Mrs. Sherwood shouts again, her footsteps thumping down the stairs.

Before I can open my mouth and yell back to her, Clint slides open the pantry door and shoves me inside, closing it behind us quietly.

"What the hell?" I mutter in the pitch darkness.

He shushes me, and I get all set to tell him off, when suddenly his body is up against mine. He nudges me backward until I bump into the shelves behind me. I remain perfectly still and keep my mouth shut, because this man has turned me into a horny ball of need, and feeling him pressed up against me fills me with all sorts of tingly anticipation.

When we hear the front door open and close, Clint finally speaks.

"Turn around."

His words are said in a low, quiet voice, and it sends shivers up my spine. I immediately do what he says, my shoulder sliding against his chest as I turn since he's still standing so close to me.

"Put your hands on the shelves and hold on tight," he murmurs close to my ear.

Sweet baby Jesus, where did this demanding guy come from?

One of his arms wraps tightly around my ribs, right

under my breasts, anchoring my back against his front. Without any warning, his free hand presses against my stomach and then quickly glides downward, dipping inside my cotton shorts, under my lace thong, and stops when his fingers are centimeters away from where I need him touching me the most.

"I've been dreaming about feeling you come on my fingers this entire week," he tells me quietly, his hand still holding perfectly still.

Everything about the night we humped like teenagers under the stars was amazing. But Clint wasn't vocal about anything, and that was perfectly fine. It was still hot as hell. It was actually almost hotter that he was so quiet and just let his actions speak for themselves.

But this? Holy shit. I could probably come without him even touching me if he keeps saying shit like this to me.

"Do you want me to fuck you with my fingers, Brooklyn?" he whispers.

My hips automatically jerk when he says something so dirty, and I swear to God I will start crying if he doesn't move his hand soon.

"Yes! Holy shit, yes," I respond in a breathy voice.

He presses his mouth to the side of my neck, gently sucking on the skin there, as he pushes his hand the rest of the way down, sliding through my wetness, and immediately plunging two of his long, thick fingers inside me.

Unintelligible words and noises come out of me that are part moans and part begging when he slowly starts pumping his fingers in and out of me.

"Christ, you feel so good," Clint mutters against the side of my neck, his hips pushing forward until I can feel his hardness pressing against my ass.

His thumb moves to my clit, and he gently starts circling it, while his thrusting fingers continue their slow assault.

I am full-on whimpering at this point, my hands smacking down on the shelf in front of me, knocking shit onto the floor as I try to grab onto it and hold on for dear life. I hear stuff spilling all over the floor at our feet and don't even care that I'm making a mess.

Everything is heightened by the fact that it's pitch black in here and I can't see a damn thing. All I can do is smell Clint's cologne that always drives me wild, and feel his hot breath against the side of my neck and his body pressing into the back of me from his chest to his thighs.

He continues to suck and nip at the side of my neck, his fingers pushing into me deeper, and his thumb circling my clit faster. My hips start jerking roughly against his hand, and I wonder if he took some sort of class on this shit. Knowing him, he did extensive research on the computer and made a whole bunch of charts and graphs about the best way to bring a woman pleasure.

I can't even believe how turned on I am right now, and how fast the ache between my legs is building and building with each and every push and pull of Clint's fingers. No one has ever made me feel this way, not even *myself* with my own hands, and definitely not without any kind of build-up or foreplay. But if I'm honest, just being in the same room with Clint is foreplay all on its own. Even when he shushed me, it made me wet.

A tingle starts traveling from my toes and quickly moves up, centering right between my legs. Clint pushes his fingers in deep and holds them there, his thumb swiping back and forth over my clit with just the right amount of movement and pressure, until I can feel myself start to pulse around his fingers.

"I'm coming. Oh, God, I'm coming," I mutter, smacking my hands against the shelf and sending more items crashing to the ground.

"That's it, baby. Fuck, you're so tight when you come," he says with a guttural moan, my orgasm exploding out of me with the force of a freight train crashing through a brick wall when he says that.

His thumb continues to gently graze over my clit, pulling every ounce of pleasure out of me, until I feel like I might pass out from how good it feels.

Swipe, swipe, swipe goes his thumb, as I continue to pulse, and tingle, and jerk my hips against his hand, this orgasm lasting longer and feeling more powerful than any that have come before it. Pun intended.

With a loud moan, I finally collapse forward, my head smacking against the back of my hand that clutches tightly to the shelf.

I let out a small whimper when he pulls his fingers out of my body. His hands press against either side of my hips, and he turns me around, leaning down and kissing one of my eyes.

He chuckles softly.

"I can't see a fucking thing in here. I was aiming for your mouth."

"What the hell was that for? Not that I'm complaining or anything."

"I can't just shove you into my pantry and give you an orgasm for the hell of it?" he questions.

"Well, sure. But I feel like there's an ulterior motive here, so spill it."

After a few quiet seconds in the pitch dark room, he finally breaks.

"Fine. So maybe I was buttering you up so you'd make another one of those pumpkin dump cake things. A dump cake I don't have to share with the girls. A dump cake *all* to myself."

I can hear the longing in his voice and I can't help but laugh.

"You just wanted an excuse to say the word *dump*, didn't you?"

All of a sudden, bright light floods the pantry and

almost blinds me when the door is flung open.

"Sugar! Are you making cookies?" Mia shouts excitedly.

"I was doing *something* with a cookie," Clint mutters.

I elbow him in the stomach and glance down at the floor where Mia's eyes are focused. Sugar, flower, rice, uncooked pasta noodles, and cereal are littered all around our feet, and right now, it's the least of my worries. If that child would have opened the pantry door a minute sooner, she would have needed therapy for the rest of her life.

"Yes! We're making cookies," I announce, stepping out of the pantry and into the kitchen.

I come to an abrupt halt, making Clint slam into my back since he was following me out, when I see Mrs. Sherwood and Ember standing by the island.

"This is just perfect. Now Lincoln will be homeless," Ember mutters.

"Looks like I'll be taking that vacation to Hawaii I've always wanted," Mrs. Sherwood says with a smile.

"You two should be ashamed of yourself," Clint scolds, pointing his finger at both of them.

You know, one of the fingers that was just inside of me. No big deal.

With a huff, he grabs Mia's hand, thankfully with his *other* hand, because *eeeew*, and starts walking her out of the kitchen.

"Come on. Let's go outside to the cupcake truck

and you can have whatever you want," Clint tells her.

"Yippee!" she shouts, as they disappear around the corner, with Clint looking back over his shoulder and giving me a wink.

Mrs. Sherwood turns to walk out after them, and I join Ember to follow behind her.

Wrapping my arm around her shoulders, I give it a squeeze.

"Don't worry. There's still a chance your kid won't have to suck dick for money," I reassure her.

Chapter 22

CLINT
Family Life

"OH. OH MY. Well, that's unfortunate."

Brooklyn doesn't even bother to hide her amusement, or the damn snort that comes out of her. She's lucky it's a cute fucking snort. And that she's wearing those sexy red cowboy boots and cut-off jean shorts.

"It's not my fault. I literally looked away for two seconds."

"Wow. She drew quite an impressive dick in two seconds," Brooklyn quips.

We both turn and stare at Mia's cheek where she did, in fact, draw a dick on her cheek with a black Sharpie. She told me it was a unicorn, but I'm not buying it. The damn thing even has hair on its balls, which Mia claims are its legs.

When I was little, the only chore on the farm I actually enjoyed doing was when my dad would have me sit with him next to the piles of recently picked pumpkins. Each pumpkin was priced according to weight. We would put a pumpkin on a regular bathroom scale, my dad would calculate the price, and he'd let me write it on top of the pumpkin right by the stem with a black Sharpie. Here's a fun fact for you. When you're carving your Halloween pumpkins and want to use a Sharpie to draw the design, but don't want all that black color to still be on the pumpkin when you finish, spray it with aerosol hairspray and then wipe it off with a rag. Ember and Brooklyn were in charge of wiping off the price up at the checkout stand when a customer would bring their pumpkins up to pay, and we still use that trick today.

Even though this farm does ten times as much business as it did when I was little, I still like this tradition and have brought the girls out here every year to let them help me price the pumpkins that will be put out in front of the store. This is the first year I let Mia help with the pricing instead of just handing me the pumpkins she could lift. Clearly, that was a mistake.

"Do you think I could spray her cheek with hairspray and it would come off?" Brooklyn asks, squatting down next to me to hold Mia's chin in her hand, tilting her head to the side to get a better look.

"Doubtful," I sigh. "So that means she just won't be going out in public until it washes off in about a week."

"Does this mean I get to call her wiener face for a week?" Grace asks hopefully, not even looking up at us from a few feet away as she concentrates on writing the price as neatly as possible on the pumpkin in front of her.

"No!" Brooklyn and I both shout at the same time.

We look at each other and laugh, but my heart fucking clenches inside my chest.

It's been two weeks since the opening of the farm, and every time the four of us are together, I forget that we aren't really a family. I forget that Brooklyn's not mine, and I forget she isn't the girls' mother.

I mean, technically she's mine in the sense that we're kind of dating, but I still have no idea what the future holds for us. The only time she's even mentioned New York was when that famous-for-doing-nothing chick did an interview, apologizing publicly to Brooklyn and clearing the air. I made a joke about how it wouldn't be long now before no one would remember what her underwear looks like and she'd be able to walk through the city without people saying something to her. I only said that shit to try to get her to give me *something* about where she was at, but she just made a little *hmmm* sound and changed the subject.

"Come on, my little hellion. Let's go inside and try to do something about your cheek," Brooklyn says, grabbing both of Mia's hands and pulling her up from the ground.

My little hellion. She said my *little hellion. Fucking hell, why does that sound so good?*

Before they walk away, Brooklyn glances over at

Grace and then gives me a wink. I told her last night that it was way past time for Grace and me to talk, and she agreed. I know this is her way of telling me that she's going to keep Mia occupied and give the two of us some alone time. I'm almost more nervous right now than I was the first time I held her after she was born and I was afraid I would drop her. There's definitely been a happiness in my girl that I haven't seen in a while, but I can tell she's still holding back, and that needs to change.

After I watch Brooklyn and Mia walk hand-in-hand over to the house and disappear inside, I turn around where I'm sitting so I can face Grace. She's bent over another pumpkin, and her tongue is sticking out of the corner of her mouth as she concentrates on writing the price on it. I watch her finish, lean back, cock her head to the side, and smile, admiring her work.

Aside from the light dusting of freckles on her nose that she got from her mother, she looks just like me. She's got my hair color, my eye color, my smile, and my dimples. Melissa used to call her my little mini-me, but she always said it in a condescending way. Like she couldn't handle the fact that there were two of us. She couldn't stand that Grace always wanted to be where I was. If I was out in the fields, walking up and down them after seeds were planted to check on things, Grace would follow behind, jumping into each of the footprints I made in the dirt. Whenever I took a tractor out to plow, Grace would sit on my lap with a pair of children's sized ear protectors on to save her ears from the loud noise. If I needed to have a meeting with the farmhands, she would be perched on my shoulders, her stomach resting on my head and her arms draped down with her hands clutched under my chin.

My eyes start to burn and there's a lump in my throat that's making it hard to swallow. I have no idea when she stopped being my mini-me, following me around everywhere, and it fucking hurts that it's all my fault and I didn't even notice. I blink my eyes rapidly when Grace puts the cap back on the marker and tosses it to the ground.

"I'm sorry," I say softly.

She pauses reaching for another pumpkin, and finally looks up at me.

"Sorry for what?"

"Sorry for not talking to you about important stuff. Like your mom."

Her eyes widen just a fraction when I say the word *mom*, and it makes me feel like an asshole.

"It... It's okay." She shrugs, quickly dropping her head and playing with a string hanging from the hole in her jeans over her knee.

Scooting forward, I grab her chin and lift it up so she'll look at me again.

"It's not okay. I never should have made you feel like you couldn't talk about her. I guess I thought if I didn't say anything, you would just forget and move on, and it would be easier on you. I didn't realize I was making everything worse by doing that," I tell her.

Her chin quivers against my fingers, and her eyes start to fill with tears. There is nothing worse than seeing your child cry and knowing that you're the cause for their tears.

"Brooklyn said she didn't leave because of anything I did," she says softly.

"Brooklyn is a very smart woman, and one hundred percent correct. It had absolutely nothing to do with you. Some people just aren't cut out to be moms."

Grace sniffles and nods her head.

"Brooklyn said that too. And that her mom wasn't cut out to be a mom either."

"You two have a lot in common," I tell her, dropping my hand from her chin. "If you ever want to know something about your mom, or want to talk about her, don't ever feel like you can't, okay?"

She nods again, rubbing her nose with the back of her hand.

In the distance, we hear the slamming of the screen door from the house, and we both turn to see Brooklyn and Mia come back outside. Their arms are loaded up with a ton of coloring books and a few containers of crayons. Brooklyn sets a blanket out a few feet from the bottom of the steps, and they both flop down and start spreading everything out around them.

"You really like her, huh?" Grace asks, as I look away and back at her.

"Your sister? Eh, she's all right." I shrug, giving her a teasing smile.

Grace rolls her eyes and leans over to lightly smack my arm, and I finally feel like I can breathe again. We're gonna be okay.

"No, duh. I mean Brooklyn. You really like her. You're always staring at her and smiling. I know you guys kiss and go on dates and stuff."

Oh, God. Maybe we aren't going to be okay.

I can feel my face heat with embarrassment, and I suddenly wonder if this is how I'm going to feel when I have to talk to her about the birds and the bees.

Shit! She'll be eleven in a few weeks. Should I have already done that? Oh, holy fuck, I am not prepared for this.

"Um… uh… yeah… yep. I like her. Is it okay that I like her?" I ask.

"Yeah, it's okay. I like her too. You can marry her if you want. That would be kinda cool."

Fuuuck.

"You know she technically lives in New York, right?" I ask gently.

I don't want Grace to get her hopes up, and then have her heart broken if Brooklyn does go back. I know there's no way Brooklyn would ever cut the girls out of her life like their mother did, though, so there's that. She puts on a good front about not liking kids, but I can see it in her eyes that she has fallen in love with my girls.

If only she would fall in love with me.

"I know. I heard Mrs. Sherwood talking to someone about it. But, Dad, she doesn't *have* to live there, you know. You just need to step up your game and make her stay."

Out of the fucking mouths of babes....

"Oh yeah?" I laugh. "And what would you suggest I do?"

She scrunches up her face and taps her finger against her chin, thinking very hard about my question. After a few minutes, a smile lights up her face.

"Just tell her you love her."

Of course I laugh when she says that, but then I immediately sober.

Just tell her I love her... like it's that simple.

Fuck. Just tell her I love her. Maybe it *is* that simple.

BROOKLYN MOANS AROUND my tongue when my hand slips under her shirt. I pull the lacy cup of her bra down and start circling my thumb over her nipple. She grinds her body down harder onto my lap, and my hand clutches tighter to her ass, helping her rock back and forth against me.

As soon as I put the girls to bed, I had every intention of having a serious discussion with her, but when she crawled onto my lap and straddled me as soon as I sat down on the couch, my dick started doing the thinking for me.

And for all those people with money in the sex pool, I'm sorry to report that if you've picked any day prior to now, you lose. My goddamn willpower is seriously being tested. I am very well acquainted with third base at this point, since we can't keep our hands off each other whenever we're alone. Or when we're not alone.

Brooklyn charged into my office the other day, the store full of customers, locking the door behind her. She dropped down on her knees in front of my chair and gave me a blowjob that almost made my head explode. Her bright blue eyes looked up at me as she wrapped her lips around the head of my cock and then fucking deep-throated me.

Her soft hands cupped and massaged my balls. She slid her fist up and down my shaft while she sucked me off. And the entire time, her eyes never left mine. It was the hottest experience of my life, and I lasted an embarrassingly short amount of time. I knocked my laptop onto the floor and cracked the screen, and spilled a cup of coffee all over the week's purchase orders when I tried to move her away and she refused, swallowing like a goddamn champ when I came down her throat.

Thinking about that blowjob isn't really helping

matters right now, so I quickly block it from my mind. Pulling my hand out from under her shirt, I end the kiss, bringing my hand up to tuck some of her hair that's curtaining our faces behind one of her ears.

She lets out the tiniest of frustrated sighs, and I really wouldn't blame her if she called me a cock block and stormed out of the house. I've stopped us every time we've gotten too close to having sex, and I know she's got to be more than a little annoyed with me. *I'm* annoyed with me, and want to kick my own ass. My dick will probably remove itself from my body and leave forever if it doesn't get to sink inside her soon. Taking it semi-slow until I know where her head is at is starting to make me a grumpy son of a bitch.

Brooklyn slides herself off my lap and plops down onto the couch next to me, reaching her hand under her shirt to pull her bra back in place.

"So, you had a good talk with Grace today, I assume?" she asks.

"I did. Thank you for giving us some time alone."

She gives me a smile and pats my thigh.

"It was a little depressing though. That girl is growing up right before my eyes. She already started giving me those half-assed, one-armed hugs with her butt sticking out so she can touch me as little as possible," I complain.

Brooklyn laughs softly.

"You know, I saw a quote the other day when I was

searching for craft projects," she states.

I hold up my hands and stop her from continuing for a second.

"Brooklyn Manning! Were you on Pinterest looking at craft projects for *kids*? What has happened to you?" I ask in mock surprise.

She pinches my thigh and glares at me.

"First of all, how do you even know what Pinterest is, Farmer Joe?"

"Hey, I'm hip with the times. I know what all the cool kids are doing with their SnapGram shit."

"You're ridiculous. *Anyway,* as I was saying, before I was so rudely interrupted. Yes, I was on Pinterest looking up craft projects to keep your daughter occupied so she stops drawing dicks on things. I saw this quote that said, *We've been teaching them how to walk away from us since we taught them how to take their first steps,*" she tells me. "Don't worry. She'll come back to you eventually."

We sit in silence for a few minutes, and that quote plays on a loop in my head, over and over.

"What if I don't want her to leave me?" I ask quietly.

"She has to. She can't stay here forever."

"I know. I get that. But there's no guarantee she'll come back to me," I say, knowing damn well we aren't talking about Grace anymore.

"She will. But she has a life to live," Brooklyn whispers.

"But *I'm* part of her life. A really important part. At least I hope I am."

She opens her mouth to respond, when a loud shriek interrupts her.

"Brooklyn! You're still here!" Mia screams, standing in the living room doorway in a pink and purple unicorn nightgown, a stuffed animal tucked under her arm, and a faded dick on her cheek thanks to Brooklyn scrubbing as hard as Mia could stand so it wasn't so dickly vibrant.

"What are you doing awake, little miss?" I ask, pushing up from the couch and walking over to her, squatting down in front of her and running my hand over the top of her head.

"I couldn't sleep. Can Brooklyn read me a story? Pretty, pretty please?" she asks.

Brooklyn quickly gets up from the couch and crosses the room, bending over and lifting Mia up in her arms.

"One story, and then lights out," Brooklyn tells her.

"One story, and three pieces of candy," Mia tries to negotiate.

"Nice try. Two stories, and no candy."

I watch them walk out of the room and down the hall, listening to them talk softly as Brooklyn carries Mia up the stairs, wondering how in the fuck I'm going to survive it if Brooklyn walks away.

Chapter 23
Love Life

WHEN I DON'T find Clint in the house, in the store, or in his office, I walk across the grass toward the stables, where a light is shining brightly out of the main door. The girls were fast asleep in the house, and Mrs. Sherwood was snoring on the couch, so I'm assuming there was an emergency Clint needed to take care of, and he asked her to come over. Thankfully, it's late and all of the workers have gone home, because it's time for us to talk, and I don't want an audience.

After the moment we shared on his couch the other night, when I told him that quote, I don't think he was talking about Grace at all. But how the hell am I supposed to be sure and not make a fool of myself? I know he has feelings for me, but are they big enough? Are they the same that I have for him, the ones that make me catch my breath every time I'm near him? The ones that make me want to cry when I even consider the idea of moving back to New York? Maybe this is just a fling for him. Maybe this is just a way to satisfy his teenaged curiosity and the crush he had on me back then.

Ember and I shared a much-needed girl's night out at the Maple Inn tonight, and when I told her all of these things, she punched me in the arm and told me I was being an idiot. Which I already knew. But this is scary shit. I am falling hard for him, but what if he's not there to catch me? There's only one way to find out. I need to suck it up and act like an adult.

Stepping into the stable, my boots clomp against the wood floor as I move down the long hallway of stalls. When I turn a corner at the end, there's a stall that takes up half of that hallway, where they put horses that are about to give birth, to give them room to move around and be comfortable. I find Clint bent forward with his arms resting on top of the gate, looking into the stall. We haven't really seen much of each other since our talk on the couch. The small handful of times we were in the same room together during the day, he seemed a little distant and moody, so I gave him some space.

I stop a few feet away from him, and butterflies start flapping around in my stomach.

God, I've missed him.

Even though I've seen him the last few days, he hasn't touched me. He hasn't joked around with me. He hasn't smirked at me with those damn dimples in his cheeks.

Fuck. I am in so deep.

As if he senses me standing there staring at him, he turns his head to the side and our eyes meet. I give him a small smile, but he doesn't return it. At least he pushes himself away from the gate and walks toward me, stuffing his hands in the front pockets of his jeans as he moves. He stops a few feet away, and I just want to scream at him to touch me, kiss me, do *something* to give me some kind of hint if I'm about to do the right thing, or make the biggest mistake of my life.

"You look good, fancy pants," he says in a low voice, looking me over from head to toe.

I'm wearing another dress from Target that I got the last time I went shopping. A short, baby doll style dress that's off the shoulder with bell sleeves. It has thin red and white stripes, with tiny blue flowers all over it, and I paired it with my red cowboy boots.

"Did you have a good time with Ember?"

"Yep! Super good time. A blast. Haven't had that much fun in ages!"

Jesus, shut up!

It wasn't that much fun, not by a long shot. Aside from me spending the entire night whining and moaning about Clint, the place was packed, and almost everyone in there came up to me to tell me what dates they picked in the betting pool and to ask if they still had a shot at winning. It took a lot of self-control to stop myself from telling all of them to go fuck themselves.

All of a sudden, something catches my eye behind him, back in the corner at the end of the hallway.

"Is that a cotton candy machine?" I ask.

"Yep," he responds, without looking back over his shoulder.

"Why do you have a cotton candy machine in the stables? Have the horses been protesting about sugar cubes, so you thought you'd impress them with something a little more upscale?" I joke.

Of course he doesn't laugh, or even smile. *Of course* he's not going to make this easy on me.

He lets out a deep sigh, pulling one of his hands out of his pocket to run it through his hair.

"You smell like cotton candy. All the time, ever since I've known you. And since I'm a goddamn glutton for punishment, I thought buying that fucking machine, putting it in the store once I have all the stuff I need for it, and being able to smell it when you leave, would make it feel like you're still here."

Son of a bitch.

I am an idiot. Why the hell have I been looking for signs, when they've been right here the whole time?

My eyes cloud with tears until I can barely see Clint in front of me.

"We should have sex now," I blurt out.

Oh, God. That's not what I meant to say. What the hell is wrong with me?

He laughs, but it's not filled with humor. His eyes, which always look at me with warm affection or sparkle with laughter, are suddenly cold and hard.

"Seriously? That's all you have to say when I just said that shit to you?" he asks angrily.

I don't like angry Clint. Not one bit. Angry Clint makes the butterflies flap even harder in my stomach and honestly kind of pisses me off. This is new territory for me. We just saw each other again after twelve years not that long ago, even though it feels like I've been back here forever. We've only been dating for like, the blink of an eye, after acting like we hated each other all our lives. Being with him romantically is the most natural and comfortable thing I've ever done, and that scares the shit out of me. The least he could do is take it a little easy on me.

My irritation replaces the nerves, and I put my hands on my hips defiantly.

"Well, Jesus! It's getting a little questionable at this point, don't you think? I'm starting to wonder if Clint Jr. even knows what to do!" I shout. "I mean, I've had a thing for a guy since I was a teenager, I think I'm in love with him, and his dick might not even work properly in a vagina!"

Oh, fuck!

I just wanted to tell him I was falling for him, not that I was *in love* with him. And I even said this shit sober, since my stomach was too tied up in knots to drink earlier with Ember. It just flew out of my mouth before I could stop it. But goddamn it, it doesn't feel wrong. It came out of me so effortlessly, and it actually felt *good*.

"What did you just say?" Clint asks quietly.

"I said, his dick might not—"

"I got that part," he cuts me off, a hint of a smirk finally tipping up one corner of his mouth.

We stand here staring at each other, and the air is so charged that if someone lit a match, the whole place would explode.

"Say it again," he orders softly.

I swallow thickly as my hands slowly drop from my hips.

"I think I'm in love with you," I whisper. "Actually, I'm 98.5-percent sure I'm—"

His mouth crashes against mine and cuts me off before I even registered he was moving toward me, his hands pressing to either side of my face as his tongue pushes past my lips. I grip fistfuls of his shirt in my hands and pull him closer, as his feet start moving and walking me backward. My back slams into the wall behind us, and Clint forces my head to change positions so he can deepen the kiss.

We both become a frantic mess of tangling arms and roving hands, trying to touch every part of each other we can reach while he devours my mouth with his skillful-as-hell tongue. I rip his flannel shirt open, and buttons go flying, pinging across the floor at our feet, sliding my palms up the smooth, warm skin of his muscled chest. His hands glide down the side of my neck, over my breasts, and don't stop until they reach my thighs. Gripping the back of them tightly, he easily lifts me up against the wall so I can wrap them around his waist. He grinds the hardness in his jeans against me, anchoring me in place as I wrap my arms around his shoulders and hold on tight.

The delicate scrap of lace from my thong is immediately ripped off of me and tossed to the side like it's made of paper. Clint's tongue swirls around mine, probing deeper and driving me crazy. I quickly drop my hands to his jeans, ripping open the button and yanking down the zipper, dipping my hand right into his boxer briefs and pulling out his hard, swollen cock. I pump my fist up and down his length a few times, until he reaches between us and takes himself in his hand, guiding himself to my entrance.

I suddenly tear my mouth away from his. He growls in protest, and the sound makes me wetter than I already am. Both of our chests are heaving, and when he starts to push the head of his cock inside me, I let out a little whimper and tighten my legs around him.

"You better not suck at this," I mutter, my heart beating a mile a minute in anticipation of what's about to happen.

"Right back at you. I hope you brought your A

game," Clint responds, before smashing his mouth back to mine and thrusting himself inside me fully, hard and deep.

We both groan into each other's mouth, and fucking hell, nothing has ever felt more perfect than this moment right here. His hands go back to gripping my ass, pulling me against him as he starts to move, thrusting roughly in and out of me. My back smacks against the wall with each of his powerful thrusts, but there's no way in hell I'd complain.

There's no other way to say it; Clint is fucking me against the wall of a horse stable, and he definitely doesn't suck at this. It's rough, hard, and dirty. After so many weeks, and months, and *years* of buildup, I wouldn't expect anything less. It's not even over yet, and I already know this is the best sex I have ever had.

Just like every time we've rounded third base in the last month, Clint knows exactly what to do to my body to make it soar, especially when he's taking it home. I don't know if it's that he's really this damn good at anything involving sex, or if it's just that it's *him*. I've never felt this way with any other man, and I'm starting to realize it's because none of them were Clint. He knows my body, but he also knows *me*. He knows everything about me, and still wants me. That's better than any aphrodisiac in the world.

His groin smacks against me each time he pulls almost all of the way out and then slams back inside of me, hitting the perfect spot every time, making me mindless with the need to come. His tongue darts against mine in the same rhythm as his cock pounding into me, and it just makes everything hotter. My legs start to shake around him, and my hips start churning against him erratically as I race toward my release that's *right there*, teetering on the edge.

My clit pulses and throbs as our sweaty bodies smack together, and Clint pulls his mouth away from mine to speak to me in a guttural voice, filled with so much need.

"Come on my cock, baby. I need to feel you."

Fucking hell, his dirty mouth.

One more rough thrust and I'm toppling over the edge, my arms clinging tightly to his shoulders as my head thumps back against the wall, and I shout his name.

"Oh, fuck… oh, fuck," he mutters, burying his head into the side of my neck.

His hips pump faster and faster between my thighs, until he drives in one last time, whispering my name as his cock pulses and twitches inside of me with his release.

Clint's body finally stills, and he collapses against me as we both pant and try to catch our breaths.

After a few minutes, he finally lifts his head from the side of my neck, and places a soft kiss against my lips.

"That definitely didn't suck," I tell him, running one of my hands through the hair on top of his head.

He chuckles and shakes his head.

"God, I fucking love you."

My heart flip-flops in my chest when I hear him say the words back. I mean, I kind of already knew at this point, but it definitely feels good to hear it out loud.

I wince a little when he pulls himself out of me, his hands on my hips as he helps me slide down the wall and put my feet on the ground.

"So, who's the winner?" Clint asks.

He fastens his jeans, grabs my hand, and pulls me down the hallway after I quickly scoop up my shredded thong, reaching over and shoving it into his front pocket.

"I have no idea what you're talking about."

"Nice try. There's no way you were at the Maple Inn tonight and weren't approached by half the town with their bets," he smiles.

"Full discloser, you need to know this is absolutely not why I told you I love you," I reassure him.

"I know. But you're eyes got all squirrelly and I can practically feel you vibrating with excitement, so spill it, Manning."

It's true. I can hardly stand it, and I can't stop the rush of enthusiastic words that fly out of me as we walk out of the stable door and into the chilly night air.

"Rita Shelby told me she traded with Katie Johnson

right after we saw Katie in town that night and now I get to take Katie shopping for dresses, and shoes, and skirts, and purses, and all the things!" I cheer.

Clint wraps his arm around my shoulder and pulls me against him as we walk toward the house, letting out a good-natured sigh.

"Rodney is gonna kill us when he finds this out."

"He won't have to spend a dime on that girl's new wardrobe. He'll be fine. Plus, Katie will look amazing at our funerals, so there's a silver lining."

Chapter 24
CLINT
Doomed Life

THE LAST FEW weeks with Brooklyn have been nothing short of amazing. We've fallen into an easy routine, and it feels like we've been doing this for years. Finding out she'd always felt something for me, just as I had for her, has been the craziest thing that has ever happened to me. It makes me want to kick myself in the ass for never vocalizing my feelings sooner. We could have been this happy for years, instead of just a few months. I realized, though, that even if I would've loved to have been with her all this time, I wouldn't have my girls. Everything happened the way it was supposed to, even if it took us a long time to get here.

"Are you gonna show me your slick dance moves tonight, or just stand here being a wallflower, waiting for some hot chick to flirt with you?"

I turn to smile at Brooklyn as she walks up to where I've been standing at the far edge of the white party tent that has been set up on the town square for the Rotary Club dinner.

Every time I see her, I can't fucking believe she's mine and that she's in love with me, and this time is no different. She's wearing the green wrap dress she wore the first day I saw her again, the soft material clinging to all of her curves and showing a generous amount of her mouth-watering cleavage with how low it dips down in front. Her long, dark hair has been pulled up into a high ponytail, and all I can think about is her neck on display and how I want to press my lips against it and taste her skin.

We've been insatiable ever since that night in the stables when I took her up against the barn wall, having sex all over the damn farm at every opportunity, each time better than the one before it. I should feel bad that our first time wasn't more romantic, but then thoughts of how good it felt to sink inside her body, how tightly she clung to me as I pounded into her, and how hard she came on my cock replace that remorse.

"Well, there's this hot chick I've got my eye on, but I don't know if she'll want to dance with a nerd like me," I tell her with mock shyness, kicking the ground at my feet with the toe of my boot.

"Oooh, are we role playing? Excellent," she mutters, closing the distance between us and pressing her body up against mine. "The khakis are a nice touch. Way to get into your nerd role, Hastings."

Even though the Rotary Club dinner is held outside, and it's a fairly casual event, everyone in town always dresses up for the most part. Some of the guys just put on their cleanest pair of jeans and a polo shirt, and others wear suits that stay in the back of their closets and only come out for funerals or weddings. The women though, they always go all out. The salon in town is busy from the minute they open until right before the dinner starts, with all of them booking appointments to have their hair done.

I decided to lose my usual uniform of jeans and a flannel for a pressed pair of khakis, a pale blue dress shirt with the cuffs rolled up, and the new pair of dark brown work boots I got for my first date with Brooklyn.

"You like the khakis, do ya? Are they making you hot?"

"So hot," she says with a wag of her eyebrows. "I feel like I'm in high school again, constantly staring at your ass in those dress pants you always wore, wondering what you were packing in the crotch of them."

I laugh, wrapping my arms around her and holding her tightly to me, as her palms rest against my chest.

"Well, now you don't have to wonder anymore. I'm packing a weapon of mass destruction in these things."

She rolls her eyes at me, but the smile on her face doesn't lie.

"I may or may not have gotten into the spirit of role playing tonight as well," she informs me, looking back over her shoulder and glancing around.

The entire town is here, either under this tent getting food, or under the other tent that has been set up right in front of the gazebo, lined with row after row of chairs, so everyone can watch the acts that have started performing under the gazebo.

We're standing in the shadows of the food tent, far away from the cafeteria tables that have been set up for dinner, and no one is paying a bit of attention to us. When Brooklyn turns her head back around to face me, she steps out of my hold, grabs the hem of her dress, and slowly lifts one corner of it, moving it inch by inch up her thigh.

When she gets it high enough and I can see her underwear peeking out from under her dress, I laugh so loudly she smacks my chest and quickly drops the skirt of her dress before anyone looks over here.

"Are you wearing bright blue Cookie Monster underwear? *The* Cookie Monster underwear?" I ask, my shoulders still bobbing with laughter.

"Not *the* Cookie Monster underwear. I'm pretty sure I burned those after I flashed the entire town. I ordered these off Amazon. Now, I'll just be flashing you tonight," she tells me with a cheeky smile.

"Oh, Cookie Brookie, you're my favorite."

Grabbing her hand, I pull her out of the tent and over to a grassy area, where a small wooden dance floor has been set up for people to use. The final act of the evening, the high school marching band, just finished their last song, and one of the seniors in charge of being the DJ for the night just started playing a slow song.

The dance floor is situated right in the middle of a small circle of trees, with strands of multi-colored lights hanging from the branches above us. I lead Brooklyn out into the middle of the floor where others have already started dancing, pulling her into my arms, the two of us slowly swaying to the music.

"Where are the girls? I haven't seen them since dinner and got pulled away for an emergency," Brooklyn asks, her arms draped over my shoulders as she searches around for Grace and Mia.

"By emergency, do you mean Katie asking you about shoes?" I joke.

True to her word, Brooklyn took Katie shopping last week to spend her winnings. They were gone for twelve hours. I almost called the police when she didn't return any of my phone calls or text messages. But then I realized she was in her element and would probably stab me for interrupting her so many times.

"Shut up! She was almost going to wear ballet flats with the skinny Seven7 jeans she got, and I had to make sure she wore the Gucci ankle boots, or her first day of senior year would be ruined," she tells me dramatically.

"I didn't understand a word of that sentence," I mutter. "Anyway, the girls are with one of many people right about now. The beauty of being out in public in a small town is that there are always built-in babysitters. Last time I saw them, Rita Clifton was taking them over to the chocolate fountain."

Brooklyn tightens her arms around my shoulders, bringing her body completely flush with mine from chest to thigh. One of her hands rests against the back of my head, and she starts lightly running her fingernails against my scalp, making a shiver run up my spine and my cock start to harden in my pants.

"So, that means we only have a few precious seconds before Rita comes running over here with a chocolate-covered Mia, who tried to swim in the fountain," she says softly.

"It would probably be wrong to disappear behind a tree somewhere so I could rip those Cookie Monster underwear off your body and fuck you silly, right?" I ask.

She trembles in my arms, and knowing I have that kind of effect on her makes it almost impossible not to drag her off this dance floor and do exactly what I suggested. It's been twenty-four hours since the last time I was inside her. Twenty-four hours is entirely too long.

"I'm really happy. You know that, right?" she suddenly asks, cocking her head to the side.

"Me too," I tell her, rubbing soft circles against her spine with one of my palms.

We continue dancing to the slow beat of the music, just staring into each other's eyes, everyone else around us completely disappearing.

"The girls go back to school next week," I remind her, the song ending and another slow one taking its place.

Our school district never starts back until the end of September. There are so many farm kids around here, that the school gives them plenty of time to help out their families with the end of summer and beginning of fall crops.

We still haven't really talked about what the future holds. I think both of us just wanted to live in the moment, enjoy every minute we have together, and not ruin anything. But with the summer coming to an end, as well as Brooklyn's "job" working for me, we can't exactly ignore this anymore. I need to know where her head is at. I need to know if I'm enough for her. If staying here in White Timber has more to offer than the life she left behind in New York.

"I can't believe Mia's going to be a full-time kinder-gartener. Her preschool teacher only had her a few days a week, for a few hours at a time. We should probably send Mrs. Knightly a fruit basket. Or a case of industrial earplugs. Or a coupon for free therapy," Brooklyn jokes, referring to Mia's kindergarten teacher.

"Mrs. Knightly taught both of us for kindergarten. If she can survive that, she can survive anything," I remind her.

We continue dancing for a few more quiet seconds, and I finally bite the bullet and just fucking come right out with it.

"Are you gonna go back to New York? It's okay if you do. We'll make it work. There's planes, and Facetime, and now that I've cut back working so much at the farm, I can take time off and—"

She cuts me off by placing her hand over my mouth, and I'm grateful for that. Each word I said to her was like a fucking knife to my heart. I wasn't lying. I would do whatever it took to make it work, because I refuse to lose her, now that I finally have her. Long distance would fucking suck. Not having her here every day, not being able to see her, kiss her, touch her, laugh with her, listen to her insult me…. I don't even want to think about it.

"I love New York. It was my home for twelve years, and it was good to me for the most part. I got to experience the place I'd always dreamed about going to for a really long time. But I realized, the only thing that made me happy there was my job. I loved what I did. And I don't have that anymore." She shrugs.

My heart thunders in my chest at the possibility that she just might stay here.

We're interrupted when Ember lightly taps on Brooklyn's shoulder.

I drop my arms from around her, and Brooklyn turns to face her, leaning her back against me as my hands rest on her hips.

"Sorry to interrupt you two love birds, but Brooklyn's phone has been ringing off the hook in her purse over at our table," my sister states, holding Brooklyn's phone out to her.

Brooklyn thanks her, looking down at her phone. Her body suddenly jerks away from mine, and I see over her shoulder that she has a ton of missed calls from someone named Nicole, and someone else named Diane Clarkson. Her phone suddenly starts ringing again in her hand, Diane Clarkson's name flashing across the screen.

"I... I have to take this," she mumbles, looking back over her shoulder at me as she starts to walk away. "I'm sorry. I have to take this."

Ember and I watch her quickly walk off the dance floor, twisting and turning her body to get through the crowds of people, pulling her phone up to her ear as she goes.

"You look really happy," Ember muses, as I look away from Brooklyn and down at her.

"I am happy. I think she's gonna stay." I smile at her.

"Of *course* she's gonna stay. She'd miss me too much if she left," my sister jokes. "But seriously, I'm happy you two finally pulled your heads out of your asses. Don't fuck it up."

"Help! Sweet mother of God, help me!"

We both turn to watch Rita rush toward us, holding onto Mia's head and guiding her to us. Mia is, of course, covered in melted chocolate from her fingers all the way up to her shoulders, a big toothy grin on her face, also surrounded by chocolate.

Ember and I laugh as Rita deposits Mia in front of us and then runs away without another word.

"I love chocolate!" Mia shouts at the top of her lungs.

"I can see that," Ember states, pinching the one part of the shoulder of her dress that isn't covered in chocolate with her fingers.

She looks up at me as she starts to tug Mia toward the direction of the library, where they kept the doors unlocked all night for people to use the bathrooms.

"Don't worry; I got this one. But you owe me big time."

I mouth a thank-you to her as she takes my messy child away, warning her not to touch anything or anyone as they go.

Sliding my hands into the front pockets of my slacks, I walk off the dance floor in search of Brooklyn. I find her walking back in this direction, staring down at the phone in her hand, not paying attention to where she's going. I quickly pull my hands out of my pockets and grab her shoulders before she walks right into me, letting out a little chuckle.

"Watch where you're going there, fancy pants."

Her head jerks up when she hears my voice, and my smile falls when I see her flushed cheeks and shocked, wide eyes with a dazed expression on her face.

"Hey, you okay? What happened?" I ask gently, pressing my palm to one of her cheeks.

"That was my old boss on the phone, from *Glitz*. She... she offered me my job back. But not really my job. A different job. A better job. Jesus Christ... she wants me to be the Editor-in-Chief. She's retiring, and she's giving me *her* job. She wants me to run the whole fucking magazine," she rambles, looking back down at her phone.

My body instantly breaks out in a cold sweat as my hand slowly drops from her cheek. My stomach rolls with nausea, and I feel like I'm getting dizzy as I watch her continue to just stare at her phone in shock. I wonder if this is what a fucking panic attack feels like. I do my best not to show Brooklyn that I'm having a goddamn breakdown right now, because I know this is huge for her.

"That's amazing, baby," I whisper. "I'm so proud of you."

"Can we go back to the farm?" she suddenly asks, looking back up at me. "I just... I just want to go home."

Hearing her call the farm *home* should make me happy, but there's a cloud of doom hanging over me right now that prevents me from feeling anything but sick to my stomach.

"Yeah. Yeah, we can go home. Let me just wrangle

up the girls, and I'll meet you out by the truck," I tell her, giving her a kiss on the head before I go, each footstep I take away from her feeling like a bad omen for the future.

Except *she'll* be the one walking away from *me*.

Chapter 25
Pros and Cons Life

I'M NUMB. THERE'S no other way to describe it. I was so fucking *happy* being on that dance floor with Clint, finally talking to him about our future, thinking about the possibilities, and then I just had to answer that damn phone call.

It's everything I've always wanted, and more. Running *Glitz*, being in charge of every article that goes in there, it's a dream come true. It's what I've been working toward since the day I was hired. I don't even have to ask myself why I'm not jumping up and down and screaming with excitement. Two months ago, I would have been. Two months ago, I wouldn't have even hesitated to pack up my shit and get on the first plane back to New York.

Now? Now, I'm torn. Going back would be the responsible thing to do. I can't just continue living with my dad, taking care of the girls when they get home from school, and let love pay the bills. I stopped cashing the checks from Clint a few weeks ago for being his nanny, much to his annoyance. I stopped feeling like their nanny a while ago, and it wasn't right to keep getting paid for something I actually enjoyed doing.

My dad worked his fingers to the bone, taking every available chance for overtime just to make sure I never had to take out a student loan for college. I owe it all to him that I have a degree in journalism and never had to pay a penny to get it. It would be a slap in the face to him if I don't seriously consider taking this job.

Clint said we'd make it work if I went back, but I could see the fear and pain in his eyes no matter how hard he tried to hide it, and it killed me knowing I did that to him. I can't just stay here and flounder, but how in the hell am I supposed to leave Clint? And the girls? And my dad? And Ember, and Katie, and Rita, and Shannon, and Mrs. Sherwood, and even Jack the Bathroom Pisser? How am I supposed to leave this town when I finally realized how amazing it is and no longer have the desire to run as far away from it as possible?

"I want more chocolate," Mia mumbles in her sleep, her cheek pressed against my shoulder as I carry her up the stairs.

I smile to myself as I hug her warm little body tighter to me, climbing the last few steps right behind Clint, who guides a barely awake Grace with his arm around her shoulders down the hall.

We separate when we get to the girls' bedrooms that are across the hall from each other. I gently put Mia in her bed, thankful that Ember stripped her out of her chocolate-covered dress before we put her in the truck. There is no way in hell I'd wake a child who crashed from a sugar high thirty seconds after Clint pulled out of town, just to put her in pajamas. Tugging the covers up to her shoulders, I tuck them all around her body.

"Snug as a bug in a rug," I whisper as quietly as possible by her ear, the same thing I've said to her every time I've tucked her in, my throat clogging with emotion as I gently kiss the top of her head.

How in the hell am I supposed to leave this?

How in the hell can I possibly stay?

Tiptoeing out of the room, I quietly pull the door closed, turning around to find Clint leaning against Grace's closed bedroom door.

After a few minutes of staring at each other in the dark hallway, he pushes off the door and comes over to me, lacing his fingers through mine and pulling me down the end of the hallway to his bedroom.

He doesn't bother turning on the light when we get inside; he just closes the door behind us and leads me over to the bed.

The room is bathed in bright moonlight shining through the window on the other side of the room, and I keep my eyes on his when he reaches for the hem of my dress and wordlessly starts pulling it up my body. I lift my arms above my head so he can pull it all the way off, tossing it to the side as I take a step forward to start unbuttoning his shirt.

Neither one of us says a word as we strip each other naked. His window is cracked, and the only sound that can be heard as he lays me down on the king-sized bed and crawls over my body is the chirping of crickets.

He rests one of his elbows on the pillow next to my head, grabbing my thigh with his free hand and pulling my leg up around his waist as he settles between my thighs. My hands press to either side of his face, and I tilt my head up to press my lips to his, as he slowly enters my body. I whimper quietly into his mouth when the hard thickness of him fills me and stretches me in the best way.

Tears prickle the backs of my eyes when he starts gently pushing in and out of me, and I deepen the kiss to try to push them away. For the first time since that day in the stables, there are no naughty words muttered between us, no quick and dirty fucking; there's just the slow and steady rocking of our bodies against each other. It's more powerful than anything I've ever felt before, and nothing can stop the tears from spilling out of my eyes and down my cheeks.

How in the hell am I supposed to leave this?

How in the hell can I possibly stay?

Clint pulls his mouth away from me, resting his forehead against mine as he continues the slow, measured strokes in and out of my body. I squeeze my eyes closed, and whisper "I love you" to him over and over. I need him to know that no matter what happens after this night, that will never change.

His hand slides up my thigh where he was holding it in place, moving it between our bodies. When the tips of his fingers start circling my clit as he slowly thrusts in and out of me, my hips jerk and I instantly push all the depressing thoughts from my mind. I concentrate on what he's doing to me, how he makes me feel, how he knows my body like the back of his hand, and how he can pull a release out of me even when I think it's impossible.

Clint peppers kisses down the side of my cheek, kissing away my tears as his fingers swirl faster and he starts pumping into me harder. He gently nips and sucks the side of my neck as my hips jerk up to meet him, taking him deeper as he drives me wild with every swipe of his fingers over and around my clit.

My orgasm quickly works its way up my body, fluttering through me and stealing the breath from my lungs as I arch my back, gasping from the pleasure. Clint's face stays buried in the side of my neck, and I smack my hands down on his ass, helping him move his hips harder and faster between my legs. He quickly finds his own release, a muffled groan vibrating against my neck as he jerks and thrusts and pulses inside me.

My arms wrap tightly around him, not ready to lose

the heavy weight of his body on top of mine. His own arms slide under my body and he hugs me close, neither one of us making any move to roll away from each other to start dealing with whatever comes next.

My eyes start to grow heavy and they flutter closed, the feel of Clint's heart beating steadily against my chest.

How in the hell am I supposed to leave this?

How in the hell can I possibly stay?

I HAVE OFFICIALLY lost my mind.

Telling Clint I needed to take a few days to think about everything was the worst possible decision I ever could have made. He told me he understood, and he's been sending me texts to check up on me, but I know I hurt him. I know he wanted me to immediately tell him I was turning down the job because I couldn't stand the thought of leaving him. It was on the tip of my tongue when I got dressed the morning after the Rotary Club dinner and quietly left the farm before the girls woke up, but I couldn't make the words come out. I was already freaked out that I'd fallen asleep in Clint's bed and spent the night with him. Even though he constantly tried to tell me it would be fine, I always refused and went back home to my dad's house no matter how late it was. I didn't want to confuse the girls if they found me in there before we woke up. And now, all I did was confuse myself.

It felt so good waking up in his arms, with his chest pressed against my back and our legs tangled together. It felt *too* good. Too comfortable. Too normal. I couldn't possibly make the right decision by being around him, which is why I told him I needed some time.

God, I fucking miss him.

And I miss the girls, even though they Facetimed me yesterday to show me all their new school supplies. Which just made everything worse. Clint took them *shopping*. Without me. That's like, a capital offense, punishable with jail time. At least he only bought supplies and didn't try to set foot in a clothing store. But he'll have to, right? If I leave, he'll *have* to take them clothes shopping, and that thought just makes my eyes cloud with tears. He'll probably put Mia in a polka dot shirt and plaid pants. Or try to make Grace wear a dress, which will in turn make her kill him, and I don't want him to die!

Jesus Christ, get it together, Brooklyn!

I angrily swipe the tears off my cheeks, staring down at the notebook in front of me that lists all the pros and cons of moving back to New York. I quickly scribble **Clint will ruin the girls' lives and die** under the cons.

I mean, he's the one who's done their school shopping every year before I came back, so I shouldn't be freaking out about this. But goddammit, it hurts. The thought that I won't be here for things like that kills me.

Sure, Clint was right. There's such a thing as planes, and I can easily hop on one and come back here, but not all the time. I'll be able to come back for the big things, like birthdays and holidays, but not for *everything*. I'll be running a fucking magazine. I can't just be like, *"Good luck with this month's issue. Gotta head back to Montana to watch the girls get on the school bus, get a look at Mia's first report card and sigh when the teacher writes a note on it that says she talks too much, and have a chat with the principal because Grace punched a boy in the face when he told her she threw like a girl. Oh, and I won't be here for the budget meeting with the art department, because Mia lost a tooth and I need to play tooth fairy. Toodles!"*

I've never said "toodles" in my life, so I start to add **Talking like a dumbass** under the cons column, naturally, but my pen runs out of ink. I smack it down on the kitchen table and go in search of a new one. I know my dad keeps a box of pens in his top dresser drawer for all those late night crossword puzzles he likes to do, so I head into his room and fling open the drawer, moving a ton of old receipts, a box of change, and a few spare crossword books aside. I don't find any pens, but I do find a large photo album buried at the bottom. Pulling it out, I flip open the front cover and gasp.

I quickly flip through the book, page by page, the tears starting up all over again at what I'm seeing. Every single article I'd ever written for *Glitz* has been neatly cut out and pressed behind the protective plastic sheets. Not only my articles, but every red carpet photo I was ever featured in from the *New York Times* and a bunch of entertainment magazines. And these aren't just print-outs from the *Times* and *Glitz* websites. These are the actual *New York Times* photos and glossy articles from magazines.

My dad subscribed to the fucking New York Times? And Glitz? And bought any other magazine I was ever in?

"I go to the VFW for one hour and come home to find you snooping through my shit. If you're looking for the good drugs, they're all gone."

I slowly turn around to find my dad standing in the doorway of his bedroom. Swiping the tears off my cheeks with one hand, I hold up the photo album with another.

"Lucy, you've got some 'splaining to do," I say to him.

He just shrugs casually.

"*Glitz* isn't completely worthless. It taught me how to properly blend my foundation, and I found out my love language by taking an easy, ten question quiz. It's really spiced things up with Arlene."

I wince a little when he says that, because it's clearly not something I want to think about.

"Did you really think I wasn't proud of you?" he asks.

"I don't know. We don't talk about shit like that.

You've never said one word to me about my job. I didn't even know you knew what I did."

"You're my kid. Of course I'm proud of you. I didn't realize you needed all that touchy feely shit all the time." He sighs.

"I don't. But, you know, every once in a while would be nice," I tell him, closing the photo album and setting it on top of the dresser.

"You gonna go back to New York?" he asks after a few minutes.

"Do you *want* me to go back to New York?"

"That's not my decision to make. But I will say, life isn't very much fun if you don't take chances. It took me a lot of stubborn years before I took a chance with Arlene. This is a big thing, this job they're offering you. But you've also got a few big things right here in White Timber. Three that I can think of right off the top of my head," he says. "And one of those big things isn't a married man whose wife will punch you in the face when she finds out about you, so I'd consider that a win."

With that, he turns and walks back down the hall.

I spend the rest of the day curled up on my bed, alternating between talking to Joshua Jackson on my ceiling and staring at my pros and cons list. My eyes zero in on "reconnecting with old friends," which I had to write in both columns.

Pushing myself up to lean against the headboard, I

grab my phone from my nightstand and pull up Nicole's contact information. I haven't spoken to her at all since I left New York. I never even responded to her texts when she sent me the link to the article for Felicity's interview. Pressing the Call button, I bring the phone up to my ear. She answers before the first ring even finishes.

"Jesus Christ, I thought you died!" she shouts, making me chuckle.

I stopped being pissed at her a while ago for the photos she provided to *Glitz*. I'd like to think I never would've done the same thing, but back then, I probably would have, just to suck up to my bosses.

"Long time no talk. How's New York?" I ask.

I have to speak loudly, since I can hear a bunch of noise in the background on her end, and looking at the time, I realize she's probably at an event taking pictures.

"Same shit, different day. Oh my God, I got to meet George Clooney tonight. He opened up a new restaurant in Midtown. He smells like honest to God sunshine and dreams," she tells me. "I heard you got offered the Editor-in-Chief position. Congratulations, hot shit! When do you get in? I'll pick you up from the airport, and we can celebrate with copious amounts of champagne."

I should be seriously offended that she doesn't even apologize for the photos, but that's just Nicole. She doesn't apologize for anything. I glance back down at my pros and cons list, thinking about Ember and what she would have done. First of all, she never in a million years would've handed those photos over. She would've lit her camera on fire and never spoken of it again. And if by some chance someone stole her camera and got to those photos, she would've felt awful. She would've never stopped apologizing to me.

"What's my favorite color?" I blurt.

"Uh, pink? Something with sparkles maybe?" she replies.

"What town am I from?" I immediately ask.

"Somewhere in Idaho? Tennessee? Fuck if I know. It's some hillbilly town in the middle of nowhere. Why are you asking me this shit?"

I sigh, closing my eyes.

"It's obviously nothing important. Look, I need to go. Got some stuff to do. I'll get in touch with you soon, okay?"

I hear Nicole shout to someone in the background, the phone call immediately ends, and I realize she hung up on me. Without setting my phone down, I quickly pull up Ember's name and press the Call button.

As soon as she answers, I ramble off a bunch of rapid-fire questions to her.

"What's my favorite color, when did I lose my virginity, the first time you ever saw me cry, who did I go to homecoming with senior year, and how many packs of Sixlets did I eat when we were ten before I puked?"

She doesn't even pause or question why I'm asking her such ridiculous questions.

"Green, because it's the color of Clint's eyes, although I always thought it was because of your favorite dress you wore one too many times in seventh grade, you whore. You lost your virginity to David Bishop junior year in the back of his pickup truck in a cornfield, and bitched about the bruises that truck left on your spine for two weeks, even though he only lasted seven seconds and you were just being a big baby. The first time I ever saw you cry, was when Clint dared you to touch the electric fence around the horse pasture in third grade, swearing to you that the main power had been turned off, when of course it wasn't. Again, big fucking baby. He always did that shit to me, and I never cried. You went to homecoming senior year with Brent Donaldson, and refused to dance with him all night when he told you Lindsay Barker looked hot in her dress. And I believe the record number of Sixlets consumed before you yacked all over the place was thirty-five."

The tears are falling fast and hard down my cheeks with every word she says.

I don't have friends like this in New York. Friends who know everything about me, and still love me. Friends who wouldn't betray me, and friends who welcome me back with open arms, even though I've majorly sucked at being a friend for entirely too many years.

"Clint's been acting like an asshole the last few days," she tells me, having no idea that I'm sitting here sobbing like a baby. "He said you were busy with some stuff with your dad, so you better hurry up and get your cute little behind back here before someone stabs him. That someone being me, FYI."

The fact that Clint didn't tell Ember what's going on makes me feel like the worst person in the world. He didn't want her to get mad at me for needing time to think. He's protecting me, even though I broke his heart by being indecisive.

I can't believe I even needed to think about this. I can't believe I let the prospect of something shiny completely eclipse what I have here, which is a thousand times better than anything I could have in New York, even my dream job.

"I love you," I tell Ember.

"You're being weird. But I love you too. Go screw my brother's brains out so he'll stop bitching at me," she demands.

I laugh through my tears as we say goodbye, tossing the phone on my bed and grabbing the notebook sitting next to me. I tear out the list I made, ripping it in half. Setting the cons to the side, I rip the pros into a thousand little pieces, letting them fall like confetti on top of my comforter.

Scrambling off the bed with the torn off piece of

paper in my hand, I take a look at myself in the mirror and cringe.

Christ, I need a shower. And a whole hell of a lot of makeup to fix this shit.

Setting the list on top of my dresser, I race into the bathroom and get the shower going, feeling a thrill of excitement and happiness rush through me that I haven't felt in days.

Chapter 26

CLINT
Simple Life

"LOOK, LACHLAN, I don't give a shit what you do with pies that didn't sell today. Dump them in the trash, feed them to some stray cats, light them on fire…. Just do *something* with them."

The sixteen-year-old who works part time in the store looks at me with wide, frightened eyes and then quickly scurries out of my office, slamming the door closed behind him.

I should feel bad that I snapped at the poor kid, but Lachlan is a dumb-as-fuck name and his parents should be pistol-whipped.

Fuck. Lachlan isn't a dumb name. It's actually kind of cool. What is wrong with me?

My eyes move over to my laptop screen, and I know exactly what's wrong with me. It's still cracked from the day Brooklyn gave me a blowjob when I was sitting in this exact same spot, and the picture of us from high school is mocking me.

Shoving aside the purchase orders I can't concentrate on, I put my elbows on the desk in front of me and rest my head in my hands. I can hear the faint sounds of a couple store workers closing everything down for the night, and I'm counting the minutes until they leave and I can go back to the house. I just want to have a nice, quiet dinner with the girls, put them to bed, and then sit in my room and feel sorry for myself, without someone interrupting me every five minutes asking me a question.

Especially when half of those questions are about Brooklyn and where she's been the last few days, because no one had seen her on the farm or in town.

I almost had a fucking panic attack, wondering if she just got on a plane and left without saying goodbye. She'd been replying to all of my texts checking in on her, but she could have been doing that from anywhere.

Thankfully, the girls begged to Facetime her, and since I was sitting far enough away so that she couldn't see me, but close enough to spy like a damn creeper, I recognized her dad's kitchen in the background.

Just hearing her voice completely gutted me. And she got choked up when Grace showed her a pile of folders. Fucking folders. I have no idea what the hell that was about, but I had to walk out of the room at that point and take a breather before I got in my truck and raced over to her dad's place to make sure she was okay.

It's been torture giving her space. Especially since

she's embedded herself in every aspect of my life in the short amount of time she's been here. Everywhere I turn, I can't escape her. I can still smell her on my sheets, I can picture her standing in the kitchen making a fucking mess while she bakes with Mia, I can see her out in the front yard playing catch with Grace, and I can hear her laughter when I'm taking a goddamn piss in the bathroom. I'm losing my mind, and I'm taking it out on everyone around me, but there's nothing I can do to stop it. I tried so fucking hard to show her that everything she needed was right here in White Timber, and I'm pretty sure I failed. And really, I can't blame her. That job offer really is a once in a lifetime opportunity, and one that she deserves. Did I really expect her to stay here and run a fucking bullshit gossip newspaper for this tiny town?

I hear my office door open and close, and I squeeze my eyes closed and grip the hair on my head so tightly I think I pull a few strands out.

"Christ, Lachlan. I don't give a damn about pie!"

"Yikes. That's gonna be a deal breaker for me. I love pie. Pie is fucking delicious."

My head whips up from my hands when I hear Brooklyn's voice. She's leaning against my closed office door with both of her hands behind her back, and it's like someone just shocked my heart with those electric paddles. My body jolts and my heart starts racing as I slowly stand up from my chair.

Wearing a pair of those tiny ripped jean shorts I love, the sexy red cowboy boots, a white Hastings Farm tee that I see she cut down the front and made into a V neck, showing off her mouthwatering cleavage, and her long, dark hair hanging loosely around her shoulders, still damp from a recent shower, she looks like she stepped right out of one of my wet dreams.

"You look like shit, Hastings," she quips, saying the exact same words I first said to her when I found her standing in my kitchen two months ago, with chocolate dripping down her leg.

"I kind of feel like shit, Manning," I tell her with a sigh, not in the mood to spar with her.

As much as I've been dying for her to be in the same room with me, and as hard as it is not to vault over my desk, haul her against me, and kiss the hell out of her, at this point, I just want her to get this over with. Rip the Band-Aid off fast and walk away, so I can grab a bottle of whiskey and drink until I pass out.

She pushes away from the door and takes a couple steps toward me, stopping right in front of my desk. I can immediately smell cotton candy, and it makes me want to cry like a goddamn baby.

I watch as she pulls her arms out from behind her back, holding a ripped piece of paper up in front of her.

"The Cons, by Brooklyn Manning," she states, looking at the paper in her hands.

"What are you—"

"Oh my God, Clint, don't interrupt me," she says in a joking, annoyed voice. "Pretend we're in high school and I just got up in front of the class to read something. But not like that time when we were in the same writing class, because I was already a brilliant journalist, you still didn't know the difference between past tense and present tense, you wouldn't shut up, and we both got detention."

For the first time in days, I feel myself smile thinking about that memory. She was reading a piece she'd written about the inhumane treatment of cows in slaughter houses, and since I was sitting at the desk right in front of her, I kept making *mooing* sounds under my breath, so only she could hear me. She continuously stumbled over her words, shooting me dirty looks, until she finally cracked and called me a fat cow who deserved to have his stomach slit and his guts spilled all over the floor. We spent a week in detention together, and I still don't regret it.

Brooklyn clears her throat, gives me one last warning look, and then drops her eyes back down to her paper.

"The Cons, by Brooklyn Manning," she repeats.

Suddenly, the confident Brooklyn from seconds ago has morphed into nervous Brooklyn. I can see the paper fluttering a little bit in her shaky hands, and I watch her throat bob as she swallows a bunch of times before she continues reading whatever is on the paper.

"No more cream cheese stuffed pancakes from the diner. No more quiet nights with just the sounds of crickets outside. No more friendly waves, smiles, and conversations walking through town. No more reconnecting with old friends, especially best friends, who know everything about me. No more getting closer to my dad, even if he's a stubborn shit who watches *Wheel of Fortune* at an unreasonable volume."

She pauses to take a deep breath, and it suddenly occurs to me she's listing all the things she would miss if she went back to New York. My palms start to sweat, and my heart starts beating even faster. Her eyes quickly meet mine before they drop right back down to the paper.

"No more sticky and messy Mia, who gives the best hugs in the world. No more coloring with her, no more baking with her, no more finding new hiding places for sugar and sharp objects, and no more tucking her in at night. No more playing catch with Grace, who can give me a run for my money in the stubborn department. No more quiet chats with her under a tree, no more watching sports with her, no more giving her advice on the cute boy from her class."

Even though there's a lump in my throat the size of the Grand Canyon, I still make a small growling sound at that last one.

Brooklyn looks up at me with tears pooling in her eyes, waving a hand at me.

"It's fine. I handled it. You still have a few more years before you need to load up the shotgun."

Her eyes drop back down, and her voice gets softer again. It immediately starts to crack with emotion with each word she continues to read from the rest of her list, the tears now falling fast and hard down her cheeks.

"No more being smartasses to each other. No more kisses that make me forget my own name. No more touches that I crave every minute of every day. No more smell of cedar and sandalwood that makes my body tingle. No more laughing. No more smiling. No more happiness. I'll miss everything important that happens with Mia and Grace. I won't get to help hand out Sixlets to kids that come to the store. Clint will ruin the girls' lives and die."

I can't help it. I laugh, even though I'm almost as emotional as Brooklyn is at this point. Quickly rounding my desk, I rush over to her, cupping her face in my hands and brushing away her tears with my thumbs.

"I draw the line at you shopping for school clothes, Clint. I can't sit back and let that happen. I don't want you to die!" she wails.

My shoulders shake with laughter, because I have no idea what the fuck she's talking about, but I don't care. I'm pretty sure she just told me all the reasons why she's staying.

I quickly dip my head down and try to quiet her with a kiss, but she pulls back immediately.

"Wait! I have a bunch more things on here. There's a lot of good ones about barn sex, and bathroom sex, and kitchen sex and—"

I cut her off with another kiss, and she immediately melts against me, the paper still clutched in her hand making a crinkling sound as she wraps her arms around my waist and squeezes me tightly. I kiss the hell out of her, making up for the last few days of not being able to touch her or feel her mouth against mine.

We finally break apart, and I rest my forehead against hers.

"I'm scared as hell you're going to regret this," I tell her softly. "You're giving up so much. You're giving up your dream job and living in your favorite city."

"I'm gaining a shit-ton more than I'm giving up, believe me. I don't need fancy parties, or hanging out with asshole celebrities, or the hustle and bustle of a big city. I just need you, and the girls, and a simple life," she tells me.

"There's going to be *nothing* simple about raising two girls. Especially when they hit puberty," I remind her. "Speaking of that, how good are you at giving the birds and the bees talk? Because I'm warning you right now, I want no part of that shit. It's already giving me nightmares."

"Do I have to use clinical terms, like penis and vagina and menstrual cycle? Or can I go all out, saying dick, and pussy, and the movie *Carrie* in your pants?"

I shudder in revolution, shaking my head at her.

"You know what, maybe we'll just rent a movie from the library that explains it all," I tell her.

"That might be the best option," she agrees.

"You're really staying? I get to keep you, smartass comments and all?" I ask with a smile.

"It's your lucky day, Hastings. The nerd finally gets the girl. And she's a pretty awesome girl, if I do say so myself."

"Cookie Brookie?" I mutter.

"Yes, Cunty Clint?"

"Shut up."

I silence her outrage with another kiss, smiling against her mouth when I think of how much fun it's going to be giving this woman the simple life she wants.

Epilogue

CLINT

Six Months Later

PUSHING OPEN THE door to *White Timber Times*, Mia and Grace look up from the back corner of the room when they hear the chime from the bell above the door, both giving me big smiles and waves. They're sitting in teal-colored beanbag chairs, on a small square of black-and-white zebra print fluffy carpet. Tucked into the corner behind them is a V-shaped bookshelf, filled with bins of Barbie dolls, coloring books and crayons, books, board games, and other things to keep them occupied when they're here. Mia is brushing a doll's hair in her lap, and Grace has a pair of earbuds in her ears, listening to music while she flips through a book about Babe Ruth.

My eyes move over to Brooklyn, on the phone behind her desk, and I give her a wink as I make my way across the room and perch my hip on the front corner of her desk. She smiles at me, rolling her eyes as she points to the phone against her ear.

"Uh-huh. Yeah. That certainly is interesting, but I'm

not sure if it's newsworthy," she speaks into the phone, rolling her eyes at me again. "Well, because Bud Moore always gets drunk and lights things on fire in his soy bean field—Wait, what? He lit the *entire* soy bean field on fire? It's March. There's two inches of snow on the ground. How is that even possible?"

Brooklyn turns her chair to the side when Mia walks up to her, holding the phone between her ear and her shoulder to scoop her up and set her on her lap. Mia leans back against her chest, and Brooklyn wraps her arm around her waist as she turns back to face her desk, my heart flip-flopping in my chest, like it always does when I watch her with my girls.

"Yes, Mrs. Marshall, I understand how dry hay and gasoline work." Brooklyn sighs, reaching her free arm out to type one-handed on her laptop.

Brooklyn is like a fucking superhero, and she amazes me every day with the things she's accomplished since she decided to stay here in White Timber. Two days after she read her cons list to me, after we'd had plenty of time to screw like rabbits all over the farm, she contacted Ed Franklin to ask about taking over the paper. He owned the building outright, and had for years, telling her she could have the damn thing, just so he wouldn't have to continue paying insurance on it. By the end of the week, she'd cleaned the dust off of everything, added her own style by painting the walls teal, hung black-framed photos of a bunch of her favorite articles from *Glitz* around the room, hired someone to come out and replace a part in the small printing press located in the back room behind the office, and set up a play area for the girls. A week after that, the first copy of *The White Timber Times* in two years was in everyone's mailboxes on Sunday morning. A copy of the front page of that issue sits in a frame on the corner of her desk, and I smile every time I see it. It's a picture of Katie Johnson surrounded by all her shopping bags, and the headlines says *"Katie Johnson: Sometimes it Pays to Take a Gamble"*.

I also have to smile when I see the other framed photo on her desk, a gift from Brooklyn's dad when she reopened this place. It's the picture from *The New York Times* of Brooklyn passed out on the ground, with her skirt up around her waist after she'd just been punched in the face. I was pretty surprised when Brooklyn decided to display it out in the open, but she said the only way she could appreciate what she has is to remember where she came from.

Like I said, fucking amazing.

Brooklyn finally ends her call, setting her cell phone down on the desk as she wraps her arm around Mia to join the other one still holding her securely.

"How was your day, dear?" I ask.

"The usual. People lighting shit on fire, people getting drunk and lighting shit on fire, and Eric Fellows demanding I put in a retraction this week that he wasn't drinking vodka when the sheriff gave him a ticket for riding one of his cows down Main Street," she tells me.

"Wait, so he wasn't drunk when he did that?"

"Oh, he was drunk. He just wants to make sure everyone knows he was drinking whiskey and not vodka, because vodka is a sissy drink, according to him," she says with a shake of her head.

"You ready to pack it up and head out to the farm for dinner?" I ask, sliding off the desk and moving around it to pull Mia off of Brooklyn's lap and perch her on my hip, so she can use both of her hands to type a few more things on her laptop.

"Yep. I just need to grab a change of clothes from upstairs," she tells me, closing the lid of her laptop.

"No need. Mrs. Sherwood washed the stuff you've left there, so you're good to go."

Brooklyn moved into the apartment upstairs from the newspaper when she decided to stay. She said it would be crazy for us to start living together so soon, and that we needed to date like normal people for a while to make sure we wouldn't kill each other before we cohabitated. I sort of understood where she was coming from, especially with the convenience of being so close to her brand new business after she got it up and running, but it's been six months. This shit is getting ridiculous.

I want to fall asleep every night with her sprawled across my chest, chattering away about the things she's putting in the paper that week. I want to wake up with her in my arms every morning, listening to her bitch and moan about how I get up at an ungodly hour to work on the farm. I know she sometimes works crazy hours, especially if a story comes in at the last minute, or there's an edit that needs to be made to one of the upcoming town functions, but just knowing she'll be coming home to the farm *eventually* is all I want.

As Brooklyn grabs her purse out of the bottom drawer, and Grace gets up from her beanbag chair to join us, I decide to wait until we get to the farm to tell her that I lied when I said Mrs. Sherwood washed the stuff she'd left there. I mean, technically she did, but she also helped me sneak up the back stairs to Brooklyn's apartment today while she was busy working, pack up *all* of her things, and move them out to the farm.

Since I told her I had a meeting with a grocery store client in the next town over, she kept the girls with her all day at the paper; they had a teacher in-service day and didn't have school. I gave Grace the job of making sure Brooklyn stayed distracted all morning while we moved stuff, telling her to cough really loudly if we accidentally made any noises upstairs.

I even played dirty by packing an entire gallon Zip-loc bag full of candy in Mia's backpack she brought with her. Since there's currently three pieces of candy corn stuck in Mia's hair, and she's practically falling asleep in my arms as the four of us head outside and wait on the sidewalk while Brooklyn locks up, I'm assuming she's crashing from the sugar high she's been on all day. She most likely drove Brooklyn slightly insane while she worked.

"Of *course* she's quiet now, when you get here," Brooklyn complains good-naturedly with a smile.

She wraps her arm around Grace's shoulders, and I use the hand that's not holding an almost-passed-out Mia against me to lace my fingers through Brooklyn's as the four of us walk to my truck.

"She ran in circles around my desk for an hour, screaming at the top of her lungs, and sat on top of my desk for two hours after that, telling me a story about her friend at school who drank too much purple Kool-Aid and pooped green for three days," she finishes.

"Two hours for a green poop story?" I laugh.

"It was a very detailed green poop story."

Brooklyn holds the back door of my truck open so Grace can get inside, and waits for me to buckle Mia into her booster seat. Backing out and closing the door, I turn and wrap my arms around her waist, pulling her against me.

"Still thinking it was a good idea to stay here and have a *simple life*?" I ask her with a smile, as she slides her hands up my chest and drapes her arms over my shoulders.

"The absolute best idea," she replies, lifting up on her toes to kiss me. "As long as you have at least three bottles of wine with my name on them in your fridge, and you put on a pair of khakis and nothing else after the girls go to bed."

I do, in fact, have three bottles of her favorite wine in my fridge. But I did that for my own protection, just in case she wants to kick me in the balls when she realizes I've moved her into my house.

I also have my kitchen table set with my mom's good china, candles lit in the middle of it, and a giant pile of cream cheese stuffed pancakes waiting for her, along with a diamond ring in my back pocket that I bought the day after she decided to stay.

And next to Brooklyn's place setting at the table are three pieces of torn notebook paper. Grace, Mia, and I each made a list of all the cons we could come up with if Brooklyn were to say no to my proposal.

I'm pretty sure she'll say yes.

And maybe after enough of that wine, she might even let me convince her that since she loves Mia and Grace so much, maybe having a child *together* at some point in the future would be an awesome idea.

Brooklyn and I separate and get into the truck. As I pull away from the curb and head down Main Street toward the farm, she looks over at me and smiles.

"You're lucky you came with a built-in family, Hastings. Shelly Bradford brought her new baby in this afternoon when she dropped off the weekly list of activities at the library for me to put in the paper this week, and when that thing started crying, my ovaries shriveled up and died," she shudders.

Orrr… maybe not.

Epilogue
Brooklyn

Two Years Later

"JESUS, YOU SURE do complain a lot. It's not that bad, you big baby."

An inhuman growl comes out of my mouth when I glare at my husband.

"I don't even understand how this happened, with you having such a tiny dick and all," I mutter, panting and groaning in pain while I squeeze Clint's hand so hard it makes him wince.

The nurse standing on the other side of my bed looks back and forth between us with a shocked expression on her face. I'm too busy wondering what the hell I was thinking when I decided to do this shit naturally to deal with her.

"It's fine. Don't worry. This is just what we do. It's totally normal," Clint reassures her, like the sweet guy he is.

The sweet guy who finally managed to convince me

that we should have a baby. And honestly, how could I say no? A perfect blend of the two of us, with my sparkling personality and his good looks? Who would turn that shit down?

"Fuck your face and fuck your mother!" I shout, as another contraction rips through me, and I clench my teeth and try to remember how to breathe, a wave of emotion immediately coming over me as my eyes fill with tears and I look over to the far corner of the room. "I'm sorry! I didn't mean that. You're a lovely woman and I adore you!"

Clint's mother just laughs softly, pushing up from her chair to come over and stand next to the nurse.

"I know, sweetie. It's fine. I said worse things to their father when Clint and Ember were born," she reassures me, reaching up to brush some of the sweaty hair off my forehead.

"She did. She called me a scum-sucking bag of garbage and told me to go fuck myself," Clint's dad adds from his chair next to where his wife just vacated.

Katherine and Sean Hastings started coming home to visit from Florida more often right after Clint tricked me into moving in with him. Katherine was always like a second mother to me; actually, she was pretty much *a mother* to me after mine left, and we've grown even closer since I married her son and legally adopted her granddaughters. I stopped caring a long time ago that my mother didn't want me, but Katherine makes it that much easier to leave all of that guilt and sadness in the past, even with her daily phone calls when she's not in town and constant meddling, which I can't help but love.

"How about we do another check and see if it's time?" my doctor asks, walking into the room and grabbing a pair of rubber gloves from the box on the counter.

"Allen, let's go get some coffee. Looks like things are heating up, and I know *I* don't want to be in here for this shit," Sean says to my dad, both of them getting up from their chairs and heading to the doorway.

"Hey!" I shout to my dad once the contraction ends. "Aren't you going to give me any kind of advice before I do this?"

"I've never pushed a kid out of my peehole, so what kind of advice could I possibly give you?" he says with a shrug. "Don't screw it up."

With that, he walks out of the room, with Clint's dad trailing behind giving me a wink and a smile, just like his son always does.

My relationship with my dad has definitely gotten stronger with each passing year. Especially when I finally came to the realization that he was an old man set in his ways and would never change. It doesn't hurt my feelings anymore that I constantly have to be the one to call him, or go over to his house to check up on him, and he never calls me unless he needs something. That's just the way he is. He's a stubborn shit, but I love him.

"All right, Brooklyn. Next contraction, I want you to push," my doctor says, his head buried between my legs at the end of the bed with the sheet pushed up over my bent knees.

I turn to the side as much as my giant stomach will allow, clutching tightly to Clint's hand with both of mine.

"I changed my mind. I don't want to do this. I don't even *like* kids!" I tell him in a panic.

He just smiles at me, resting his arm on the pillow above my head as he leans down and presses his forehead to mine.

"Liar," he whispers. "You love Mia and Grace more than anyone."

"Yeah, but I had to grow to love them. I can't just *grow* to love my own kid!" I argue.

"Quit your bitching and push my new niece or nephew out of you already," Ember complains, walking into the room to stand next to her mother. "I didn't even *like* Lincoln the first four months after he was born, due to the postpartum depression. What you really need to worry about is that thing ripping you open from vagina to asshole, and shitting on the table."

"I hate you right now." I glare at her, my eyes widening when I feel another contraction start to tighten my stomach, and feeling like my ovaries are being ripped from my body.

"Go ahead and push, Brooklyn," the doctor instructs, his head dipping back down and getting right up in my business.

Clint puts his arm around my back and helps me sit up, and Ember and Katherine give me words of encouragement as I try to push this thing out of me.

Squeezing my eyes closed, I bear down as hard as I can, doing everything to try and forget about the pain, but it's fucking impossible. This shit hurts!

"We are never having sex again. Ever," I grunt, panting heavily when the contraction ends. "Your penis is too close to me *right now*. It needs to be at least ten to fifteen feet away at all times from now on."

Clint kisses my sweaty forehead and just chuckles, the bastard.

"Here comes another one. Push as hard as you can, Brooklyn. You're doing great," the doctor tells me.

"Dad, Mia wants—Oh my God, my eyes!" Grace shouts, coming to an abrupt halt in the doorway, smacking one hand over her own eyes, and the other over Mia's standing next to her, before she continues to scream. "I can never unsee that!"

"I want to see!" Mia complains around a mouthful of Kit Kat, trying to smack her sister's hand off her face.

"Sorry, Brooklyn!" Mrs. Sherwood apologizes, coming up behind the girls and wrapping her arms around both their shoulders. "Mia wandered off, and when we found her, she insisted she needed to see you to make sure you were okay."

In between breathing heavily and trying not to kick the doctor in the face just to give me something to do other than think about how much this fucking hurts, I glance over to the doorway and do a double take when I see Mia.

"Mrs. Sherwood. Is that... blood all over the front of Mia's shirt?" I pant, looking at the red splatters all over her lavender shirt.

I should probably stop calling her Mrs. Sherwood now, since she officially became my stepmother last year when she married my dad, but old habits are hard to break. It feels weird to call a woman who practically raised me by her first name.

"Brooklyn, I need you to concentrate and push," the doctor orders.

"I'm a little busy here, Doc. I think one of my kids snuck into an operating room to play in a body cavity," I mutter. "Can we just... pause this thing for a minute?"

Another contraction rips through my body and I can't help it; I scream at the top of my lungs, throwing in a "fuck this bullshit" and a "I will murder all of you assholes if you don't get this thing out of my right now" just for good measure.

"It's fine! Everything is fine!" Mrs. Sherwood shouts from the doorway over my screams of pain. "Mia was chewing on the end of a red pen and it broke and exploded all over her. No blood, no foul. She didn't *draw any blood*."

She laughs at her own dad jokes, and I'd laugh too that my father has rubbed off on her, but there is currently a small human being trying to chew its way out of my uterus.

"Why don't you girls go back down to the cafeteria and find your grandfathers?" Katherine suggests, as she runs her hand soothingly over the top of my head.

Grace immediately yanks Mia back, her eyes squeezed tightly closed, and practically runs away, as Mrs. Sherwood gives me an encouraging smile and races after them.

"Remember what that looked like, Grace! This is what happens when you let a boy touch you!" I shout after them.

Clint just raises his eyebrow at me with a smile.

"Shut up. She's thirteen. She needs to learn now," I tell him, groaning loudly through another contraction and pushing as hard as I can.

It only takes two hours of the worst pain in my entire life before Clint Allen Sean Hastings, or Cash, comes screaming into the world.

Thank God I finally managed to remember that Clint's father's name was Sean long before they first came home to visit us. Not only because it would have been a little awkward, but because I don't think Clint Allen Old Man Hastings is a good name for a little boy.

Katherine and Ember left a little while ago to give half the town that has been sitting out in the waiting room the good news, leaving Clint and me alone with our son.

Our son. I have a son. Holy shit.

Clint is lying next to me in the hospital bed, with his chin resting on my shoulder, staring down at the most beautiful baby in the world, who's wrapped in a blanket, fast asleep in my arms.

"I still don't like kids," I whisper softly. "But your sisters are pretty cool. And I really, really like you. Don't be too much of an asshole, okay?"

Leaning forward, I kiss the top of his soft head full of dark brown hair the same color as mine. Cash smirks in his sleep, his father's dimples indenting both of his cheeks.

"You're incredible, you know that?" Clint asks softly.

I turn my head to look at him.

"Really? A compliment? How boring," I quip with a smile.

"Just keeping you on your toes, fancy pants. Give me an hour for this euphoria to wear off, and I'll tell you that you look like shit." He smirks.

"Ahhh, much better."

Tucking my head into the crook of his neck with a smile, we stare down at our sleeping son.

At least I'll never be bored, living in this tiny town,

with my nerd-turned-cowboy, running a newspaper and raising three kids. Clint promised to give me a simple life, and he did his best to make that happen, but craziness seems to follow me wherever I go.

My life is amazing.

The End

Tara writes in a bunch of different genres because her brain is completely ridiculous. There's a lot of screaming, things are sometimes on fire, and there's usually a squirrel wearing a sweater running around. She's got a little something for everyone: Romantic Comedy, Romantic Comedy/Mystery, Romantic Suspense, Psychological Thriller, Emotional Contemporary Romance, and New Adult Drama.

You can check out all of her books here:

tarasivec.com

You can also stalk her all over social media:

Monthly Newsletter:
http://bit.ly/2n5wLeS

Instagram:
instagram.com/authortarasivec

Twitter:
twitter.com/TaraSivec

Private Reader Group (Tara's Tramps):
http://bit.ly/2hig52F

Amazon:
http://amzn.to/2wSPBfu

BookBub:
bookbub.com/authors/tara-sivec

Recipes

*I did not create the yummy goodness I mentioned in this book, nor am I claiming ownership of them. These were my mom's recipes, and I have no clue where she got them. I'm sure you can find them somewhere out on the interwebs. If you find the original creator, make sure you thank them! Enjoy!

Monkey Balls
- 2 cans Pillsbury Flaky Layers Buttermilk biscuits
- ½ cup sugar
- 2 ½ tsp cinnamon
- 1/3 cup melted butter

Instructions
1. Preheat oven to 400 degrees.
2. Generously grease 8x4 inch loaf pan (do not use dark-coated pan)
3. In small, shallow bowl, combine cinnamon and sugar; mix well.
4. Separate dough into 10 biscuits; cut each into quarters.
5. Dip each quarter into melted butter; roll in cinnamon/sugar mixture.
6. Arrange in greased loaf pan.
7. Bake at 400 degrees for 19 – 27 minutes.

8. Cool for 2 minutes.
9. Loosen edges; remove from pan. Place on serving plate.
10. Serve warm.

Candy Corn Cupcakes

- 1 package white cake mix
- 2 tsp. pure vanilla extract
- Yellow & red food coloring

Candy Corn Glaze
- 1 bag candy corn, 11-ounce size
- 1/4 cup water

Instructions
1. Prepare cake mix as directed on package, adding vanilla.
2. Divide batter in half.
3. Tint one batch yellow with 1/3 teaspoon yellow food color. Tint second batch orange with 1/4 teaspoon yellow food color and 1/8 teaspoon red food color.
4. Fill each paper-lined muffin cup 1/3 full with orange batter. Gently add yellow batter on top of orange batter, filling each muffin cup 2/3 full. Bake as directed on package for cupcakes. Cool cupcakes on wire rack.

Candy Corn Glaze
1. Reserve 1/4 cup of candy corn then place the remainder of the 11-ounce bag in a medium saucepan. Pour in 1/4 cup water and heat on low

for about 10-15 minutes. You will want to candy corn to be melted completely.

2. Remove from heat and allow to cool slightly. (You will want to cover cupcakes while glaze is still warm, but not hot.)

3. Using a spoon, drizzle glaze over frosting.

4. Decorate tops of cupcake extra candy corn pieces.

Pumpkin Dump Cake

- 1 package yellow cake mix
- 1 5oz. can pumpkin
- 1 can evaporated milk
- 3 eggs
- 1 ½ cup sugar
- 1 tsp cinnamon
- ½ tsp salt
- ½ cup chopped pecans
- 1 cup melted butter

Instructions

1. With a hand mixer, mix together pumpkin, evaporated milk, eggs, sugar, cinnamon and salt.

2. Pour mixture into a 9x13 baking dish.

3. Sprinkle bag of yellow cake mix evenly over top of mixture.

4. Sprinkle pecans evenly over top of yellow cake mix.

5. Drizzle melted butter over top of everything.

6. Bake in a 350 degree oven for 50 – 55 minutes.

7. Serve warm with whipped cream or vanilla ice cream on top.

CPSIA information can be obtained
at www.ICGtesting.com
Printed in the USA
LVHW010811011118
595603LV00018B/859/P

9 781724 146960